Playing With The Bad Boys

A Mia Ferrari Mystery

SYLVIA MASSARA

License Notes

Published by Tudor Enterprises
Australia
(61) 419 492 623

Revised edition 2016
First published by
Tudor Enterprises in 2011

ISBN-13: 978-0-9875475-0-7

Cover photograph by Franny Carufe

Dedication

To my brother, John Massara.

*And in loving memory of my parents,
Michael and Norma; and
four-legged children,
Lofty, Henry and Mitzy.*

Titles by Sylvia Massara

Romantic comedy:

Like Casablanca
The Other Boyfriend

General fiction:

The Soul Bearers

Mia Ferrari mystery series:

Playing With The Bad Boys
The Gay Mardi Gras Murders
The South Pacific Murders

Sci-fi romance:

The Stranger

For more information on Massara's novels, both in eBook
& paperback editions, plus participating retailers;
or for latest novels or to contact the author, please visit:

www.sylviamassara.com

CHAPTER 1

I expelled a big sigh as I gazed at David Rourke. He weaved in and out of the crowd, stopping here and there to chat with various guests.

"What's that for?" Thorny spoke over my shoulder. Her real name was Jo Hawthorne, but I called her Thorny—as did all the chefs who worked under her. The woman was renowned for her temper.

I turned to her, still following David with my eyes and feeling rather melancholy, and sighed again. "The one who got away."

Thorny glanced at David and then back at me. She threw me a comforting smile and patted my shoulder before placing her chef's hat on her curly mop of a head. I thought she looked like a teenager rather than the thirty-five-year-old head chef of Rourke International Hotel in Sydney.

"Time to check on the buffet." She pushed a couple of errant, ginger curls back under her hat and grinned. "Imagine, the most important night of the year and I have half the team off with the freakin' flu. Someone's got to keep the temp staff under control. Good luck with lover boy." She winked at me and walked off with purposeful strides before I could come back with a smart rejoinder.

I turned away from her retreating back and for a heart-stopping moment my eyes suddenly met David's as he regarded me thoughtfully from across the room. Thankfully, my beeper vibrated at that precise moment and I was jolted out of my trance-like state. It was a triple zero, which meant we had an emergency. I immediately telephoned the switchboard from my mobile, all other thoughts forgotten.

"Mia," a shaken female voice answered. "Get to the piano bar now. Some woman's plunged to her death and the police are on their way."

I felt as though a bolt of lightning struck me and dropped the phone from my slack fingers. When I went to retrieve it I found David standing in front of me with my phone in his hand. "Something wrong?"

The deep timbre in his voice always sent butterflies to my stomach; tonight was no different, but I had no time to waste. "David … I mean, Mr Rourke." I was always unsure of how to address him in a formal situation. "There's been a death at the piano bar. The police will be here shortly."

I must've swayed with delayed shock because the next thing I knew I was being propelled by David's hand on my arm as he led me toward the lifts. He punched the call button and addressed me with concern on his face. "I'll meet you there in a few minutes. I just have to excuse myself from the guests."

I nodded and stepped into the lift when it arrived. David held out the phone to me. "Don't forget this." He had just enough time to hand it over before the lift doors slid shut.

I took a deep breath to calm myself on the way down to the lobby and when the doors opened upon arrival, I stepped out looking cool, confident, and official. Let's face it—I felt like I was going to puke at any moment, but to all outward appearances I looked in control as I made my way to the bar. My black pantsuit, sleek and elegant, made a stark contrast to my white-blonde and scruffy short hair. All that was missing was a badge and a gun. Damn it! I should've joined the cops when I had the chance. Now it was too late.

Thankfully I had no time to ponder on this as I neared the bar and its hive of activity. The police had already arrived and cordoned off the area with crime tape to keep onlookers away from the scene, and from what I could see over the top of people's heads it wasn't pretty.

I started to push my way through the throng while I called out, "Excuse me, hotel duty manager. Please make way."

It took me a few minutes to reach the perimeter of the tape and as I went to duck under it, a uniformed police officer placed a restraining hand on my arm. "I'm sorry, madam, but this is a crime scene. You can't come in here."

I snatched my arm from his grip and threw him a look of disdain. He seemed to be in his early twenties and, though cute, a bit dumb. He obviously hadn't had time to take in my name badge.

"First of all, boyo," I addressed him firmly, "I am not *madam*. *Madam* is for whorehouses or for *Driving Miss Daisy*. Second of all, if you take the trouble to read my name badge, you'll see that I'm in charge of this hotel. So move it!" The officer looked stunned, and I took full advantage of the situation. "Mia Ferrari," I introduced myself, "duty manager of the hotel."

Before the officer had a chance to respond, Guy Dobbs, the hotel's security manager, appeared next to me. "Mia," he said uneasily with a strong American accent. "Let Constable Johnson get on with his job. I'm handling this with Smythe."

I wrinkled my nose at the name. Detective Sergeant Phil Smythe couldn't stand my guts, and I hated his. So it was my tough luck that he happened to be on duty this evening. "Dobbs," I addressed him in a stern voice for the benefit of the still-stunned Constable Johnson. "Unless Mr Rourke joins us I'm in charge right now, so you better fill me in on the situation."

I caught the raised eyebrows on Constable Johnson's face; then he turned and walked away, leaving me alone with Dobbs.

"What's the matter with you, girl?" Dobbs flew at me when the young cop was gone. "Can't you see we have a dead body on top of the piano?"

My ego had a way of taking over when my authority was questioned, but now I came down off my high horse. "Sorry, Dobsy." I reverted to my usual, friendly way. "You know how I get around cops."

Dobbs could never stay mad at me when I called him by his pet name. He simply sighed and led the way toward Smythe, making sure we stayed close to the crime tape so we wouldn't interfere with the scene around us. The progress was slow, but it gave me time to take in what was going on.

There were at least ten uniforms walking around the place, some taking photos; others talking to eyewitnesses and taking down notes. The forensics team hadn't yet arrived, but it didn't take an Einstein to work out what had happened. It was obvious the person on the piano had jumped from one of the high floors and plunged down the hotel atrium, landing straight on top of the baby grand. The only thing that registered in my mind was the fact that there was barely any damage to the actual piano, but the body on top of it told a different story. It was splayed in a grotesque way across the top of the instrument's lid with the head at an impossible angle. The arms and legs were spread apart and blood had leaked out of the mouth, nose, and ears.

The body was that of a young Asian female with long black hair spread out all around her, some of it caked in semi-dried blood. The victim was dressed in a pink satin robe; but she was barefoot and naked save for the flimsy garment, and one small breast peeked out from her open neckline.

"Oh, my God!" I was still somewhat shocked despite my earlier bravado. "What happened? Who is she?"

Dobbs's crinkled black face looked back at me for a moment. "She's a suicide. I talked to a few guests who saw her jump from the top floor. That's all we know so far."

I shook my head in disbelief. In all the years I had worked at the Cross we'd never had a public suicide like this. We had heaps of guests who came to the hotel to commit suicide in one of its luxury rooms, but most of them went in style—a drug overdose while stretched out on a plush, quilt-covered bed or cut wrists in a bubble bath. Never, ever, had I seen such a mess before—not at one of the most luxurious boutique hotels in Australia. I mean, why pay a fortune for a room you didn't intend to enjoy? May as well jump off the Harbour Bridge for free and be done with it.

"Ferrari!" A grating male voice called out, making me wince. "I might've known you'd be on duty tonight."

It was Smythe—my archenemy. I felt Dobbs place a placating hand on my shoulder, but it was too late. "Listen, Smythe," I spat out and planted my slight five-foot frame in front of his athletic six-three. "I don't need your crap tonight of all nights, okay? We have a big function upstairs, commemorating the tenth anniversary of Rourke Hotels and filled with VIPs of all kinds; then, we have a guest who decided to take a leap onto the piano down here. So cut me some slack and buzz off!"

I registered Dobbs's sigh of resignation. He knew how much I hated Smythe and the only option open to him now was damage control; and like the good man he was, he went straight into it. "Mia, if you'd be kind enough to manage some of this crowd of onlookers and make way for the forensics team, I'll finish with the detective."

I aimed a look at him that would have instantly withered a camel in the desert, but when I saw the pleading look in his eyes, I backed down. He was right. No point getting into an argument with that pig Smythe while I had a job to do. Besides, David would be coming downstairs at any moment and I had to report to him on what had happened.

I took a deep breath and threw daggers at Smythe with an icy glare; then I addressed Dobbs as if Smythe didn't exist. "Very well. I've got to wait for Mr Rourke, in any case; so I'll hook up with you later."

I didn't even acknowledge Smythe when I turned my tail and walked off, but not before I heard him comment to Dobbs: "How do you put up with her?"

I never heard Dobbs's response but left him to it. He was an ex-cop and knew how to deal with smartarses like Smythe. Not only this, but he had been my father's best friend when they were both on the force years ago and I trusted him.

David wore a frown on his face while he waited for me by the lifts.

"We're not sure who she is, Mr Rourke. Dobbs is trying to find out, but she's definitely a guest." I reported when I reached him.

"How do you know?"

"She was wearing some kind of robe," I replied, "so unless she's a local hooker who sneaked in, she's got to be a guest."

David sighed tiredly and ran fingers through his wavy brown hair. His green eyes looked directly into mine with concern. "Are you okay?"

My heart leapt with joy. He still cares for me. Shut up, Mia! There's a dead body less than twenty feet away, and you're behaving like a silly virgin. "I'm fine," I responded in as grave a tone as I could muster. "We'll know more when we identify her. My advice is you return to the function and try to keep your guests in there until we clear all this up. I'm sure they won't appreciate any undue exposure when the press get here." I was rewarded with a smile that could have launched a thousand ships and sighed; but then I remembered where I was and stood ramrod straight.

"What would I do without you?" David remarked, looking relieved. "I'm glad you're on the job tonight."

I nodded but didn't trust myself to speak.

"I will take your advice. There are many important people here who'd be grateful to you for your foresight. Please ring me if you need anything." He cast one last look at me, perhaps to ascertain I was truly okay, and then stepped into the first lift that arrived.

At that moment, the sliding lobby doors swished open and two forensic officers walked in. I made my way over and led them to the scene through the crowd. Dobbs approached me after the forensics team thanked me and set to work.

"Still checking for identity. Smythe wants to talk to every guest on the tenth floor. He thinks someone must've seen something or that maybe one of them will come forward and identify her."

I felt my blood boil but knew I couldn't stop Smythe from investigating. After all, he had the authority to do so. I was only the duty manager of the hotel and my role was to cooperate in any way possible. Normally, I would have been more than happy to be of help, but Smythe was one of the reasons I hadn't got into the force and this still rankled even after twenty-something years.

The last thing I wanted now was a major disruption with our in-house guests. It was bad enough we already had the bar patrons looking on, and there was still the risk that some of the guests from the function might leave early and stumble upon the scene. I wanted to avoid having the police knocking on every door and asking questions. I was happy to do this with Dobbs and his guys, but somehow I knew Smythe would never stand for it. Therefore, the only thing I could do until the body was taken away and the scene cleared was stall.

"Tell Smythe before we go around disturbing everybody, he should take a look at the CCTV footage," I suggested, glancing at my watch. "It's past ten o'clock and some of the guests will be asleep. It'll come as a shock if we go pounding on their doors."

Dobbs looked doubtful. "Hey, you forget I'm not a cop anymore. Why should Smythe listen to me?"

"Because you saved his arse a long time ago when he almost got stabbed by that crazed druggie," I reminded him. "So he owes you."

"Mia, I'm done calling favours from him on that account," Dobbs pointed out. "I think he's repaid me over and over."

"Tough!" I replied, wishing the druggie had stabbed the bastard after all. "He owes you his life and he should never forget it."

Dobbs's eyebrows lifted with skepticism and almost touched his graying and frizzy hairline. "Whatever you say, but I don't think—"

"Don't worry about anything. Just try to persuade him, at least until we clean up this mess. Later, he can go and talk to the guests." I hoped to pacify him, but of course I had no intention of giving in so easily. With Smythe and his lot out of the way, I was going to talk to the guests discreetly, and hopefully find the identity of our dead woman before the cops had a chance to finish checking out the CCTV footage.

Dobbs still looked unsure and I knew it was time to work my charm. I threw an arm around his shoulders and started to steer him in Smythe's direction. "Come on, Dobsy. You know Smythe respects your opinion, so he'll listen to you. After all, you have years and years over him on the force—both here and in Five-O." I knew this would do it.

Smythe admired Dobbs because he had been a homicide detective in Hawaii before emigrating and joining the local force in Sydney. Smythe had grown up with the likes of Steve McGarrett and he positively idolised the older man for having worked over there. I knew this and shamelessly took advantage of it whenever I could.

A white smile in a black face told me Dobbs saw right through me. "Okay, I'll do it, Ferrari." He always called me by my surname when he knew I was up to no good. "I'll send a few of my guys to give you a hand, too. I want you to post a couple of them at the door. Don't want the press coming in."

I could have kissed him but didn't want to embarrass him. So I gave his shoulders a tight squeeze and sent him on his way to call in yet another favour.

I waited patiently around the lobby and within half an hour Dobbs disappeared into the back-of-house area with Smythe and some of his officers. Meanwhile, the forensics team was preparing to take away the body. It seemed they were satisfied it was a clear case of suicide, at least for now.

I made a call on my mobile. "Richard, any press lurking about?" He was one of the guys Dobbs had sent me to post at the door.

"No, Mia. All clear out here."

"Okay, stay put until the cops leave." I rang off and motioned for one of Dobbs's other guys to join me.

"Nat," I instructed the young, stocky security officer, "stay here with the guys and make sure everything is tidied up when the forensic team leaves." Nat nodded and strode off. This left the way clear for me to go and start my inquiry on the tenth floor.

As it happened, however, I needn't have worried about disturbing the guests. As soon as I exited the lift on the top floor, I saw a man in a tuxedo rushing toward me. He was tall, around forty, and rather good looking if you were into redheads. "Sir?" I had a vague feeling of recognition going through me.

"I'm James Geering," the man stated, stopping short in front of me and looking rather frazzled. "That, down there, is my wife."

CHAPTER 2

I knew the woman did not commit suicide the moment I stepped into James Geering's suite. Of course I wasn't going to share this information with Smythe—not yet, anyway. Let him do his own investigation and waste hours of unproductive time. He deserved it after his treatment of me earlier in the evening.

The fact that I was even in the room was a miracle in itself. After bumping into Geering, I had immediately notified Dobbs, and within minutes he joined me along with Smythe and a couple of uniforms. Dobbs asked Geering if we could go to his room to talk, and as the two men started to walk down the corridor I made to follow, but a hand shot out and strong fingers wrapped themselves around my wrist.

"Not so fast, Ferrari," Smythe spoke two inches from my face. "This doesn't concern you anymore."

I took a deep breath in order to control myself, for as much as I wanted to punch his nose and break it, this wouldn't do. "Listen, Smythe, I know you don't like me, and the feeling is mutual. The fact is, however, in the space of a few minutes I was able to identify the victim while you boys were watching videos. And thanks to me, we now have the husband to question. So I'd say this pretty much puts me in the playing field."

The thunderous look this elicited from Smythe told me he wanted to throttle me for being a wisearse, but I didn't care. The guy was a scum bucket and reminded me of my ex, so I disliked him even more. Therefore, if I could make trouble for him, I would do so at every opportunity.

I shook my arm free of his hold and threw him a scathing look. "This is my hotel and if you don't want me in on the questioning, then I suggest you take Geering to the cop shop instead. But as long as he's under my roof, we play this my way." Of course I was bluffing. Smythe could've overruled me at any time. After all, I had no right to obstruct a formal police investigation.

"Okay," Smythe acquiesced, totally taking me by surprise. I was so sure he was going to refuse that I was almost disappointed. "But you stay quiet, you hear?" He didn't wait for me to respond but turned on his heel and made off toward Geering's room with his two uniforms in tow. I followed after them, still not believing my luck.

Geering was sitting on a sofa chair, head between his hands, while Dobbs opened a small bottle of Johnnie Walker from the mini-bar, poured the contents into a glass, and handed him the drink.

"Mr Geering, my condolences," Smythe began upon entering the room.

Geering simply shook his head in acknowledgement, and Dobbs gazed in my direction and motioned with his head for me to stand by the closed door. I did so and remained quietly in the background taking in the whole scene as yet again I was hit by the fact that Mrs Geering could not have committed suicide.

Smythe took a seat opposite Geering while the rest of us remained standing. "Mr Geering, I'm Detective Sergeant Phil Smythe from the Kings Cross police. Sir, I know this is a huge shock, but I need to ask you some questions if you don't mind."

Geering looked up, his eyes red from crying, and took a sip of his whisky. "I understand, Detective. Please excuse me for the state I'm in."

"There is nothing to excuse," Smythe replied. "Just a few questions and we'll leave you in peace. We can finish the rest at the station tomorrow."

Geering nodded. "Very well."

"Please tell us what you know," Smythe stated while he jotted something down in a small leather-bound notebook. Meanwhile, the uniforms stood side by side and Dobbs was not too far away from me, taking his own notes.

"Well," Geering began, "my wife, Linda, and I were to attend Mr Rourke's function tonight, but she said she had a headache and insisted I go alone." Geering paused to sniff and I immediately stepped forward and handed him a small packet of tissues I happened to be carrying with me. "Thank you." He gave me a weak smile as he took them.

Smythe threw me a warning look, communicating I should stay where I was and not interfere. This got my back up—how inconsiderate could a person be? I mean, the poor man had just lost his wife and needed tissues to wipe his tears. If Smythe didn't like what I had just done, he should've had one of his lackeys fetch the tissues.

"You were saying?" Smythe prompted Geering.

"Well, I attended the event on my own but decided to come back early to check on Linda, and that's when I saw the commotion in the lobby. I ..." At this point, Geering broke down and cried into the wad of tissues he was holding.

Smythe waited patiently until Geering got a hold on his emotions. I rolled my eyes but kept my sarcastic thoughts to myself. Heaven forbid someone should feel pain of any kind in front of him. Smythe reminded me more and more of my ex-husband, and I had to squash a strong desire to reach for a gun and shoot the bastard through the head—something I should have done with the ex as well.

"I'm sorry." Geering's words broke into my thoughts as he dried his tears and then took a large gulp of his drink. "I looked down on the commotion in the lobby and that's when I saw Linda's body on the piano. I ... I just went into shock. I didn't know what to do."

"So what happened then?" Smythe scribbled in his notebook while he spoke.

"I ran into our room first. I thought maybe I'd made a mistake. I thought Linda would be in bed, but she wasn't."

"Did you notice what the time was?"

"I left the function at around nine-thirty, so it was probably around quarter to ten by this time." Geering seemed more in control now. His tears were gone and so was his drink.

"Okay, please go on." Smythe went on scribbling.

"Well, I went back out with the intention of going down to the lobby to talk to the police, but then I came across the duty manager lady." Geering nodded in my direction. "I told her it was my wife down there, and she immediately called you."

At this point, I had to ask myself whether Geering had gotten his times mixed up. The body was still on the piano just after ten and the forensics team didn't give the go-ahead to take it away until around half past the hour. This was when I'd finally gone to the tenth floor to carry out my inquiry and bumped into Geering. In my estimation, the man was about forty-five minutes out of kilter.

"Mr Geering," Smythe spoke, breaking into my thoughts, "do you know of any reason as to why your wife would commit suicide?"

Geering sighed and placed his head back in between his hands. "Linda lost her father a few months ago. They were very close, you see. Plus she discovered certain things about him that came as a shock. Since then she started taking anti-depressants, but I'm not sure she would've committed suicide. I really don't think she had it in her."

Smythe did not ask about Linda's father. Everybody knew about him. It had made the headlines not so long ago. Geering's wife was Linda Liu, daughter of the Chief of Narcotics for the Hong Kong police. According to the news, Mr Liu was assassinated after he allegedly made a deal to testify against the leader of a major drug ring. There were rumours Mr Liu had been connected to the organisation and involved in money-laundering activities. With Liu dead, the Hong Kong police had lost their key witness in the prosecution against one of the biggest drug lords in the country.

Married to Geering, a successful Australian businessman, Linda had been ignorant of her father's activities, but after Mr Liu's assassination the Hong Kong police wanted her to testify in the case. They still had reason to believe she may have possessed information about some of her father's associates.

Smythe snapped shut his notebook. "I think this'll do for now," he informed Geering. "As you know, an autopsy will have to be carried out."

Geering nodded, probably not trusting himself to speak. I imagined how terrible it must be for him to have a loved one autopsied, but this was police procedure and couldn't be helped.

Smythe stood and shook Geering's hand. "I'm sorry we had to put you through this tonight. We will have more questions for you, but they can wait until tomorrow. Is this where we can contact you?"

"I'm in the hotel for the whole week. I have business regarding the launch of a new restaurant, but in light of what's happened I'll extend my stay." Geering drew out a business card from his jacket pocket. "Here's my mobile number."

Smythe thanked him, and he and his uniforms took their leave. Dobbs saw the cops out while I remained in the room with Geering.

"Mr Geering, please accept my condolences."

Geering regarded me with interest. "Thank you. You've been very helpful, and I appreciate it. What's your name?"

"Mia Ferrari, sir," I responded and drew out my business card. "If you need anything, day or night, please feel free to contact me. I'll be happy to be of assistance in any way I can."

Geering took the card, glanced at it, and gave me what appeared to be a smile. "Thank you, Ms Ferrari. I won't forget your kindness."

"May I get you anything before I go, sir, or do you wish me to contact anybody for you?"

"No, thank you," he replied. "I'm going to get some sleep now. I'm very tired."

"Um... Sir, would you like for us to change your room?" I felt uneasy asking this, but I couldn't see how the man was going to be able to relax in the same room he had shared with his wife only hours ago.

"No need," he answered. "Goodnight for now."

I nodded and stepped out of the room quietly, leaving him to his thoughts, and went in search of Dobbs. I found him in his office, tidying up his desk in preparation to go home. It was past eleven and our shifts had long finished. "Hey, fancy a drink?" I called out from the doorway.

Dobbs gave me a tired smile and nodded. "If you don't mind being seen with an old man like me."

"C'mon, Dobsy," I returned flirtatiously, "you know you're still a stud at sixty. Mrs Dobbs told me so." I grinned.

Dobbs perked up at this and let out a belly laugh. "Ha! I knew my old lady still had the hots for me."

"Well, you'd better ring her and tell her you're going out with a hot, younger chick," I teased.

"Didn't I tell you, girl? Eileen's in Hawaii visiting our daughter."

"Oh, that's right. When's the baby due?" I asked, knowing this was the reason why his wife had gone to be with their only daughter. Dobbs hadn't been able to take the time off as we were short-staffed, but he planned a quick visit back home after the baby arrived.

"In the next two days or so. At least that's what the doctor says."

"Well then, it looks like I'm going out with a soon-to-be grandpa." I chuckled. "And to think I never had it on for older men."

Dobbs threw me a fatherly look and wasn't joking anymore

when he remarked, "Maybe you should consider someone older, Mia. Look at the bad luck you've had so far."

"You mean with younger men?" I couldn't help but sound bitter about this. My ex had been five years younger than I, and David Rourke was ten—except David and I had never been in a real relationship. "Hey, don't worry about me. The ex was an arsehole who couldn't even find himself with a GPS," I replied with false gaiety. "In any case, I like them younger. You know, easier to train." I smirked.

Dobbs gazed back at me with a frown. "You're forty-eight already, though you look much younger, but when are you going to stop playing games?"

"Okay, *Father* Dobbs, don't worry about me. Older men bore me—except you, of course." I gave him a saucy look and was rewarded with a reluctant smile.

"You're a real smartass, girl. But I guess you know what you're doing even though you like playing with the bad boys. C'mon, let's go and get that drink." He locked the filing cabinets and switched off the office light.

I knew Dobbs cared for me as a father and didn't want me to get hurt, but his view was clouded. He thought all marriages were happy simply because his had been blessed from the start. In this respect Dobbs was a bit naïve. He'd never had to contend with the secrecy and infidelity of a spouse.

My thoughts soon changed to other matters as we hit the streets of Kings Cross around midnight. Though the place had been cleaned up in the last few years, it still remained Sydney's red-light district; and it seemed this went hand in hand with tourism. Rourke International had selected the right location when they opened their Sydney hotel a decade ago. Of course security was always a problem in the area, but this only meant we had a bigger budget and more manpower. It also meant that unlike other hotels downtown we always had some sort of occurrence, and there was never a dull moment at work.

The streets were still teeming with people at this time of night as we weaved our way toward Bill's Café Bar through a mix of tourists out on the town along with the seedier side of life, which included members of different biker gangs, druggies, and prostitutes. Bill's was a popular twenty-four hour hangout frequented by cops, the nearby navy personnel at Garden Island, and local hotel staff such as ourselves.

We settled on a couple of stools at the bar, seeing as all the tables were packed with people, and ordered two beers. I was quite hungry, having had little time to eat earlier in the evening, and ordered one of Bill's famous pizzettas. Dobbs followed suit but decided on nachos. Our beers were served and we chitchatted about work matters until the food arrived.

"So what gives?" Dobbs finally turned the conversation to real business through the noise and jazz music blaring in the background. "I know you didn't drag me here just for a hot date."

I came straight to the point. "I don't think Linda Liu committed suicide," I remarked while taking a bite of the delicious ham and pineapple pizzetta.

Dobbs frowned. "Mia," his tone held a hint of warning, "what are you up to? We had like a hundred witnesses that saw Linda jump. Besides, we caught the whole thing on CCTV."

"Well, I don't care," I insisted. "Something's not right."

"What's not right, Ferrari?" His gaze narrowed while he regarded me with a suspicious look that was akin to a frown with a look of alarm thrown in.

I ignored the gaze he usually reserved for me when I was up to something of which he did not approve and finished eating my pizzetta. I took a long swig of the cool beer before I responded. "Something happened this afternoon, and it wasn't until after we entered Geering's suite that I realised I'd been there hours earlier; and then I knew for sure."

Dobbs sighed and popped a corn chip laden with sour cream in his mouth. "I'm going to regret this, but I know you're going to tell me anyway. So what is it you know for sure?"

I moved closer to him so I could speak directly into his ear. Despite the noise around us, I didn't want to risk anyone hearing what I had to say. "Linda Liu saw me walking past when I was doing some room checks today and called me into her suite. She asked me to make her an appointment with the hotel's hairdresser for that afternoon." I let this sink in and knew I had Dobbs's full attention when the white of his eyes grew large.

"You mean—" he started to say.

"Yes. She had every intention of attending the Rourke function.

Besides, even if what Geering tells us is true, that she got a headache, why would someone who's contemplating suicide make a hair appointment?"

"So why didn't you tell Smythe, for God's sake?" Dobbs reprimanded me.

"Why should I help that arsehole?" I took another swig of my beer.

Dobbs shook his head, trying to reason with me. "Mia, this is an official matter. If you have information that can help the police, you can't withhold it."

"I'll tell him when the time is right," I said smugly. "Let the bastard do some work on his own for a change. I mean, I already helped by finding out the identity of the victim, didn't I? Do I have to solve the case for him, too?" The thought of helping Smythe was enough to make the pizzetta I had just ingested threaten to come back up.

"You really have to let go of this animosity between you." Dobbs tried to appeal to my better judgement. "Not only can you get into trouble for concealing information, but you're only hurting yourself by being hateful to the man."

I finished my beer and motioned the barman for another. "I will never forgive Smythe for interfering with my application to the force."

"They had height restrictions in those days," Dobbs pointed out.

"Yes, I know. But it was all about to change and I would've made it in. Smythe just didn't like me for some reason and he talked the panel into rejecting me on some pretext or other," I replied in a resentful tone.

"Okay," Dobbs reasoned, "but you could've reapplied at a later date. Why didn't you?"

I gazed at him and took in his tired eyes. Time to go home and get some sleep, I thought. I wasn't exactly bouncing with energy myself. "God knows," I sighed. "I guess time got away from me, and then I married that prick and put it all aside for good."

I couldn't help the anger that still coursed through me every time I thought of my ex-husband. I had been such a fool to give up so many of my dreams for him; but I didn't want to think about this now.

"Come on, let's get out of here." I took some money out of my wallet. "This one's on me." Dobbs and I usually took turns at paying.

We were back out in the street, walking toward the hotel at around one in the morning, when I realised I had an early shift starting at seven. I would be lucky to get five hours of sleep, if that.

"Mia," Dobbs said when we reached the car park at the hotel, "what about this information regarding Linda Liu? When are you going to tell Smythe?"

I unlocked my car door and turned to him. "When I know more. If he's the big shot cop he thinks he is, then maybe he'll have the brains to figure it out for himself."

Before Dobbs could say anything else to persuade me to talk with Smythe I was in my car and driving out of the car park with a simple wave of the hand.

CHAPTER 3

I was having breakfast the next morning in Thorny's office and could barely keep my eyes open as I watched through the window at the frenzied activity in the main kitchen. "How many for breakfast this morning?"

Thorny sipped on her cappuccino but kept an eagle eye on her crew. She never allowed herself to become distracted by anything while on duty. "Over a thousand covers."

"That many?" I exclaimed. "We usually do around six hundred at most."

"Big tour group from Japan." Thorny sighed with frustration. "God, they're driving me insane. They're staying here for a whole week and all they ever eat is bloody steak!"

I laughed. "You mean for breakfast?"

She rolled her eyes. "And dinner, too. On top of that, I've got the purchasing manager sourcing around eight hundred frozen beef packs for them to take back home."

"You know the Japanese; they love their beef." I laughed again. It was fun hanging around the kitchen. One thing was for sure, it was never boring; and one was usually well fed, I thought, tucking into my freshly prepared scrambled eggs and strongly brewed coffee, compliments of my friend.

Thorny drained her cup and leaned across the desk, her chin propped on one hand. "So what gives with this James Geering business?"

I stifled a yawn, feeling absolutely exhausted. It had been around two by the time I got to bed, and after much tossing and turning I finally fell asleep only to be awakened by the alarm at six o'clock. In total, I had had around three hours of shuteye.

"Man, your eyes look positively bloodshot," Thorny observed.

I wanted to hit her. She was twelve years younger than I. At her age, I could go all night without a wink of sleep and still come up looking like a dewy English rose. In my late forties, however, I could no longer pull this off, and even if I tried I'd probably come up looking like a *spewy* rose—albeit an Italian one, I thought with amusement. I looked around for a mirror so I could check out my baby blues but couldn't find one. Perhaps this was a blessing. I was willing to bet they were swimming in the Red Sea by now.

"What about James Geering?" I shot back at her—better to forget about my eyes. I was surprised when I caught a soft blush on her face or perhaps I imagined it.

"Just wondered what happened last night," Thorny said. "I mean, the guy's so well-known and all."

"And rather good looking if you like the Robert Redford type," I added.

Yes, she did blush; her cheeks had taken on a rosy hue. Thorny had a crush on James Geering. It was weird to see her go like this over a man. The only times I saw her with a flushed face was when she was in a rage and terrifying some poor junior chef or a careless kitchen hand.

"What exactly happened?" Thorny was back in control, her eagle eye once again trained on the main kitchen.

"Well, we're not really sure." I finished eating and pushed back my plate. "Geering's wife allegedly threw herself from the top floor of the hotel and landed squarely on the baby grand. The police ruled it a suicide, but they need to wait for confirmation from the coroner." This was all I was willing to divulge about the case. Much as Thorny was a dear friend, I only ever confided my suspicions to Dobbs.

"It's kind of creepy, don't you think?" Thorny remarked. "From all the media reports they're supposed to be happily married. Why would she commit suicide?"

"God only knows. Maybe he's doing the housekeeper or something," I replied. "I suppose we'll find out more if the police decide to come back to us as a matter of courtesy. Once the cops get involved, our responsibility's pretty much over."

"What did Rourke have to say?"

Now it was my turn to blush. Thorny always referred to David as "Rourke". I had the impression she didn't exactly like him, but I didn't know why. David was a good boss to all his staff. "What could he say?" I drank the rest of my now cooling coffee. "I gave him the report last night and as far as the hotel is concerned, case closed. Of course, the media is all over it this morning. David is making some sort of formal statement to pay our condolences to Geering and his family. Any other questions will have to be directed to the police."

"You still care for him," Thorny observed, obviously not interested in what David had to say to the media.

I sighed. "Sure I do; but it could all be an illusion, you know."

"How so?"

"Well," I explained, "remember the film *Sliding Doors*?"

Thorny nodded.

"It was the same for David and me. In the film, Gwyneth Paltrow misses the train because the doors slide shut in her face. As a result, her life takes a different turn from the one she would've followed if she'd caught the train."

"I know all that. So what's your point?" Thorny sounded impatient, and by the look in her eyes I could tell she was ready to go back to the kitchen to crack the whip.

"When I met David, I was thirty years old and he was ten years younger than I. I was looking for commitment and he was barely starting his education in hotel management. Then, along comes Nathan and sweeps me off my feet. He was closer to my age, ready to settle—or so I thought at the time—and I went for the wrong guy, didn't I?" I frowned while I ran the whole episode inside my head. "The worst part," I added, "is that David ended up marrying a girl my age, only a few months after I married Nathan, and they had a child almost immediately. As for me, I had nothing but trouble. How ironic is that? And now I'll always wonder what would've happened if I'd married David. I loved him more than I did Nathan, you know," I confessed.

Thorny regarded me with sympathy. "So why go for Nathan in the first place despite his so-called readiness to settle?"

I felt tears rise to my eyes but blinked quickly and made them go away. "I guess I was too afraid to take the risk with David. He was so young." I made as if my pager vibrated. "Look, I have to go." Better to make a hasty exit. I hated talking about what might have been. "Thanks for breakfast. I really needed it."

Thorny smiled. "You're welcome as always; but Mia, don't beat yourself up over the sliding door factor. You did what you thought was right at the time, you know. We all come to a crossroads in life and have to choose what path we will take. Whatever you chose at the time was obviously right for you."

This was very Zen-like coming from someone who loved ruling with an iron fist and conjuring terror in her staff. "You mean the lies, the infidelity and the final betrayal were right for me?" The sarcasm in my voice was unmistakable, but I just couldn't get rid of the bitterness that came up every time I thought of Nathan.

"I know you've heard this a hundred times before, but I'll say it again to remind you—*what doesn't destroy me makes me stronger.*" She grinned and patted my arm. "You're the person you are today because of what happened in the past; and I think that person's pretty wonderful."

I felt a warm feeling towards her. "Thank you for your friendship," I returned, almost getting emotional again.

"Don't mention it," Thorny said in her usual no-nonsense manner. She grabbed her chef's hat and popped it on her head. "I'm off to check on the troops." She then left the office and I watched her out in the kitchen, yelling at a young Asian chef who had burned an omelette. I smiled in sympathy at the poor guy and made my way out of the kitchen and toward the hotel lobby.

"There you are!" A commanding female voice brought me to a stop as I was halfway up the stairs from the back-of-house corridor, which led to the public area of the hotel. I looked upward and found Elena Rourke standing on the top landing, looking like a catwalk model in a white designer pantsuit. She was reed-thin with long blonde hair and the brightest blue eyes I had ever seen.

I squashed rising feelings of animosity and responded in a professional manner. "Good morning, Mrs Rourke. How may I help you?"

Elena flicked a strand of hair from her face and regarded me with cat-shaped eyes. "My husband sent me in search of you." She placed emphasis on the last word as if she couldn't understand why David would ever need to see me.

I felt like slapping her beautiful face, wiping off her superficial smile that revealed her perfect pearly whites. "He's finished with the press then?" I maintained a cool demeanour.

Elena shrugged her slim shoulders. "How should I know? I'm only delivering the message because I'm on my way to speak to the head chef about dinner tonight. We have a VIP function and I want to go over the menu with her." She came down the stairs and walked past me, all five feet ten inches of her, and I felt like a dwarf by comparison. "He's in the lobby somewhere. Please don't keep him waiting," she called out without even turning back to look at me.

I didn't bother to reply and made my way up the stairs and out to the lobby where I espied David talking with Dobbs by the reception area. For a moment I had to wonder why David had married the "ice queen" as Elena was known throughout the hotel. The woman threw orders at the staff left, right, and centre without caring about the fact that, although married to the boss, she was not a hotel manager.

"Mr Rourke," I uttered when I reached them, keeping my eyes downcast so they wouldn't give me away. "Mrs Rourke told me you were looking for me."

I heard David sigh but didn't search his face to find the reason. Perhaps he was frustrated with his wife throwing orders about. But no, she'd said he had asked her to give me the message. No use analysing this to death; whatever the reason for his sigh, I was here now and waiting for what he had to say.

"Mia, I've just been discussing with Dobbs about debriefing the staff regarding what happened. I don't want anyone talking to the media."

"I'll get human resources to organise a couple of groups so we don't have everybody off the floor at the same time," I suggested, and nodded toward Dobbs for his feedback.

"We can do it in the ballroom," Dobbs remarked.

"Good job." David's tone held praise. "I knew I could count on the two of you. Shall we say at ten and eleven respectively?"

I glanced at my watch. "It's only eight now, so yes. This should give us enough time to do all the check-outs and get the staff ready." I risked a brief peek at David just then and caught him smiling down at me. That smile could melt icebergs! So how come the lovely Elena was such a cold bitch? I pushed the uncharitable thought out of my head.

"Oh, another thing," David added, "tonight we're hosting a dinner party for a few of the top CEOs in Sydney. James Geering was invited, but under the circumstances I'm not sure if he'll be attending. I thought—"

"Don't worry, sir," I interrupted. "I'll call on Mr Geering and see how he's faring."

"Thank you for that. I'll see you both at ten." He turned and walked off.

Only after David left did I notice Dobbs's eyes on me. "What?" I asked, feeling irritable.

Dobbs let out a deep, rich laugh. "Are the 'reds' due to lack of sleep or because you had to deal with the ice queen?"

"Fuck off," I whispered, and started to make my way to human resources with Dobbs in tow. He was still laughing good-naturedly; he knew I didn't mean it when I swore at him.

"Oh, I love these Italians. They have such a temper. By the way, any relation to Enzo Ferrari, the car manufacturer?" He loved teasing me.

"Much as I love Ferraris, the answer is no."

"Okay. And didn't you once say you were descended from the Medici?"

"Shove off, Dobbs." I maintained my pissed-off façade. "You know the Medici died out sometime in the 1700s."

We were in the back-of-house area again, and he let out a loud whoop of laughter when he asserted, "That's the Medici born on the right side of the blanket, Ferrari; so this would make you a bastard."

I cracked up then and laughed along with him. "You're incorrigible, you know that?" I mock-slapped him on the head. "Hey, any word from Smythe?" I was serious again.

"Not a one," Dobbs replied. "Give me a few days and I'll get something out of him on poker night."

I stopped walking and turned to him. "You play poker with that scum?"

Dobbs seemed bewildered at the hatred in my voice. "What's wrong if I fleece him out of a few dollars?"

"But he's always lording it over us, Dobbs," I argued. "Even when you and my father were on the force he was like that. Dad never liked him."

"Like father, like daughter," Dobbs returned. "Mia, the guy's not that bad. Honestly. He's done us a number of good turns in the past."

"Only because you saved his arse that time!" I protested.

"Whatever the reason, I intend to keep him on my good side. There may come a time when we might need him."

I threw him my own brand of "ice" by pinning him with my bloodshot eyes. "Dobbs, I'd rather chew glass than reach out for help from *that* person!"

Dobbs grinned. "Well, you're improving, at least. You're no longer calling him scum." He laughed again.

"I don't need to listen to this. I'm off to HR. You go check the bloody ballroom!" I walked off in a huff with Dobbs's laughter following me.

CHAPTER 4

It was early afternoon by the time I got around to checking in with James Geering. He answered the door to my knock but didn't invite me in.

"Good afternoon, Mr Geering," I greeted him, taking in his frown of impatience. "I hope I'm not disturbing you, sir."

Geering's frown turned into a smile all of a sudden and he cleared his throat. "Not at all, Ms Ferrari or may I call you Mia?"

He was all charm as he suddenly swung open the door and motioned for me to enter the room.

"Mia's fine; thank you, sir." When I walked in I was hit with the unmistakable scent of vanilla. A crazy thought crossed my mind and for a moment I thought Geering must be baking a cake. I shook my head softly to dispel such a silly notion.

"Can I offer you something to drink?" Geering asked as he made his way to the mini-bar.

I was about to refuse when from the corner of my eye I saw the door leading to the bedroom move slightly and I sensed we were not alone. "I'll just have a Coke, thank you."

"No drinking while on duty, right?" Geering teased.

I smiled and made like I was looking around the room while he fixed the drinks. In reality, I wanted to see if there was someone behind that door. Of course there was no way I would be able to confirm this, unless I came on to the man and suggested we have wild, passionate sex on his bed. I almost laughed. I could just imagine the look on his face if I were to suggest something so outrageous.

"This is one of our nicest suites," I remarked. "It's so full of natural light." I cast my eyes around once again and was hit one more time with the vanilla scent. I was trying to think whether there were any flowers that smelled of vanilla, but before I could focus on this Geering appeared in front of me, offering me a glass of Coke. I took it and thanked him. Unless he had some kind of exotic flowers in his bedroom that I didn't know about, I would never find out the source of the scent. I guess I could have asked Geering, but this wouldn't be a good idea in case it had something to do with his deceased wife.

"So what can I do for you, Mia?" Geering asked as he took a seat on a sofa chair and indicated with his head that I should do the same.

I remained standing. "I'm sorry to barge in on you like this, but I won't stay long. Mr Rourke asked me to check on whether you will be attending the CEO dinner this evening. He wasn't sure if you'd be up to it under the circumstances." I looked down out of respect in case he became teary-eyed.

His response surprised me. "Well, why shouldn't I? Of course I'll be there. Business is business after all." He downed the whisky he had poured for himself and got up to go for another.

I drank my Coke as quickly as possible, trying very hard not to burp from all the bubbles. "Very well, sir. I'll inform Mr Rourke you'll be attending." I held out the glass when he came toward me with his own drink in hand. "Thank you for the drink. I'll leave you in peace now."

Geering held my glance for a moment, and I thought he wanted to say something else. Instead, he nodded and took the glass from my hand. "Thank you, Mia," he simply replied.

I smiled and let myself out of the room, but not before I caught another whiff of the lovely vanilla. I realised then I was starving. I hadn't yet had time for lunch and it was already past two in the afternoon. I was almost at the end of my shift and all I'd had to eat was the breakfast Thorny had prepared for me early this morning. My stomach grumbled in protest.

Two hands covered my eyes then, and I almost jumped out of my skin. "Guess who?" A male voice exclaimed and I relaxed, shaking myself free and turning on the owner of the hands.

"Chris, you gave me the fright of my life!" I admonished a younger-looking version of David Rourke—tall, athletic frame, wavy brown hair, green eyes, and delicious dimples when he smiled. He could have been my son. The boy was only eighteen, though he looked nothing like a boy now as he stood eyeing me with mock-hungry eyes.

"Ms Ferrari, you look sexier every time I see you," he declared with an impish smile that had the same effect on me as his father's.

I told myself to get a grip and stop my cradle-snatching thoughts. "You're a little devil, Christopher," I chided him but smiled a welcome. "When did you get back from holidays?"

He smoothed down his white shirt and black pants, and threw me a boyish grin. "This morning."

"And you're working already? Man, your dad doesn't waste any time," I jested.

Chris was home on semester break from university and he normally worked in the functions department on a casual basis during his time off. Being the son of the hotel owner had nothing to do with Chris's decision to work. His father was well able to keep him, but Chris believed in earning his own way—a belief shared by his dad.

While attending university Chris lived on campus, but during breaks he came to stay at the hotel. David lived in one of the penthouse suites with his wife; though Elena was hardly ever in residence these days, jetsetting all around the world while hubby ran the hotel empire.

"I heard about the suicide," Chris commented and fell into step beside me. "It sounds like it was a bad one."

"They're all bad ones, aren't they? Nothing pleasant about taking one's own life," I remarked.

"Oh, come on, Ferrari," Chris returned. "You know this isn't a garden variety suicide. So what gives?"

I suddenly stopped walking and turned to him, looking up at his handsome face. "You've been talking to Dobbs!" I accused.

I then resumed walking and opened a door that led to the back-of-house area and to the service lifts. I had to get some food into me and my intention was to head for the staff restaurant. "You didn't tell me how your holiday was," I changed the subject, hoping to end the discussion about Linda Liu's apparent suicide. We stepped into the lift together and I pressed the ground floor button.

"I got some skiing done," Chris replied, but it was obvious he wasn't in the mood to talk about his trip to the snow. "Hey, can I help with anything?"

"What makes you think you can help? There's nothing to help with." I was going to kill Dobbs. This could only have come from him.

The lift doors opened and I turned left on the long corridor leading to the restaurant. Chris followed me. "C'mon, Mia," he implored, trying to appeal to my lighter side. "If you think this is a murder, I'm sure I can help."

I said nothing, furious with Dobbs and his big mouth. I walked in silence, with Chris still following, and when we arrived at the staff restaurant I headed for the service counter. "Cheeseburger and fries," I ordered from the attendant.

"Make that two," Chris put in.

I sighed. "Don't you have some work to do?"

He grinned. "Sorry, Ferrari, but I finished a luncheon function, and I'm now on a short break."

"Well, don't let me hold you up," I said dismissively.

He laughed, and if I closed my eyes it could have been David laughing right beside me. A sudden image of Venice flashed into my mind, but I forced it out almost before it took shape. "How are your studies going?" I asked my companion in the hope I could dissuade him from asking more questions about the case. *The case?* Who said this was a case? God, I needed some food.

"Just finished mid-year exams and going great guns," Chris reported cheerfully.

"Your dad must be pleased," I observed.

"Yes, I guess he is. You know, he always wanted me to follow in his footsteps, but he took it well when I told him IT was my world."

"That's a good thing, isn't it? Some parents get upset if their kids don't follow them into the business."

Chris smiled. "Not Dad. I'm lucky that way. But if we're talking about Elena, then it's a different thing altogether." His smile faded and before I could question him further, the attendant came back with our orders.

We took our plates to a table in the far corner of the room and grabbed a couple of sparkling mineral waters from the drinks counter along the way. At this time of day there weren't too many employees in the restaurant, but I didn't want to run the risk of being overheard. Everyone knew Chris was the owner's son; and though well liked, there were always those who enjoyed gossiping about him.

"Chris," I said, biting into my burger with relish. "Why do you call your mother by her first name?" He'd been doing this since I knew him, some five years or so, but it never occurred to me to ask him why. I always thought it was none of my business; but Chris liked me, and I was sure he looked upon me as a kind of pseudo-mother.

"I don't know," he replied, his face giving nothing away. "I guess I never felt close to her. She certainly never made much time for me."

I caught the slightest hint of resentment in his voice but decided not to pursue it further. "So how long are you with us this time?"

Chris shoved some fries into his mouth. "About a month or so."

"That long? I thought the July break was only for two weeks."

"It is, but I'm exempt from some of next semester's units, so I don't need to start until mid-August."

While we ate, Chris and I chitchatted about general things and soon we parted company as we both had to get back to our duties. I bade him goodbye at the lifts and made my way to the security office, my temper rising with every step I took. Dobbs was alone, working on his computer.

"Dobbs!" I called in a loud enough voice to make the man jump up from his chair.

"What the—"

I entered the office and slammed the door shut before I spoke. "How dare you fill Chris Rourke's fertile mind with the facts of the *apparent* suicide?"

Dobbs sighed, looking frustrated. "Ferrari, what's got into that brain of yours? Do you think I'm stupid enough to blab our suspicions to a young, impressionable boy?"

I noticed straight away that he said *our* suspicions, and my temper cooled right down. I took a seat opposite his desk and eyed him with excitement. "So you admit you think there was foul play."

Dobbs's eyes bore into mine. "Now listen here, Ferrari. First you accuse me of blabbing, and now you're taking an interest in my opinion. What is the matter with you, girl?"

"I'm sorry." I managed to look contrite. "I should've known you'd never say anything to Chris, but he seemed to know it wasn't a suicide—and who else knows about this besides you and me?"

"Good question," Dobbs answered thoughtfully.

I made a mental note to speak to Chris about this. I had immediately jumped to the conclusion that Dobbs had said something, but I believed him when he said he hadn't. Therefore, it was apparent someone else agreed with my opinion even though I hadn't shared this with anyone outside of Dobbs.

"Do you think someone overheard us at the bar last night?" My mind was already going through the different possibilities at a hundred miles per second.

Dobbs shrugged. "Anything is possible; although it was quite noisy, and we were careful to keep the conversation close to us."

"Hmm." I searched for other potential answers.

"Maybe the boy put it together from the information he received," Dobbs offered.

"But how could he?"

"Who knows, but just imagine the gossip that ran through this hotel when the suicide happened."

A sudden thought occurred to me. "My God! What if someone saw something but didn't come forward?"

Dobbs nodded. "That is a possibility we can't dismiss. It's only natural if a staff member saw something they may be too afraid to come forward or they simply don't want to get involved."

"Damn!" I felt annoyed with myself. "I should've questioned Chris further when I had the chance. Now, I'm going to have to bring it up with him again and he's already talking about helping me."

Dobbs laughed. "Helping? Who does he think you are; Five-O?"

I threw him an irritated glare. "Be quiet, Dobbs. We might not be the cops, but we can still get to the bottom of this."

"Mia, I'm telling you to leave this alone and let Smythe in on what you know so far."

The mention of Smythe made me writhe in anger. "Stop it! I already told you I'll tell Smythe when I'm good and ready. And if you should get any ideas about saying anything to him, I'll never speak to you again."

"Whoa, there!" Dobbs held up a placating hand in front of me. "You know I don't approve of what you're doing, but I'm willing to go along with you just for now. However …" He paused when he saw my countenance change into one of glee. "*However*," he said with more emphasis on the word, "if things look like they're going to get dangerous you have to promise me you'll go to Smythe. And if you don't, I will."

I mulled over what he said for a few moments. This meant

Dobbs was going to help me. Yes! We were going to crack this case wide open and then throw it at the useless cops. Smythe would have to eat humble pie after this. The thought was almost arousing.

"Very well," I stated in a serious tone. No need to let Dobbs know how I truly felt.

The telephone rang and Dobbs picked up while I ran a movie in my mind of us presenting Smythe with all the facts of the case and handing over the murderer. I saw Dobbs and I dressed in our best hotel uniforms, accepting a medal of honour from the Mayor of Sydney for valour and our undying commitment to civic duty.

"All right!" Dobbs's jubilant exclamation broke through my mental movie and I brought my focus back on him. "What time?" he said, a wide grin on his face. I waited, wondering what was going on. "Okay. I'll make the arrangements," he stated and then lowered his voice and whispered something into the phone, which I didn't quite catch but guessed was of a personal nature.

When he rang off he turned to me, and from the happy look on his face I knew. "The baby."

He nodded and let out a whoop of joy. "I'm a granddaddy!"

"Woo hoo!" I shouted and came around the desk to give him a hug.

Dobbs engulfed me in his arms and almost squeezed the breath out of me. When he let me go, I noticed tears of joy in his eyes.

"So tell me all. What time, boy or girl, how are mum and baby doing?" I peppered him with my eager questions.

"Maggie gave birth to a healthy baby girl about half an hour ago. They're naming her Rose, after my mother," he reported. "It's a shame she's not alive to see her great-grandchild." There was a pause filled with sadness in his joy and I knew he was thinking of the passing of his mother, which had taken place just as Maggie had become pregnant. I sighed with resignation. Why was it that joy always seemed to come laced with some sort of pain? For the sake of my friend, I put on a bright face.

"So when are you off to Hawaii?"

"I'll try to leave this weekend and have next week off."

"Wish I could come with you," I sighed wistfully. Nathan and I had planned a trip to Hawaii as a kind of second honeymoon; only he'd dumped me for another woman just before we were meant to leave. The bastard took our tickets, had mine changed into her name;

and that's how he replaced me within five minutes. He still had his honeymoon, only not with me. At the time, I wished he would drown in one of those large Hawaiian waves. Unfortunately, he made it home ten days later and proceeded to make hell for me in terms of the financial split of our assets.

This had been almost a year ago, and we were still waiting for a court date. All my attempts at trying to negotiate with him had been met with arrogant disdain and a big refusal. He was under the illusion that our home should go to him complete with my equity, which had come from a legacy left to me by my father.

I wasn't sure what the outcome would be in court, but I would as soon shoot the fucking bastard through the head before I let him touch my dead father's money.

"So I guess I'll be back by the week after next." Dobbs had been talking, but I only caught the tail end of what he'd said. This always happened to me when I thought of that piece of scum that had posed as my husband for so many years. Still, I didn't want to spoil Dobbs's moment of happiness; therefore, I forced a smile to my face.

"Well, then, it's all settled. Go home and clean up. Tonight, I'm cooking you dinner at my place and we'll celebrate."

The smile he gave me was all I needed to restore me to a good mood.

"I've got something to finish up in the office and then I'm off duty. I'll see you around seven?" I asked, opening the office door.

"Seven, it is."

I had to get back to David about James Geering's confirmation for the CEO dinner. On my way to the office, I started planning the menu for the evening meal with Dobbs but came to an abrupt stop as I passed the Concierge desk. Something was not right. I looked around the lobby, but all seemed normal.

Then it came to me. The vanilla scent. I could smell it again. I turned slowly around and finally honed in on the source of the scent. Standing by the Concierge desk, talking to one of the boys, was Elena Rourke.

CHAPTER 5

Dobbs attacked his penne primavera with gusto. "I can't believe Elena Rourke is having an affair with Geering," he remarked, pausing just long enough to take a sip of his red wine.

I fidgeted with my hair, my appetite gone. "I don't have another explanation," I observed. "This vanilla scent is obviously some kind of perfume. Elena reeked of it in the lobby."

Dobbs helped himself to salad and a piece of crusty Italian bread. "Well, if it's some kind of perfume what's there to say some other woman wasn't wearing it?"

Good point, I thought, but what were the chances? I figured in a hotel with over two hundred rooms it was possible some other guest may have been wearing the same perfume—or it could have been someone that dropped in to console the grieving Mr Geering, I reflected with suspicion. Even if it wasn't Elena, what was Geering doing with another woman in his room so shortly after his wife took a plunge into oblivion?

I pushed away my plate and got up from the table to put on the coffee. Dobbs finished eating, but I was sure he still had room for espresso and tiramisu.

"You're right, Dobbs. It could have been anybody in that room, but I'm still not letting Elena off the hook as a suspect."

Dobbs finished the last of his wine. "A suspect to what?"

"To murder." I switched on the stove for the espresso maker.

"I still think you're reading too much into this," Dobbs argued. "We have the whole thing on video, remember? No one pushed Linda Liu over the banister. She jumped of her own accord, and don't forget we have a whole bunch of witnesses that saw her do it."

What Dobbs said made perfect sense, but there was still

something nagging away at me. I couldn't say what it was; I just knew things weren't quite what they seemed. "Any news from Smythe?"

"Not yet," Dobbs replied while he cleared the table for me. "If I don't catch him at the poker game I'll ring him before I fly out. I couldn't get a flight until Monday so I'll be dropping by the game on Friday night."

The espresso maker started bubbling and I inhaled the wonderful aroma of freshly ground coffee. Dobbs didn't even wait for me to get dessert. He went straight to the refrigerator and took out the tiramisu slices I had placed on two plates prior to his arrival, one for each of us. I smiled. If I left him to it he'd probably eat both pieces. He had a sweet tooth and his paunchy stomach was a testament to it.

We sat back down at the table. "So how are things with Nathan?" he asked, taking me by surprise. Why bring up the subject of my psychopathic ex when I had better things to think about?

"We're still playing lawyer tag, but I'm putting the apartment on the market," I informed him with a sigh of frustration. "The bastard won't pay his part of the mortgage so he's forcing me out. God, what I'd give for a gun!" I cast a look around the near-new apartment I had purchased with Nathan only months prior to our break up and thought what a waste it had all been—both the marriage and the property investment.

Dobbs gave me a look of sympathy. "I'm so sorry, Mia. Who would've thought he'd turn out to be like that—and after eighteen years of marriage. At least, there weren't any kids."

"Yes, that's a good thing. I guess Nathan, for all his narcissistic tendencies, couldn't make the grade as far as his sperm count was concerned." Then I added bitterly, "And he wouldn't even consider adopting."

"But surely there must've been some good times." Dobbs looked like he regretted having brought up the subject—he frowned, but at the same time he kept stuffing his mouth with tiramisu.

"You know, Dobbs, I just don't know anymore," I replied and sipped my coffee. My dessert remained untouched, and I noticed him casting his eye over it. I smiled and pushed the plate his way. "You have it." I grinned wickedly. "But Eileen isn't going to think you're so hot if you put on any more weight."

We laughed. "I intend to walk it off by carrying my new

granddaughter around for all my friends to see." Dobbs looked happy as he dug into the second dessert with enthusiastic abandon.

I let him enjoy it and sipped my coffee quietly. When was the last time I'd been happy with the ex? To my surprise, I couldn't remember; and it dawned on me that I'd never been truly happy with him. I'd gone for the illusion of happiness, not for the real thing. Unfortunately, at the time, I hadn't been able to tell the difference. I thought about the sliding door factor and expelled another sigh—this one, however, was infused with melancholy.

"Hey." Dobbs patted my arm. "Don't worry, girl. Things will work out in the end."

"I hope you're right. You know, Nathan's the one who dumped me and did all the lying and cheating, and yet he seems to hate me so much. He's out to fight me legally every way he can to get his hands on my money; but it should be the other way around. I've tried to negotiate with him so many times to no avail."

"Well, let's hope the court can do something," Dobbs tried to comfort me.

"It's been close to a year now so I hope they won't keep me waiting much longer." I really didn't want to talk about Nathan anymore. The man should be at the bottom of the ocean with cement shoes on and not living with the floozy he picked up from heaven knows where. I drained my cup. "Want more coffee?" I asked a tired-looking Dobbs. It had been a long day for both of us.

He patted his stomach. "I'm stuffed. That second slice of tiramisu really did it, I'm afraid."

"Isn't gluttony one of the seven deadly sins?" I teased.

He smirked unabashedly. "I'll walk it off, I promise."

I poured myself another coffee and brought the topic back to the suicide. "There's one thing that really bothers me. It's the time lapse between when Geering said he saw the body and when he ran into me."

"How's that?" Dobbs looked curious.

"Well, he said he left the function at around nine-thirty, right? Then he saw the body down below but had to check to make sure he didn't make a mistake, and that it really was Linda down there."

"So?"

"When he met me, it was ten-thirty. How come it took him so long to make sure it was really Linda down there; and why wait to

39

come forward until the forensics were taking away the body?"

Dobbs's brows drew close in thought. "He admitted to the police he left the function early to check on her. When he saw the commotion in the lobby, he went to the room to see whether he was right—that it was indeed his wife down there. So maybe he simply lost track of time."

"Well, let's assume he got his time right about when he left the function. It doesn't take someone forty-five minutes to check whether their wife is in the room."

"Huh? Now you've lost me."

My eyes widened with excitement. I had such a strong feeling we had a murder on our hands. "Don't you see? He leaves the reception at nine-thirty or so," I explained slowly so he could take it in. "I mean, it's like five minutes to take a lift up to the tenth floor from the function room on the mezzanine level, right?"

Dobbs nodded, a look of understanding dawning in his eyes.

"Okay, so he apparently sees the body on top of the piano on the way to his room. He rushes in and sees Linda isn't there. By this time, he says it's probably around quarter to ten or so, and then he rushes back out and bumps into me. But he didn't meet me until ten-thirty, Dobbs. I remember this quite clearly because it was at this time that the forensics team took away the body."

"I'm with you," Dobbs said, more alert now; his look of tiredness gone. "But there is still a chance he got his times mixed up with the shock of it all. It's possible, you know."

I hated it when Dobbs made sense, but he was right. Geering could have gotten his times mixed up. His wife had just committed suicide. Anyone could make a mistake under such circumstances. But there was one way to check this out. "We have to go back to the hotel," I declared.

"Say what?" Dobbs looked at me as if I'd lost my mind.

"Don't you see? We have to check the CCTV footage. If it recorded Linda jumping over the railing, it would have caught the time Geering headed back into his room."

Dobbs frowned. "You're not going to like this, but the police took the tape as evidence."

"Fuck!" I exclaimed and noticed Dobbs's look of surprise. "Bloody Smythe always has to throw a spanner in the works, doesn't he? Well, we just have to get that tape back."

"Are you mad? Smythe won't release it. It's police property now."

I wanted to scream. "Dobbs, why didn't you have them make a copy?"

This time, Dobbs regarded me as if I had truly taken leave of my senses. "Ferrari, how many times do I have to tell you? We're not the cops! This has nothing to do with us anymore."

"So we're going to let that bastard Smythe keep us from investigating this?" I challenged him. "Come on, Dobbs. You know we can still get the information from him. Ask him at the poker game."

"Man, you're one pushy broad," Dobbs protested, and I noted, as I always did, that despite his many years in Australia his American accent was very pronounced, especially when he was frustrated with me.

"Dobsy, come on," I coaxed. "You're off to Hawaii on Monday. Just do this tiny little thing for me and I promise I'll be good."

He cast me a look of disbelief. I smiled and waited. "Oh, okay!" He gave in. "I don't know why I'm doing this, but I'm doing it."

I wanted to throw my arms around him, but showing too much enthusiasm would make him more concerned for me. He already knew I had every intention of looking into this case further and he probably didn't want me to do too much in his absence.

Hmm. *Case* again. Yes, it was a case. This time I could finally call it a case. I could smell it.

The funeral for Linda Liu was arranged surprisingly quickly. She plunged to her death on Tuesday evening and was supposedly autopsied the following day, on Wednesday. The body was then released on Thursday in preparation for a Friday morning service.

David called me into his office when I started my shift on Thursday morning. He was standing behind his desk as I entered and the smudges under his eyes were the first thing I noticed; even so, he still managed to look gorgeous.

At that moment, I would have given anything to be transported back in time to that fateful night in Venice where we'd made love—the one and only time.

"I'm sorry, Mr Rourke. What did you say?" I realised he had been talking while my mind was miles away.

David smiled and suddenly I felt the need to sit down, my legs

41

having grown weak at the knees.

"Mia, you can call me by my first name when we're alone, you know." He seemed amused.

"Of course. Sorry, Mr Rour ... I mean, David." I felt like an idiot. "Um, what did you want to see me about?" I did my best to mask my feelings at the awkward moment.

"Please, sit down," David offered, and took his own seat behind an antique walnut desk in the elegant and classically furnished office. I sat opposite him in one of the visitors' chairs. "James Geering called me this morning to let me know his wife's funeral will be held tomorrow. Unfortunately, I'll be away for a few days meeting with the managers of the other Rourke properties. It's budget review time as you probably know." I nodded and waited for him to continue. "I fly out to Melbourne this evening, so I would like for you and Dobbs to attend the funeral in my place seeing as you were both here when the incident occurred. I'll email you the details."

"Very well," I replied. "When will you be back?"

"In about a week. I also have to cover the New Zealand properties."

Rourke International owned five hotels in Australia and three in New Zealand, so David was in for a very busy time. He was a hands-on CEO, and this probably explained the reason for the smudges under his eyes. Although he had competent managers at each property he always maintained an active interest in the operation of his entire company.

"Will there be anything else?" I asked as I got up from my seat.

He seemed to hesitate for a moment, but then shook his head. "That's all. Thank you, Mia."

I nodded and left the office, but not before the ice queen pushed her way past me to address her husband in a loud enough voice for everyone to hear.

"Do you have a few minutes from your precious schedule?" Her voice was full of sarcasm.

"What do you want, Elena?" I heard David respond with a sigh of exasperation.

"I want some money, David. You know I'm off to Switzerland for the next month and—" She slammed the door behind her, and I couldn't hear anything else. I raised my eyebrows at David's secretary, who smiled at me from behind her desk, which was located outside his door, and walked out of the executive offices only to bump right into Chris.

He put out both hands to steady me. "Mia, sorry; I didn't see you."

"If you're after David you'll have to take a number and get in line," I replied with a cheeky smile.

"Why's that?"

"Elena's in there," I informed him.

"The ice queen." Chris grinned. "Let's get out of here before she comes back out."

"How do you know what the staff call her?" I asked as we walked down the corridor and toward the lifts.

"Oh, please! Everyone knows," he answered in a matter-of-fact tone and did not seem upset.

"Hey," I uttered, suddenly seizing the chance to ask him about his reference to Linda Liu's suicide. "Got time for a cuppa?"

He nodded and we went down to the Lobby Café, which was located opposite the unfortunate site where Linda Liu had jumped to her death. I noticed that sometime in the last couple of days the bar had obtained a new baby grand.

We took a corner booth and ordered cappuccinos. "The other day," I remarked as the waitress walked away with our orders, "what made you say the Linda Liu thing was a murder? Do you know something I don't?"

Chris smiled knowingly. "I knew it!"

"Hey, don't get excited. I didn't say it was murder. You implied it." The last thing I wanted was for the kid to run away with his imagination.

"Look, I've been hanging around you and Dobbs long enough to know that you guys are always suspicious of stuff. Remember the time we hosted the jewellery exhibition, and you uncovered the drug dealer trying to pass off his drugs as some kind of rare crystals?"

I flashed him a warning look. "Be quiet, Chris. It was just a fluke. We caught the guy on camera while he was trying to deal drugs among the confusion of the exhibition. That's all it was."

"Yeah, right," Chris responded with disbelief in his tone. "Anyway, no one said anything about the suicide. I simply thought there was more to it."

Our coffees arrived and we waited until the waitress went on her way. "There must be something that sparked the thought," I finally said while stirring one sugar into my cup.

Chris looked around to make sure no one was listening and then leaned across the table toward me. I waited tensely. "The day I was doing that luncheon function," he whispered, "I saw Geering with another woman."

My heart stopped for a moment and I remembered the vanilla scent. I hoped to God Chris wasn't going to tell me it was his mother he saw with the man. I waited, barely drawing breath.

"I was making my way to the back-of-house area across the mezzanine floor and happened to catch him from the corner of my eye," Chris added and paused to take a sip of his coffee.

"And?" I could barely stand the suspense.

"He was near the entrance to one of the other function rooms, but my view was partially blocked by an open door. All I saw was Geering kissing somebody and a woman's arms wrapped around his neck."

I swallowed hard, preparing myself for what came next.

"That's all," Chris concluded.

"Huh?" I exclaimed almost rudely. "How can that be all?"

Chris shrugged his shoulders. "That's all I saw. He was kissing someone; and I got to thinking a man who barely lost his wife twenty-four hours earlier wouldn't be in the arms of another woman."

I had news for the naïve young man, I thought sarcastically as I pictured Nathan with his cheating bimbo, but now was not the time. "Did you get a look at her?" I felt like shaking him as if this would somehow make him reveal some deep, dark secret that would lead us to the murderer.

"No," Chris replied, and my hopes for a good clue dissolved into thin air. "All I saw was a flash of white. She was obviously wearing a white top or something."

I felt like screaming. We had nothing. Well, not exactly, but it was all conjecture. Geering may only be guilty of having an affair, and though this was bad enough it wasn't murder.

Chris must have noticed the chaotic expressions fleeting across my face and guessed my thoughts because he smiled mysteriously before pointing out, "I know it doesn't necessarily mean murder, but it could be a motive."

CHAPTER 6

Friday was my day off and I didn't relish the thought of having to attend a funeral service. I tried to swap with one of the other duty managers so I could attend during work time. Unfortunately, no one could accommodate me. I knew I could take a day in lieu at some other time, but we were extremely busy and this would have to wait for a while.

I looked out of my bedroom window and took in the dark grey sky—a perfect backdrop for a funeral. Any minute now, it was going to pour with rain. I dressed warmly in black pants and a black turtleneck top, then slipped on black medium-heeled boots, and pulled out my cashmere long coat of the same colour out of the wardrobe. I grinned, thinking all that was missing were the sunglasses and I could almost pass for the guy in *The Matrix*.

The telephone shrilled and almost made me jump out of my skin. It was only seven in the morning; who could be calling at this time? I picked up the receiver. "Mia Ferrari," I answered formally before remembering I was not at work. I shook my head for letting suspicions and thoughts of foul play, which were always on my mind, distract me so much.

"On the job even at home," teased David at the other end of the line.

I was surprised to hear from him, especially as I didn't recall giving him my home number. He must've read my thoughts. "Dobbs gave me your number when I couldn't reach you on the mobile."

This was strange. I fished my mobile out of my handbag and noticed it was switched off. "I must've forgotten to charge it," I told him. "Is anything wrong?"

"No. I only wanted to catch you before I go into my meeting. I hope I'm not calling too early."

"That's okay. I was just about to make coffee," I replied, still waiting for him to tell me the reason for his call.

"Mia, I'm sorry about making you go to a funeral on your day off."

"How did you—" I started to say, but he went on before I finished.

"I rang the hotel, thinking you'd started your shift, and they told me it was your day off today. I guess I should've checked with you when I asked you to attend."

A feeling of warmth spread through me. How sweet of him to care. "It doesn't matter," I reassured him, thankful he couldn't see my blushing cheeks. "I think it's important that I be there to represent the hotel."

"Well, thank you for doing this; and please take tomorrow off," he said, his tone sincere.

"Too busy. We have the Thorpe wedding in the evening," I informed him. "I want to make sure all goes off without a hitch." I was still waiting for him to tell me why he'd tried to call me at the hotel in the first place.

"I ... um ..." He hesitated for a moment and then continued, "Look, I know this is probably an imposition, but I called to ask if you wouldn't mind keeping an eye on Chris while I'm away. Elena's gone to Europe and he's staying in the penthouse on his own."

"You don't even need to ask, David. I'll make sure he doesn't have any wild parties." I laughed to cover my confusion at being asked to do what was obviously a very personal favour to him.

He seemed relieved. "Thank you so much, and ... well, I owe you dinner when I get back."

Now I had to sit down. Was he asking me out? "I ... You ... What I mean to say is you don't have to feel obligated. I truly don't mind keeping an eye on Chris."

"I don't consider this to be an obligation." There was warmth in his voice.

I flashed back to Venice and then forced myself back to the present. "Well, in that case, you're on." I accepted casually, as if we were mere acquaintances trying to tee up a time for coffee.

"Then I'll see you toward the end of next week," he sounded pleased.

"Have a good trip," I uttered and rang off. Memories of Venice refused to be squashed into the dark vortex of my mind and a bittersweet feeling in my heart made me cry out for just a moment.

I always played the *what if* game with myself and hated going down this road as it achieved nothing. *What if I hadn't married bastard Nathan? What if I'd married David instead?* Then I'd be transported to that one glorious spring night in Venice when David and I made sweet love. At age twenty, he hadn't been as experienced as I, my being ten years older than he. Still, our lovemaking had been passionate as well as sweet, and it had the promise of so much more—that is, until I fucked it up. I frowned. Yes, I really did fuck up because at thirty I'd been looking to meet someone more mature; someone who could provide me with security and stability.

When I'd met Nathan, I had been sure it was the real thing. The interlude with David had been simply that—a holiday romance—but Nathan represented a more solid future.

Little did I know at the time the arsehole was going to turn into a dream-stealer, a tightfisted and self-centred SOB; and finally, a cheater. Aaaarrggghhhh! Time for coffee. Whenever I allowed myself to sink into my *what if* scenarios, only coffee saved me from going stark raving mad.

Dobbs arrived at my place an hour later, very smart in a black suit and crispy white shirt with a navy blue tie.

"You're early," I commented as I let him in.

"I know." He grinned and held out a small, white cardboard box toward me. "I thought these would go just right with some of your great coffee."

I took the box from him with a smile while he followed me into the kitchen where I opened it to find six mini-cannoli—my favourite Italian sweets, in the shape of a small tube made of pastry and filled with vanilla or chocolate custard.

Dobbs had brought four of each. A wide smile spread across my face and the images of Venice dissolved while my suspicions of foul play returned, ready to be stimulated further by coffee and cannoli with Dobbs.

"Oh, Dobbs," I gave him a hug, "how did you know I'd be hankering for something like this?"

He threw me a knowing look. "Ferrari, you're always hankering after food, especially pizza, cannoli, and loads of coffee."

I laughed and set about making more of the stuff. This would be my second cup for the morning. I felt Dobbs's eyes on me and turned to him with a querying look. "Yes?"

Dobbs said, "I don't know how you do it, girl. You eat, eat, and eat, and yet you never put on any weight. Now me, I only have to look at food and I pack on the pounds."

"This is the secret not many people know about," I remarked in a conspiratorial tone. "It's called 'nasty-ass' divorce with a 'nasty-ass' cheating prick. It's not very good for the heart, but it does wonders for the figure." I grinned as I delivered this with an imitation of Dobbs's American accent.

Dobbs broke into a spasm of laughter from which he had difficulty recovering while I shrugged my shoulders and simply served the coffee. We sat out on the paved terrace of my lovely garden apartment and I tried not to have poisonous thoughts about Nathan, whose selfishness was forcing me to place the apartment on the market. I figured right now my Italian forebears would have put the obligatory horse's head in Nathan's bed before shooting him in the balls.

"Sorry, what was that?" I became aware that Dobbs had said something, and I didn't catch it because of the disturbing scenario in my head.

"I asked why we are eating out of doors on such a horrible and rainy day," Dobbs responded.

I looked about me and noticed it was drizzling. "Well, we're under cover," I remarked but realised it was rather too cold to be outside. "I'm sorry. I guess I didn't notice it was quite so chilly." I added, "Let's go back in."

Back in the warmth of the apartment we devoured the cannoli, washing them down with the lovely, aromatic coffee.

"What's on your mind?" Dobbs suddenly asked.

I assumed he meant in terms of the death of Linda Liu and not my *what if* scenarios. "Chris told me something interesting yesterday." I then filled him in on Chris's remarks about Geering, and how he saw him kissing some mystery woman.

Dobbs looked thoughtful. "I wonder if this is the same woman you say was wearing the vanilla scent."

"We have no way of knowing this, of course," I stated while trying to finish off a third cannoli even though I felt stuffed.

Dobbs leaned back in his sofa chair, obviously sated after having downed his four cannoli like there was no tomorrow. "It's certainly a motive for murder," he remarked.

I eyed him with interest. "I don't necessarily believe an affair is enough of a motive for someone to commit murder," I commented, and then thought of how I would love to kill Nathan for cheating on me. Even so, I didn't feel this was a strong motive for someone like James Geering, unless he stood to lose something. "What I think," I said aloud, "is if Geering was trying to get rid of his wife the motive must go beyond a simple affair. It has to do with money. Linda was his legal wife and if he was planning to leave her, he'd have to pay her a huge amount in maintenance. It could've even ruined his vast business empire."

Dobbs's eyes were wide as he looked into mine. "Now, there's a thought."

I glanced at my watch and jumped out of my chair. "Shit! It's quarter to ten," I exclaimed. "If we leave now, we might just make it in time."

Dobbs struggled to his feet, and I noticed he wasn't as nimble as I. Too much good food in that tummy of his, I smiled secretly but hoped he meant it when he said he would walk off some pounds in Hawaii.

"I have the car outside already," Dobbs announced. "We'll go in mine and I'll drop you off later."

I nodded, grabbed my coat, and we rushed out the door. The funeral service was being held at Holy Cross in Bondi Junction and we made it just as it commenced. The place was jam-packed with what I assumed were Geering's friends and business colleagues in Sydney. Family and close friends would have had to fly down from the Gold Coast, where Geering and his wife made their home. Dobbs and I stood at the back of the church as there were no seats to be had.

While the priest droned on, my mind started to wander and I cast my eyes around the crowd. The first thought to pop into my head was that Linda was getting a Catholic service even though she was Chinese. This didn't matter too much as a number of Asian people were Catholic or belonged to some other Christian denomination.

I didn't see anyone I knew in the crowd with the exception of

Geering. I noted he was sitting at the front with an elderly Chinese lady to his left—perhaps Linda's mother—and what looked like a middle-aged man to his right; probably one of Geering's friends or colleagues.

The priest went on and on and I didn't hear a word he uttered until Geering was suddenly standing in front of the crowd, addressing them from a lectern to the left of the altar. I focused intently on what he said. First, he thanked his family, friends, and colleagues for attending the service; and then he launched into his eulogy.

"Linda was my life," he stated, and then paused briefly to wipe at one eye with his finger. Crocodile tears? I wondered. "We were married for close to fifteen years and our love remained fast throughout all that time." Once again, I had to wonder whether the guy was for real or simply a consummate actor.

"I don't know what happened when Linda made the decision to end her life." This time he sniffed and wiped at his eyes with a handkerchief. "All I know is that I will always ask myself whether I could have prevented this if she'd said anything; if she'd reached out. I can't forgive myself for not noticing that perhaps things weren't right with her, and now it's too late."

There was a pause here as if he was trying to control his emotions. I noticed the whole congregation was silent, spellbound by his every word. I waited quietly until Geering was ready to resume speaking; and it was then my eyes landed on Smythe, who was standing beside an interesting-looking Asian man near the front pews, but leaning against the sidewall of the church. They must've arrived late because I hadn't seen anyone standing there earlier.

I didn't pay any attention to Smythe, though he looked rather dashing in a navy blue suit with white shirt and yellow tie. A thought flashed through my mind that this was the first time I'd ever seen him wearing a full suit; and he didn't look half bad. Smythe reminded me of a young version of Tom Selleck minus the moustache. Oh, my God, get a grip, Ferrari! I mentally reprimanded myself. Smythe was my archenemy and I didn't intend to forget it.

My eyes then slid across to the man standing next to Smythe. There was something about him reminiscent of a bad martial arts movie. He wore a charcoal-grey suit with white shirt and burgundy tie, his outfit impeccably cut to his slim figure. However, it wasn't what he was wearing that arrested my attention, but the way he looked.

He seemed somewhere in his thirties, with a thin face framed by straight black hair reaching past his shoulders and a rather long goatee that almost touched his chest. He had small slits for eyes and, as he smoothed down his goatee with one hand, I noticed he sported an incredibly long fingernail on his pinky. I was mesmerised by how long it was—at least three inches. My initial thought was how he kept it from breaking off. I knew the growing of long pinky nails with Asians was a sign of wealth and the fact the person did not do manual labour. I'd seen heaps of Asian men with long pinky fingernails before, but there was something about the whole appearance of this man that gave me the creeps.

Just then I realised Geering was going back to his seat, and I had missed the rest of his eulogy. I felt Dobbs nudge me with his elbow and looked around while the crowd started to slowly disperse. "Smythe's here," Dobbs announced in a whisper.

I raised my eyebrows at him in response. "Big whoop."

Dobbs ignored my childish remark. "I'll meet you in the car in fifteen minutes. I want to catch up with him and see whether he's got any information for us."

"Good idea," I replied and started to move away before Smythe could spot me. No use antagonising him if Dobbs could draw some details out of him.

It was raining heavily when I exited the church and I made a run for Dobbs's car. Good thing he'd left it unlocked. I opened the passenger door and slipped in, all the while keeping my gaze fixed on Dobbs while he stood chatting to Smythe under the portico at the front of the building.

I thought Smythe looked up a couple of times in my general direction, but I couldn't be sure. In any case, even if he couldn't spot me, he'd know I had attended the funeral with Dobbs. He knew me too well to believe I would stay away. I smiled and acknowledged that at least I had a cluey nemesis to pit my wits against.

The driver's door was suddenly flung open and Dobbs landed his butt on the seat.

"That didn't take long," I remarked.

He started the car and pulled off the kerb. We drove in silence for two minutes before he spoke. "I'm starving. How about some lunch?"

I stared at him and asked impatiently, "What did you find out?"

He grinned. "I knew you'd want to go home without lunch if I told you what I learned. So first, we eat."

I laughed. "You're nuts, you know that? What do I care if you want to stop for lunch?"

"Because, Ferrari, you're always at me about my weight."

"Just trying to keep you looking sexy for the *missus*," I teased.

He smirked and took a left into Ocean Street and a right into Queen. We were in the centre of Woollahra, a fashionable suburb with trendy shops and cafés. Dobbs parked outside Puccini's.

"God, you must be really hungry," I exclaimed. Puccini's was one of the best Italian Café Restaurants in the eastern suburbs and they were renowned for their famous homemade pasta dishes.

Dobbs did not say a word to me until we ordered lunch—fresh spinach and ricotta gnocchi for me and penne with pancetta and cream for him, with cappuccinos all around. I sat quietly until the waiter walked off with our order and then I spoke. "Dobbs, you're going to have to jog all the way up to Diamond Head crater and back before you walk this one off."

He frowned. "Hey, get off my case. "

I smiled. I knew he was just pretending to be mad at me. "But come on, pancetta with cream? Why not go for a tomato-based sauce? Less fattening, and you can still enjoy the pancetta." I knew how crazy he was about the Italian version of bacon.

The only response I received from him was a closed look, meaning he wasn't going to continue with this particular subject. I shrugged and changed the topic to what I really wanted to discuss. "So what did Smythe have to say?"

"He told me the CCTV tape showed absolutely nothing. The boys watched it in its entirety several times."

"Yes, but how much did they watch prior to the time Linda actually jumped?" I queried, once again wondering whether Geering had lied about the time he went to the room and how long he had stayed in there.

"The tape had about a half hour on it before Linda is seen coming out of the hotel room to take the final leap," Dobbs replied.

"Hmm," I remarked thoughtfully. "This may not be enough time."

"Enough time for what?" Dobbs sounded impatient. "We have

nothing on tape and we're simply speculating that this is a murd—"
He stopped talking when the waiter arrived with our cappuccinos.

I watched Dobbs as he stirred three sugars into his coffee, and I winced but didn't say anything. I only hoped the man had enough sense to go on a diet or that Eileen kicked his "sorry ass" once she saw how much weight he'd gained since she left for Hawaii.

"What else?" I asked.

"Well, Smythe said the autopsy showed nothing except traces of her regular anti-depressants and some drug for treating insomnia."

"Insomnia? This never came up before. Geering only said Linda was on anti-depressants when he was questioned on the night of her death."

"I know, but don't forget he was questioned more at length by the cops afterwards, and we weren't present."

"True," I agreed, beginning to doubt my theory about this being a murder. If Linda was on so many drugs, it's possible she simply decided to end it all. Even so, something kept spurring me on; and there was still the question as to why she would make a hair appointment on the day she planned to take her life.

"That's about it," Dobbs concluded, cutting into my thoughts. "That's all Smythe had to report."

I sighed and looked into my coffee. This couldn't be all. "Did he tell you who the Asian guy was?" I asked suddenly.

"You mean the one with the goatee?"

"That's the one."

"His name's Kwon Lee. He's Geering's business partner from Hong Kong."

I glared at him. "So Smythe told you more after all."

"Hey, take it easy, Ferrari. I simply happened to ask him if he knew the guy. I mean, you don't forget the appearance of someone like that easily."

"True," I concurred, wondering why I felt so jumpy.

The pasta arrived and Dobbs attacked it with relish, wiping away at drops of cream sauce now and then with his serviette. I ate at a more sedate pace, with new questions ticking away inside my mind.

Geering had a business partner from Hong Kong. Linda was from Hong Kong. What were Geering's business interests over there? Linda's father had lived in Hong Kong. He had been corrupt and involved in money laundering. He'd been assassinated before he could testify against a major drug kingpin; and then the police had wanted Linda to testify, but she committed suicide. But perhaps she was simply killed off so she wouldn't talk to the cops. After all, the Hong Kong police had reason to believe she might have had some information about her father's associates.

A gnocchi suddenly got stuck in my throat and I coughed and spluttered. Dobbs stopped eating and poured me a glass of mineral water. I drank a few sips and gave myself time to settle down. Then, just as Dobbs was about to shove another forkful of penne into his mouth, I remarked, "Dobbs, what if Linda Liu was assassinated so she wouldn't testify, just like her father?"

CHAPTER 7

My lawyer telephoned on Saturday. I was surprised seeing as lawyers never worked on weekends, and I winced at the thought of how much this was going to cost me. I wondered whether they charged weekend rates.

"Good news," Arthur Boyd announced when I answered the call.

I rolled my eyes even though he couldn't see my face. What possible good news could a person get from a divorce lawyer? It was all bad news as far as I was concerned. "So what's so good that makes you ring me on a Saturday, Arthur?" I asked with skepticism.

"I heard from Nathan's lawyer late yesterday. He's agreed to drop the whole thing if you don't pursue the maintenance issue."

I felt like reaching through the phone in order to throttle him, if that were possible, but it wasn't Arthur's fault. Don't shoot the messenger, Mia. "How magnanimous of him," I responded, my voice dripping with sarcasm. "I bet the bastard suddenly realised how much it's going to cost him to go to court and he'd rather keep the money to buy his new woman a big diamond ring."

Arthur cleared his throat and it struck me the guy was probably a little afraid of me. I certainly hadn't been a very patient client, and he'd had to cope with my numerous calls and emails because I wanted to expedite the process. "You know I've always advised you against going to court, Mia. It would have cost thousands more in legal fees, and for what? The court isn't going to give you much maintenance seeing as you work fulltime and can support yourself— not to mention the legacy from your father."

I wanted to scream at the injustice of it all. It wasn't the money; it was simply the fact that Nathan was going to get away with it. The system sucked. The law sucked. We had a "no fault" law in Australia, so getting maintenance was difficult unless one was unemployed, had kids, or was too ill to work. "So the bastard walks away—just like that!" I tried not to grind my teeth at the fury I felt sweeping through my body.

"What can I say? Sometimes you have to cut your losses," Arthur replied.

Yeah, right—cut my losses while Nathan and my lawyer get fat on my money. How I wished I could organise one of the biker gangs from the Cross to break Nathan's every bone and give his floozy a good "what for" at the same time.

It took all of my willpower to remain calm and collected, but I somehow managed it. Although I knew I was going to pay for this later by getting a tension headache, there was no point in continuing with this farce of a case against a worthless SOB. "Okay, Arthur," I uttered, cool as ice. "Let them know we accept. I guess it's a good thing that prick didn't go for my father's legacy. I wouldn't put it past him, you know."

There was a sigh of relief from the other end and I could already feel the pounding pain starting at the base of my skull. Great! Just what I needed when I had to go to work and stay through the Thorpe wedding. I finished with the call and paced around the apartment while I tried to breathe deeply in order to relax. If this didn't work I would resort to strong painkillers and Valium.

I was going to miss my lovely apartment filled with natural light and every possible modern convenience; then there was the evergreen foliage of its garden with the many Lilli Pilly bushes, the creeping ficus vines, the abundant and aromatic star jasmine plants, plus my favourite white frangipani tree, which I had planted with my own hands. All were lost because Nathan couldn't keep his dick in his pants.

At this point, the painkillers and Valium seemed the better option and I turned to make my way to the bathroom to take the tablets. Just then, my eyes fell on a photo of my father, which rested on a bookshelf alongside framed photos of my entire family—now all deceased except for a couple of cousins in Italy. My mother had passed away when I was a young child and my father brought me up pretty much on his own. His entire family had lived in Italy, but they died off one by one as I was growing up and I never met any of them. My only true family had been my dad and Dobbs, his best friend.

I picked up the framed photo of Dad in his police uniform, his arm thrown casually around the shoulders of a younger-looking Dobbs. They were in their prime, though Dobbs was the younger of the two by around twelve years. Tears welled in my eyes and rolled slowly down my face. Dad had passed on in his early sixties, his body riddled with bone cancer. This had been ten years ago, when I was with Nathan and still happily married. Dad had gone to his grave with the belief his only daughter would be taken care of by the man who'd promised to do so as Dad lay dying.

"Dad," I spoke to the photo, "you were taken in, just like me. We both thought Nathan was a good man, but he turned out to be a con man instead. At least I got to protect most of the inheritance you left me." I kissed the photo and put it back on the shelf.

My headache started to fade away without the tablets, and I felt more relaxed. Despite the fact that Nathan had taken some of my money and invested it in shares under his name didn't matter anymore. Dad's legacy to me, which came from the proceeds of the sale of his home, had left me with enough money to buy a small apartment and have some to spare. So it was prudent to cut my losses now, as Arthur had put it. No sense in handing over more money for legal fees. Let Nathan keep the money he took from me. One day he would come to regret it. Karma had a mysterious way of evening things out in the end. Now, I simply had to convince myself this was true. It was sometimes difficult to believe things would turn out well with so much injustice in the world.

Oh, crap! I caught the time on the wall clock in the kitchen when I went to make myself a coffee and knew if I didn't hurry I'd be late for my three o'clock shift. I rushed through a late lunch of salami and cheese on Italian bread, and strong black coffee. After this, I jumped in the shower and by two-thirty I headed out the door in my tailored black uniform. The hotel was only a ten-minute drive from where I lived.

I picked up my pager upon arrival and checked through the morning shift logbook entries; nothing untoward, except a minor incident with valet parking where a guest's car incurred a small scratch. The hotel insurance would take care of it. I dropped by security to pick up the master keys and was told Dobbs had decided to take the weekend off in preparation for his trip on Monday. I would give him a call later to arrange his ride to the airport; I had decided to roster myself off so I could drive him in.

The afternoon dragged on and after a couple of room checks I tackled my emails and ordered a cappuccino from room service. The duty manager's desk was tucked away in a stuffy little cubbyhole behind the wall that separated the back office from Reception. My desk phone rang and I picked up on the second ring. "Mia Ferrari speaking."

"Mia, this is George Walsh," said a male voice at the other end of the line. George was my real estate agent. "We received an offer on your apartment."

My heart jolted—an actual offer. The apartment had been on the market for a short time and had attracted much interest, but this was the first formal offer to come in. George told me the amount, which was below the asking price. "Too low," I stated, still trying to process the fact that it was all happening way too fast for my liking.

"That's what I said to the buyers," George informed me. "I told them to come back with something more realistic and after a couple of hours they increased the offer by ten thousand. This is only a few thousand below your asking price, but in the current market I'd have to say it's as good as you're going to get."

I wanted to slap the little turd. He simply wanted me to accept so he could take his commission with a minimum of fuss. On closer consideration, however, the offer wasn't too bad, and what George had said was right. The market was beginning to slow down, and this was a good price. Fuck it, I thought, just take the damn offer and finish this off. "Okay," I uttered, sighing for the loss of my lovely home.

"That's a yes?" George could barely keep the excitement out of his voice. I really wanted to strangle him. He reminded me of a ferret sniffing for food, except he was sniffing the money instead. Turd with a capital T.

"Yes, George," I confirmed, "tell them yes."

He rang off before I could change my mind and I went back to checking my emails. Well, it was over. Legal case settled, home sold, Nathan getting off lightly—and me, still nursing a broken heart. Let's face it, all the hate and resentment was simply a defence mechanism. I still had feelings for Nathan; this was why I barked at most people.

I had to take it out on someone after all and that someone, I decided, was Smythe. Not only had he messed up a promising police career, but he looked a little like my ex. Tall, athletic, handsome, and a total bastard. God, I hated his guts—almost as much as I hated Nathan and that bimbo of his. If I ever got my hands on her she'd be minced meat. I suddenly flashed on my younger years, when I used to do martial arts. I had a black belt in Tae Kwon Do, and though I hadn't practised in years, I could still inflict enough harm on someone to put them out of circulation for a while.

The telephone rang again and I answered it, sounding none too friendly, "Ferrari here."

"Hey, whatever it is, I didn't do it," teased Thorny.

I relaxed. "I'm sorry. I just received an offer on my home and … Well, you know how it is—it brought everything back." I felt the pinprick of tears in my eyes, but hell if I was going to cry. "So what's happening?" I changed the subject abruptly. "Getting ready for the Thorpe wedding?"

"Sure am," Thorny replied. "Come down and we'll have coffee before bedlam breaks loose."

I didn't need a second invitation. "I'll be right there." I stood and put on my jacket.

"So who's this Thorpe family, anyway? If we have four hundred guests for a sit-down dinner, they must be pretty rich," I commented to Thorny a few minutes later while sipping coffee in her office and munching on a custard cannoli.

She smiled. "You don't know about Thorpe wines? They're only one of the largest wineries in the Hunter Valley."

"Okay, and?"

"And we're going to have our work cut out for us. They decided on a six-course dinner with choice of entreé and mains," she explained. "Plus they want silver service for the side dishes, instead of serving platters; and Gueridon cooking for Crêpe Suzette and Pineapple Flambé."

"Ouch!" I remarked. "That's going to be hard on their pocket."

"Then it's just as well they have very deep pockets," Thorny replied. "I've had to put on twice as many chefs, just for the dinner, plus four extra chefs who can do Gueridon. Not everyone knows how to do it these days, especially the younger ones."

Gueridon cooking was a bit of a lost art, unless one went to a five-star French restaurant. This was where the chef prepared certain food out of a trolley by the table while diners looked on. Most hotels had phased this out, unless they ran a true silver service French restaurant, but Rourke's, being a boutique chain of hotels and offering more personalised service, catered to all tastes and budgets.

"Well, save a Crêpe Suzette for me," I said, finishing the last of my cannoli. "I'll be by later to check out the ballroom."

I got up to leave at the same time as Thorny and almost collided with her. It was then I was hit by the soft aroma of vanilla.

"What is it?" Thorny asked when I leaned over to take a whiff at her.

"You smell of vanilla," First Elena and now Thorny, I thought, and wondered whether this was the latest rage in perfume.

A rosy blush spread across Thorny's face. "It's my perfume ..." She seemed a little fazed. "Well, there's this guy ..."

I eyed her with a smile on my face. "Oh? Do tell, you dark horse."

She smiled back. "Promise you won't say anything?"

"Promise," I replied in a conspiratorial tone.

"I'm having a bit of a fling with my sous chef."

I grinned. "You wicked woman! But which one—Tony or Frank?" I was teasing, of course. I knew it would be Tony. He was the typical tall, dark and handsome type while Frank was short and built like a beer barrel.

"Out of my office!" Thorny made like she was affronted.

I blew her a kiss and left with a laugh. I would never have guessed she was having an affair with someone who worked directly under her. But then, I smiled, he was *under* her after all. How delicious!

Later in the evening, after I dropped by the ballroom to ensure the Thorpe wedding was going well, I decided to check on young Chris Rourke. He had worked the day shift, so I had missed him earlier. I assumed he would be in the penthouse now, probably watching a DVD with his dinner.

I was crossing the lobby to make my way to the lifts when I saw Geering and Kwon Lee having drinks in the cocktail lounge. I halted for a moment and held my mobile to my ear, pretending I was talking on the phone. How could Geering handle sitting in the same bar where only a few days before his wife had jumped, landing on the baby grand? Just at that moment, as if he could sense my thoughts, he turned to me and nodded a greeting. I nodded back, still carrying on a fictitious conversation on the mobile, and slowly started to move away toward the lifts. During all the time I felt Geering's eyes and those of his business partner boring into me. The hair at the back of my neck stood on end and I couldn't wait until the lift arrived.

When the doors slid open I tried to look casual as I stepped in and pressed the button for the penthouse. Only once the doors shut did I put away the phone and lean against the lift wall, expelling a sigh. I still couldn't explain why I felt this way, but something didn't seem right.

When I knocked on the door, Chris called out for me to enter. He was on the computer.

"Hey," I greeted him as I walked into the expansive lounge room with wall-to-wall windows overlooking the city skyline in the distance. "What's happening?"

Chris smiled warmly, happy to see me, and I thought of his father. Stop it, Ferrari!

"I knew that'd be you. You missed the best pizza ever," he said. "I ordered from Giuseppe's up the road."

"I had dinner in the kitchen," I informed him, still feeling full. "Leftovers from the Thorpe wedding plus a very nice Crêpe Suzette."

Chris laughed. "Yeah, but nothing beats Giuseppe's pizza."

I grinned back at him. "You're right."

"Want a drink?"

I glanced at my watch. It was almost ten. "No, thanks. I only dropped by to check on you so I can report to your father that there are no wild parties going on in his absence."

"I knew it!" Chris tried to look like he was insulted by his father's lack of trust; but he had a great relationship with his dad, and this was just a put-on for my benefit. In any case, Chris was a bad actor. He was too open and easy for me to read. "Okay," he confessed when he saw the look in my eyes, "I'm only messing with you."

"I know you are, my friend. So what gives?" I took a seat opposite him at a walnut desk where he had his computer.

"I've been doing a little checking on Mr Geering and his very interesting business partner, Kwon Lee." My face must've looked like I'd just seen a ghost because he laughed hard. "C'mon, Ferrari, I know what you're thinking."

I recovered my composure. "How do you know about Kwon Lee?"

"I didn't. His name came up when I started to do a background search on Geering."

I tried not to look too enthusiastic. After all, I didn't want Chris involved in this. What if Linda Liu had really been murdered? I could be placing Chris in danger. "Chris, you have to stop this," I warned him. "The case is closed. Linda Liu committed suicide."

It seemed I was just as open as Chris because he simply smiled knowingly. "Don't you want to know what I found?"

His tone was enticing and I couldn't resist. I shook my head, as if to say *fuck caution*. "Okay, give it to me."

He grinned. "That's better." He brought up a screen on the computer and scrolled up and down before he spoke. "Geering owns five theme restaurants: two in Australia and three in Asia, namely Hong Kong, Singapore and Malaysia. The theme is gangsters and molls, emulating the Al Capone era."

I nodded. So far nothing I didn't already know. Chris continued, "The Sydney restaurant is supposed to open in a week's time, but due to construction problems the opening date's been delayed. The funding for the restaurants came partly from Geering's previous business in property development. He opened the first restaurant on the Gold Coast, where he lives now, and Sydney's the second one. The three in Asia are a joint venture between Geering and Kwon Lee."

"There's nothing suspicious there," I remarked. "I knew all this already. Geering's a wealthy businessman."

"True," Chris replied, "but where did all the money to fund the openings come from?"

"What do you mean? Geering was in property development. He probably picked up the buildings for a song. With so many businesses going broke there are heaps of commercial properties to be had."

He nodded. "Yes, I know, but Asia is a different story. Property prices over there are premium due to the shortage of land, and the restaurants are all in prime locations."

"So what are you saying?" I felt my heart thumping against my chest. If Chris had found some sort of link to illegal activities we might have something solid with which to work.

"I'm looking into Kwon Lee's background. It's a little more obscure than Geering's, although he's also into property development, mainly in Hong Kong."

"And?" I prompted.

"And there seems to be some scandal in his family. His brother was involved with drugs at one stage."

"Dealing?" I held my breath.

"No," Chris said, and I sighed with disappoitment. "Using. He died of an overdose."

"Oh."

"I know this isn't much, but it could lead us to something else. I'm still researching."

I didn't like what I heard. "Chris, you really have to forget about this. The case is closed. Don't meddle anymore."

He threw me a knowing smile. "Yeah, right, as if you're going to drop it, Ms Ferrari."

I gave him a serious look. "I have dropped it. There is nothing for us to go on with. Smythe told Dobbs it was a case of suicide. That's it."

"Ferrari, tell that to the Pope; though I don't think even he would believe you." He laughed and I wanted to hit him.

Damn! How was I going to solve a murder if I couldn't even bluff my way past a teenager?

CHAPTER 8

"Thanks for the ride," Dobbs said on Monday morning while I meandered in and out of peak hour traffic toward the airport in my little Hyundai Getz.

"No problem. What are friends for?" I threw him a smile. "Now, did you pack the gifts I'm sending for your daughter and baby Rose?"

"Of course. Maggie's going to love the little outfit you picked out for Rose, and that body lotion for Maggie is yummy."

I laughed and quickly glanced sideways at him. "Trust you to think of food."

Dobbs raised his brows and remarked innocently, "What do you mean, Ferrari? It smells really nice and reminds me of something fruity."

I grinned. "Well, at least it's not fattening." I espied Dobbs's lips and they were set in a firm line. "Hey, I'm only teasing you," I added. "In fact, I agree with you that the aroma's fruity or floral, anyway. It's called Japanese Cherry Blossom."

He seemed pacified and changed the subject. "So Mia, you stay out of trouble while I'm away, you hear?" His tone held a warning.

"Of course," I responded quickly; too quickly, unfortunately, and I felt his eyes on me. I didn't dare look, but I knew there would be frown lines furrowing his forehead. "Okay, Father Dobbs, I promise." This time I tried to sound sincere; and Dobbs must have bought it because he didn't add anything else and changed the subject once again.

"Any more news on the sale of your place?"

I shrugged my shoulders. "Not yet. But as far as I know the sale's going through. I'm waiting to hear from the agent about the settlement date and then I'm going to start looking around."

"Are you going for the standard settlement of six weeks?"

"Yes," I replied. "And I thought I'd invest the money and rent instead of buying."

"How come?" He sounded surprised.

"Because it's too soon for me to make a decision about where I want to live, so I thought I'd rent something nice and close to work, like in Potts Point, and see whether I like the area."

He nodded. "I guess that makes sense, but don't rent for too long. It's dead money."

"True, but at the same time I don't want to get bogged down with something I don't like simply because I rushed into it."

I felt his eyes on me again. "Can this be the Mia Ferrari I know?" He was being sarcastic.

"What do you mean?" I wasn't sure if I should take offense.

"I mean you always rush into things without thinking."

"Hey!" I protested.

"Oh, all right," Dobbs remarked. "It just doesn't sound like you, that's all."

"Well, it's the new me, Dobsy baby, so you better get used to it," I returned forcefully. I really didn't care what he made of this. Life was too short to constantly please others.

He laughed. "Now, *that's* the Mia I know. For a minute, I thought I'd lost you."

I laughed with him. "You're incorrigible." Then I turned the conversation back to the Linda Liu case and told him about Chris's findings regarding Kwon Lee.

"And?" Dobbs queried.

"What do you mean 'and'? This could be a vital clue. If we can find a link from Geering and Kwon Lee to the drug world, then we'd have a clear motive as to why Linda had to be killed off. They just didn't want her to testify in case she gave the game away for them."

Dobbs sighed. "Honestly, Ferrari, you keep away from all this and wait until I get back. I mean, I hope your theory is wrong and it was only a case of suicide; but if it isn't, then you could be in danger. Tell Chris to stop snooping, too. The last thing we need is to get the boss's son into trouble."

"It's okay, Dobbs," I said to calm him down. "I've already told him to stay out of it. Anyway, there is nothing much I can do right now. The only shame is we didn't get the CCTV tape back from the police."

"I told you that's evidence. The cops aren't going to release the tape back to us, so forget about it."

I sighed with frustration. "Yes, but couldn't you just have a quiet word with Smythe when you return?"

Dobbs didn't reply; he simply glared at me. I shut up then; switched on the radio, and kept driving. When I pulled up at the departures gate at Kingsford-Smith airport a few minutes later, I stepped out of the car to bid Dobbs farewell. He enclosed me in a big bear hug that almost squeezed all the air out of me. "You mark what I said, okay? Stay away from this whole thing."

I nodded. "I will. Don't worry. Kiss Eileen for me. Congratulate her on becoming a grandma and send my love to Maggie and baby Rose."

Dobbs smiled from ear to ear and it was obvious he couldn't wait to get to Hawaii and meet his new granddaughter.

On the way home I decided to do some grocery shopping, so I stopped off at Woollahra, the suburb next to where I lived but the trendier of the two. I had a weakness for trendy things, be they clothes, restaurants or groceries, and I loved Woollahra's gourmet food stores where one could find imported ingredients from all around the world.

I parked the car on Queen Street, the main shopping drag, and headed straight for Salumeria Giorgio or Giorgio's delicatessen. The place was to me like a candy store was to a child. Giorgio was from Parma, and he imported a whole bunch of items from that region plus the rest of Italy; and the prosciutto from his hometown was to die for.

"Ciao, Giorgio," I greeted the diminutive and rotund man as I walked into the store.

"Mia! Ma come stai?" Giorgio called out with a wave of the hand.

"Bene, bene, grazie," I replied. Greetings out of the way, Giorgio went back to serving his many customers while I browsed.

I was a good cook—my father had seen to this when I was growing up; and we used to cook our meals together. These days, though, I worked such long hours at the hotel I rarely indulged in preparing something nice, especially when I was on my own. When I had been with Nathan I'd made the effort to cook more often. Nowadays, however, I usually made a quick plate of pasta and threw some pesto on it, which came from a jar. I only ever made an effort to cook something special if Dobbs dropped by for dinner; and it was at times like this I was reminded of how much I actually enjoyed cooking. So tonight I was going to reward myself by preparing a meal made with fresh ingredients from Giorgio's.

When I thought about it, it was really rotten that just because I'd gone through a nasty break up I had stopped looking after myself properly. Well, it was time to change this; and let's face it—I deserved it. If I didn't care for myself nowadays, who would?

I picked up some superfine Arborio rice to make the famous Venetian dish *risi e bisi*, which was dialect for rice and peas. This was not just any rice and peas, though. There was a certain art to making a good risotto so the end result was a creamy texture of tender and plump rice grains flavoured with a variety of ingredients that made your mouth water. Mmm. Just thinking of it made me feel hungry and I glanced at my watch. It was lunchtime. No wonder I was starving. Oh well, once I finished up here I would treat myself to lunch down the road at a new Italian place called Rosetti's.

Before I left Giorgio's I picked up some fresh figs to go with the succulent, paper-thin Parma prosciutto I would be having for antipasto. I kept picturing my dinner while I made my way to Rosetti's and was sharply brought back to reality when my eyes met those of Phil Smythe, who was sitting on the sandstone verandah of the restaurant glancing through a menu.

I was about to keep walking and find another place to eat, but it was too late. Smythe called out, "Ferrari, what are you doing in this neck of the woods?"

I didn't make any attempt to get closer to his table but forced a smile to my face with great effort before replying, "Just been to Giorgio's." I made as if I was going to keep walking, but suddenly he was out of his chair and walking toward me.

"Hey, I didn't know you lived around here," he said when he reached me.

"I'm next door in Edgecliff, but I do my shopping around here." God, was I going to have to chitchat with the enemy now? My stomach growled with hunger and I thought I might go farther up the road to Puccini's where I'd had lunch with Dobbs after the funeral;

but it looked like Smythe had other ideas.

"Is this a day off for you?"

I nodded and volunteered, "Just came back from dropping Dobbs off at the airport."

"That's right," Smythe remarked. "He's off to Hawaii today. He told me and the boys on poker night."

Smythe had become Mr Chatty all of a sudden and I gazed at him with unveiled suspicion. "Okay, what's going on, Smythe; what's with the garden party chitchat?"

Smythe almost smiled in amusement, but I was glad he didn't; otherwise, I would have walloped him over the head with the Arborio rice I was carrying in my shopping bag, which was quite heavy.

Perhaps Smythe sensed my impatience to be on my way, but for some reason he wasn't going to let me off the hook so easily. Instead, he said, "Have you had lunch yet?"

I was about to lie and tell him that I had, but he caught me off guard and I shook my head. What an idiot. Now I was stuck with him.

"Why don't you join me?" he asked smoothly.

Oh, but he could be a charmer when he wanted. I had to make an escape from this hateful male of the species and was about to open my mouth to refuse when suddenly it struck me that if I had lunch with him I might be able to get him to tell me more about the findings on the Linda Liu case. This was an opportunity that, while distasteful, I couldn't afford to miss.

"Very well," I responded before seeing a smile lurking about his lips, "but we're going Dutch."

"Why, of course," he replied sarcastically. "I wouldn't want to come across as being a gentleman where you're concerned."

I let that one pass with a roll of my eyes, and we took a seat at the table. Smythe asked for a second menu while I ordered a much-needed cappuccino.

As we scanned our menus I couldn't help but think about the time Smythe pretty much single-handedly had me rejected from being considered by the force all those years ago. Granted, the height restrictions had just been discarded, but not within the mentality of the recruitment panel. Smythe had been a member of that panel and I was sure he had something to do with the rejection of my application.

My father had never really liked him. He'd never told me why and I never asked. Dobbs couldn't remember exactly why enmity existed between the two men, but he thought it had something to do with the fact that Smythe was vying for a higher position in the force at the time and he'd come up against my dad for the role. The younger man won. So it seemed it wasn't just height discrimination in those days but also age. In any case, my dad was never able to let go of the fact that he was passed over and he took a dislike to the man who was given the job. My assumption was that Smythe remembered my father's dislike of him, and he, in turn, rejected my application.

"Ready to order?" The object of my thoughts asked.

"Sure." I nodded even though I hadn't taken in a single item on the menu. Just then, my cappuccino arrived and I had the chance to quickly scan the fare on offer. "I'll go for a pizza," I stated. "A small one."

The waiter who brought my coffee took out his order pad. "Which one, Signora?"

I felt myself bristle. What was it with these Italians, who automatically assumed I was a Mrs? Couldn't they see I wasn't wearing a wedding band? I fixed the man with a glare. "It's *Signorina* actually, and I'll have the Capricciosa, please."

The waiter nodded apologetically and took my order. I noticed Smythe grinning from the corner of my eye and felt like punching him in the mouth. Meanwhile, he addressed the waiter. "I'll have the spaghetti puttanesca and a glass of house red."

When the man walked away Smythe turned to me with a serious look in his eyes. "By the way, I only just heard about your break up. I'm very sorry."

I was in the process of taking a sip of coffee and almost spat it out. Dobbs and his friggin' poker night with the boys! Outwardly, however, I remained calm and simply gazed at Smythe with coolness. "Thank you," was all I said.

"I've been divorced for a few years now, so I know what you're going through," he added with what seemed to be genuine sincerity. Even so, this wasn't going to soften me toward the man who'd cost me my police career. "Any kids?"

I shook my head.

"Me neither; although I would've loved to have some."

"Yes, well, what are you going to do, right?" I commented with disinterest, hoping he'd get the hint that I didn't want to talk about personal things. I simply wanted to pepper him with questions about the Linda Liu case, but I didn't know how I was going to introduce the subject.

We chitchatted some more, mainly about Italian cookery. I found out he was an enthusiastic cook himself but, like me, he didn't get much time to potter around the kitchen. Our food arrived then and we ate silently for a few moments, until it suddenly occurred to me how I was going to broach the subject.

"Remember Mr Geering?" I commented casually.

Smythe looked up from his pasta. "Of course. What about him?"

"It looks like he's staying on in Sydney indefinitely—something to do with a delayed deadline on the opening of his new restaurant."

Smythe received this with faint interest, and I was dying to know what he was really thinking. I had only found out the day before from the reservations manager that Geering had taken up the same suite he had shared with his late wife for another month or so.

"Perhaps the man wants more time to get used to the death of his wife," Smythe offered.

Great, I thought. This is all he's going to divulge; and here I am, trying not to get indigestion while I eat with my archenemy. "But then again," he went on, "he's probably dealing with delays, as you've said."

Oh, shit! What now? "I find it surprising he didn't arrange for the body to be taken back to the Gold Coast. You'd think he'd want his wife buried where her family is."

Smythe savoured his wine for a few moments; then he replied, "Didn't you know? He had the body cremated after the funeral service. So I'm sure he'll be taking her back with him when he goes."

Good God! This had never even occurred to me. "How could I know?" I shrugged. "I was surprised at how fast the police released the body, though."

"Don't be," he said. "You know very well there were no suspicious circumstances whatsoever."

Damn! He knew Dobbs would have shared the information with me. No use playing this silly game anymore. I wasn't going to catch him out, so I decided to be direct. "Dobbs told me they found traces of anti-depressants and some other drug she was taking for insomnia.

Do you know what the drug was?"

Smythe sighed. "Ferrari, you know I'm not going to discuss any of the details with you, but you can rest assured the coroner knew what he was doing."

Fuck! I had just sat through what could have been an informative lunch only to hear this. Smythe obviously caught the look of annoyance on my face because he added, "Unless there's something you know and you're not telling."

His eyes dared me to divulge any information I may have had, but I would rather drop dead on the spot than tell him anything. Had he been a bit more forthcoming, I might have shared my theory. Now he could go and take a flying leap for all I cared, and I smiled at him with a look of innocence. "No, I know nothing other than what you told me. I don't know where you get the notion that I might know something more than you guys, anyway." I threw the ball back in his court.

Smythe grinned, and I hated his guts. "Nice try, Ferrari, but I don't share."

I felt like throwing the rest of my pizza at his face, but I controlled the impulse and finished it while engaging in more inane chitchat, all the time wondering why he'd taken the trouble of asking me to join him for lunch when he was going to be such an arsehole.

CHAPTER 9

The real estate agent telephoned the following day to inform me the sale was definitely going through and the buyers were happy with the usual six-week settlement period. This meant I had less than six weeks to search for a place to rent and move.

I was back at work after my day off and during my lunch break I searched rental listings on real estate websites to see what was on offer around Potts Point. The location was perfect; I could walk to work from there, and it was very close to Bill's Café Bar—the place we usually frequented with hotel personnel. This meant I could relax after my late shifts and have a few drinks without having to worry about driving home.

I found a few places of interest, which I saved into "my favourites", and I checked the roster for the next couple of weeks so I could slot in times to go and see a few apartments. In this part of town, one had to be very quick to grab a place. Potts Point was a really popular place with singles and professional couples due to its close proximity to nightlife and the busy hub of Kings Cross and the city.

I was marking down some dates so I could arrange for viewings when the phone on my desk rang. I picked up the call. "Mia Ferrari."

"Always on the job, I see." David's voice sent a shiver of anticipation through me. I hadn't thought about him for a while, but now I remembered the dinner he'd promised me upon his return and I found myself looking forward to it. I hadn't been out on a single date since Nathan and I broke up, and it would be nice to have dinner with an attractive man who wasn't totally fucked up in the head.

"Hello, David; I'm happy to report Chris is still alive and well. No wild parties in the penthouse; at least, not ones I haven't attended," I joked.

David laughed. "You're a worry sometimes."

"Sometimes?" I remarked, feeling lighthearted. "You mean all the time, don't you?" God, I was flirting with my boss and ex-lover. The ever-recurring image of Venice popped into my head, and I shooed it away. It was amazing how I could still remember something so vividly after eighteen years, but right now I wanted to avoid going into my usual *what if* scenarios.

"Yes, I guess you are trouble, Ms Ferrari." David's voice held a tone of fondness, but he soon reverted to a businesslike manner and gave me a rundown on his trip, informing me he would be returning Friday morning. "So I was wondering if you have any plans for Friday night. I'd like to take you out to dinner."

I couldn't help feeling excited at the prospect, but I didn't want to show my enthusiasm too readily. "I'm not sure about my roster; I may be working. I'll call you back and let you know."

"Okay, Mia, but call tomorrow. I'm about to pop into another meeting, and I have a business dinner to attend tonight."

We rang off and I went back to checking out real estate listings. I wasn't working on Friday evening, so I should simply have accepted nicely. I didn't understand what was holding me back, except I was still very much attracted to David and the last thing I needed right now was to get involved with an ex-lover—especially one who was married.

I lived by a strong code, which was not to get involved with a man if he was with someone else. Not even if he swore on the Bible that the relationship he was in had gone down the gurgler. Nine times out of ten the relationship had gone down the gurgler only inside his head, and I wasn't going to be "the other woman".

I thought with distaste about Nathan's new woman. She had been in this thing all along with him, despite my still being in the picture. It was obvious she was a selfish tart who didn't have a sense of the sisterhood. Had she held off from getting involved with my husband, he might have gone to couples counselling with me and perhaps I'd still be married today. Not that I blamed her entirely; after all, it takes two to tango, as they say. Regardless, she was as bad as my ex. She obviously couldn't keep her legs from spreading and she'd welcomed Nathan's advances with more than open arms. Slut! Well, I only hoped one day she would get a taste of the same bitter fruit I'd been forced to bite into.

My thoughts turned back to David as I dismissed Nathan and his bimbo in a puff of mental smoke. I certainly wanted nothing to do with David as long as he remained married to the very attractive Elena. Loving him the way I had—and I still loved him in my own way—I couldn't understand why he kept up the pretense of a marriage. It was easy for anyone to see that David and Elena had finished their marriage long ago. He worked endless hours in his business while she was always jetsetting off to some exotic destination or other. I often wondered if she travelled alone and if David trusted her.

In any case, while I looked forward to having dinner with him, this was as far as it would go. Even if David came on to me, I would not allow anything to happen. But I didn't think I had to worry on this account. David had too much honour to simply jump my bones, so I was safe—disappointed, but safe in the knowledge that both he and I were doing the right thing. Therefore, for the time being David would remain a friend—just as he had been all these years I had known him.

I did my rounds in the afternoon and carried out a few room checks. All was in order and by three o'clock I started to get ready to leave for the day. I was logging off my computer when Annie, the reservations manager, popped her head into my cubicle. "Mia, Jason called in sick," she announced.

Damn! Jason, one of the duty managers, always left it to the last minute to call in whenever he knew he wouldn't be coming to work. It was now too late to call on any of the other duty managers as Jason's shift started at three, so I was stuck with a double shift. Honestly, I would have to do something about this and made a mental note to speak to the general manager of the hotel. If he couldn't keep his duty managers under control he would have to run the shift himself next time. I was exhausted from working extra long shifts already.

"Let the GM know, Annie, if you please. I'll cover Jason's shift for this evening, but tell Peter I'm going to pop in and have a chat with him later."

Annie nodded and went back to her duties while I decided to

drop in on Peter, the general manager, sometime before he left for the day and tell him a thing or two.

It was almost six-thirty by the time I finished with the afternoon duty manager's to do list. I carried out a few more room checks; dropped in on the executive housekeeper to ensure she had enough staff for the evening turndown service; and I checked in with the kitchen. Reporting she was fully staffed, Thorny added it would be a slow evening and invited me to join her for dinner in her office.

"Come back at seven," she said. "I'll get one of the boys to throw in some pasta for us."

I nodded and went on my way to handle a customer complaint at Reception. By seven-thirty that evening I sat back in one of Thorny's visitors' chairs and stretched my arms over my head. "That was great, thanks. Just what I needed." I was referring to the pasta carbonara one of the chefs had whipped up for us. Now, we were having coffee and cannoli.

"So how are things going with you and Tony?" I asked, noticing he was not on duty this evening.

A smile played around Thorny's mouth. "Delicious." She gazed at me with a wicked glint in her eye.

"Good God, woman! You're one for secrets, I tell you. I never would've thought you two would get together," I remarked.

"Why not?" Thorny sounded curious.

"Well, he works with you for one, so it can get rather messy. I mean, what if you have to dismiss him or something?"

Thorny simply smiled dreamily at me, ignoring my question. "What else?"

"Aren't you worried this'll all come out? People love gossip, you know; and then where will your credibility be?"

"I'm just using him for sex," Thorny confessed, much to my surprise. She was my friend, but she usually kept her personal life to herself.

"What's that supposed to mean?" I queried. If she simply wanted to use someone for sex, it would be safer to look for a man who didn't work in her department.

Thorny's face wore a frown. "It means I've recently gone through a break up and I'm now on the rebound."

I was intrigued. "I'm sorry to hear that. But of course, your being a dark horse, I didn't even know you were in a relationship in the first place."

"That's because I don't like to talk about my love life," she replied. "It makes me uncomfortable." Her lips formed a firm line and I knew this was the end of it. It meant the subject was no longer open for discussion. She could be a real strange creature at times.

I drained my coffee cup and stood. "Well, I hope it all works out for you," I said, feeling rather put out. I had confided in her about David and my fling with him in Venice, but it was obvious she didn't trust me enough to share her problems. Perhaps I was being unfair; some people truly found it awkward to open up, and Thorny seemed to be one of them.

I was almost at the door when she laughed merrily and remarked, "You know, we almost got caught a couple of nights ago."

I turned back to look at her. "What do you mean?"

"We were in one of the function rooms on the mezzanine level. There was no one there, of course, and the lights were off. So we started fooling around; but then I remembered the security cameras. I mean, there's one pointing right at the entrance to the room we were in, and the door was wide open. Anyway, thank God we didn't switch on the lights; otherwise, I'm sure I would've been in a lot of trouble."

I froze.

"What is it?" Thorny asked when she saw the look of stunned realisation on my face.

I shook my head. "Nothing, nothing." I changed the subject abruptly, "I just remembered I forgot to do something quite important. Thanks for dinner, but I really have to go."

She shrugged her shoulders. "Don't mention it. See you tomorrow."

I rushed up to the mezzanine level as fast as my legs would carry me, all the time thinking how stupid I'd been to overlook this clue. Chris had told me he'd seen Geering kissing a female on the day after his wife's death, but he hadn't been able to make out who the woman was. It had never occurred to me to check the cameras on that floor. If luck was on my side, I would be able to find out the identity of the mystery woman.

When I reached the mezzanine floor I looked around for the cameras. There were two, one pointed toward the lifts; the other toward the three function rooms located on this level. Chris had never told me which function room it was where he'd seen Geering hanging around, but the camera swivelled between all three rooms and there was a possibility it may have caught something on tape on the day after the murder. My only fear was the boys in security might have used the video tapes again. They often recycled the same tape over and over if nothing of interest was caught on video. I prayed the tape I was looking for had not been re-used.

I went down to the security office and found Richard on duty. "Hey Rick, how're things without the boss around?"

Richard looked up from his desk and smiled. "Hi Mia, it's been quiet. And not a word from Dobbs, either. I think he must be having a grand time in Hawaii.

I laughed. "He's only been there for a couple of days. Were you expecting to hear from him?"

Richard grinned. "Are you kidding me? Dobbs is never off the job, even on holidays. He usually rings in every day to make sure things haven't fallen apart."

"Well, this time around he's got a granddaughter to engage his attention, so you should be grateful to the baby," I remarked.

"Oh, we are. Believe me, we are," he said cheerily. "Anyway, what can I do for you?"

I told him about the tapes I was looking for and we spent about an hour trying to track them down. Richard was fairly sure the tapes were not re-used for at least a month in case the hotel needed to review something. This was welcome news.

We went into a small storeroom at the back of the office and had to move a number of boxes in order to get to the tapes, but after a while we found what I wanted. In fact, there were four tapes I was going to have to sit through. They each ran for about six hours, but I wanted to cover footage for the whole of that day.

It also occurred to me there should be some footage from the previous night, when Geering claimed he left the function early in order to check on his wife. If so, I might be able to catch him coming out of the function room and waiting to take the lift up to his suite. This would confirm the time issue as to when he made his way to the room. I only hoped the cops hadn't taken this particular tape.

Richard gave me all the tapes in question and I knew I was going to spend the whole night watching dull footage that would be as entertaining as watching paint dry, but I had to do it. I wouldn't be able to sleep until I went through every single tape; and if I found something I would have a clue to work with.

I left the security office and went to my own to write up a few entries in the duty manager's log in preparation for the graveyard shift. Usually, the night manager looked after the time between eleven at night and seven in the morning. It was now close to nine and I started to feel the effects of working a double shift.

I knew I was going to have to stock up on coffee if I intended to stay awake all night watching the tapes. The kitchen was still running and I thought I'd see whether Thorny wanted to have coffee with me, but first a quick visit to the general manager. He had been working late tonight and I wanted to catch him before he left.

It was almost ten by the time I got down to the kitchen, but I was happy in the knowledge that Jason had it coming to him for ringing in so late. I was sure he was hung over rather than sick. He had a reputation for doing this and I knew his time with the hotel was getting short. Served the little shit right! He should know better than to party all night and let down his co-workers.

"Sorry," I said when I met Thorny in her office. "I got held up with Peter for a while."

Thorny poured out the coffee from a silver pot that was ready and waiting on her desk. "Black and strong as you ordered," she replied. "So what's up?"

I told her about Jason calling in sick at the last minute. "Oh man," she commented, "he always does this. When are they going to sack him?"

"Who knows, but I'm exhausted. I've been on my feet pretty much since seven this morning." I sipped the aromatic coffee and almost immediately felt my energy return.

"You know, coffee's just a quick fix. You really need to get fit," Thorny suggested.

I looked at her as if she'd lost her marbles. "Oh yeah? And since when does the day have forty-eight hours?"

She smiled. "Come on, it's not as bad as all that. You know, I've been going to yoga for a few months now and it's made all the difference in the world for me. I used to get really tired before, but now I feel revitalised—even when I pull long shifts. All you have to do is make the time."

I raised my brows with interest. "Really? I never thought about yoga. It may be just what I need."

"You should try it. I'll give you the number for the place where I go; it's not far from here."

"So how come you're doing yoga?" I asked, thinking it was probably to calm her temper. She certainly needed it if her terrified staff were anything to go by.

"It keeps me young and supple," she answered, "and now we're learning a kind of self-hypnosis technique that's wonderful."

"How does it work?" I felt sudden interest, thinking I could self-suggest myself to become superwoman.

"We do visualisation exercises and affirmations, which have a better chance of entering into our subconscious if we're in a relaxed state."

"Sounds great. So what kind of things do you affirm to yourself?"

"You know, general stuff like *I am in excellent health* or *I am calm and relaxed*. Anything you like."

"How about *I'm a sex goddess and scores of younger men are after me?*" I grinned.

Thorny grinned back. "Hey, you can try it, Ferrari. You never know your luck in a big city."

I glanced at my watch and finished off the coffee. "Maybe I will, but right now I'm going to get ready to go. It's almost eleven."

"I'll catch you later, *sex goddess*," Thorny teased, a wicked glint in her eyes.

I smiled at her and left the office. Sex was the last thing on my mind, especially since the break up. I was still trying to process all the emotions brought on by the separation: resentment, anger, sadness, hurt, and a whole host of others I couldn't believe I had inside me.

On the way home I realised it could take years to recover from this wretched break up, and I hated Nathan all the more. Everything I did with my life these days was tinged with the residue of some negative emotion. The only time I felt more like myself was when I was with someone I liked, such as David, or when I was trying to solve a mystery.

When I arrived at my apartment I had a quick shower to refresh myself and then changed into pyjamas. I put a pot of coffee on the boil and took out some leftover pizza I had in the fridge. It was going to be a long night and I needed fortification.

It was really difficult keeping my eyes open while watching the boring CCTV footage, but the good thing was I could fast-forward the tape whenever there was no action. The first tape I watched was the one from the function on the night of Linda Liu's death. I saw many people go into the function room, including Geering. Then, for the next three to four hours, there were people going in and out at all times: waiting staff, guests going to the restrooms, the functions manager flitting about, kitchen staff delivering platters filled with food, and so on. Unfortunately, I never caught Geering coming back out.

He had told the police he left the function at around nine-thirty. I watched and re-watched the timeframe between nine and ten but found nothing. I could only assume the camera must have missed him, and it seemed he had also slipped by unnoticed on the camera pointing at the lifts.

It was about one in the morning by the time I got to the other tapes. I ran through them fairly quickly because the only thing on them was a breakfast function for a business group, a few people simply passing by the mezzanine floor and finally, the lunch Chris had worked. This was where I slowed down and watched very carefully.

Again, there was a hive of activity with guests going in and out and waiting staff carrying on with their work. After this, all was quiet. I fast-forwarded the tape, but no other activity came up until the late afternoon, which was out of the timeframe I was examining.

I yawned and noticed the time on the video player clock. It was past four in the morning. I was badly in need of sleep and very disappointed I had found nothing. I decided to pack up and go to bed. What a waste of a night. Just before I shut off the video player, though, I decided to rewind to the lunch function one last time. Chris had mentioned his view had been obstructed by a door that stood open and I didn't remember seeing this on the tape.

I ran through the entire lunch once more, with my eyelids feeling as heavy as bags filled with sand, and then I saw it. On the bottom right of the screen there was part of a door that stood partially open. The camera had not caught the entire door. I rewound back to where the door appeared on camera and then hit play. What I saw made my eyelids fly wide open.

CHAPTER 10

I was fully awake as I rewound the tape and watched the segment of the couple embracing and kissing by the function room door. I must've watched it ten times before it finally sunk in that I had discovered the identity of the mystery woman. The attractive figure, the long blonde hair, and the supermodel looks, obvious even on the grainy black and white footage, proved there was no mistake—I was watching Elena Rourke on screen sharing a passionate kiss with James Geering.

I thought of the vanilla scent in Geering's room and of Elena at the Concierge desk later, reeking of the stuff. It all fitted in. But how? Even before I had time to digest it all, I rummaged through my telephone directory and dialled Dobbs's number in Hawaii.

"Hello," Dobbs answered the phone, and I could hear a baby crying loudly in the background.

"Hey, baby Rose has a real set of lungs on her," I said cheerily.

"Ferrari! How the hell are you?" Dobbs greeted me. "Rose is having her bath and she doesn't like it," he explained. "But wait, it must be like five in the morning over there; what are you doing up so early?"

It was indeed five in the morning, but I felt as energised as if I'd just got out of bed after a good night's sleep. I knew this was nervous energy and I was going to feel like death warmed up later. Thank God I was on the afternoon shift today.

"What's wrong?" Dobbs continued. "Did you get yourself into trouble, girl? I told you to wait until—"

I interrupted him. "I'm not in trouble, Dobbs—at least not yet," I responded while I wondered how I was going to handle this.

81

The baby kept crying in the background and I couldn't think. Dobbs must've read my mind. "Let me transfer the call to another room. Hold on a moment."

When he came back on the line I related what I had found on the CCTV footage. Dobbs expelled a long whistle. Then he said, "But are you sure it was Elena?"

"Of course I'm sure," I snapped impatiently. "I'm not stupid, you know."

"Okay, okay," he returned in a placating tone. "This complicates matters."

"Duh!"

"Now, Ferrari, don't get smart with me. I'm trying to think this out, too, you know."

"Sorry, Dobbs." I sighed. "It's just that I've been up all night going through these tapes, and this was after I had to pull a double shift. So right now I'm not the best of company, but I had to discuss this with you."

Dobbs agreed. "You did right to call me."

"So what do I do now?" I certainly had no idea on how to proceed and I wanted his feedback.

There was a moment of silence at the other end of the line and I thought I'd lost the call, but then Dobbs spoke. "Well, it's certainly suspicious, of course. But, Mia, this is circumstantial, to say the least. I mean, maybe Elena is cheating with Geering, but this doesn't mean they committed murder."

"True, but Geering lives on the Gold Coast, so when did the two meet? How long do you think they've been together? This could prove they've been planning it all along." I thought of poor David and wondered whether he knew what his wife was up to.

"Geering's been a guest in our hotel many times before. He always stays with us when he's on business in Sydney," Dobbs argued. "He could've met Elena at one of the many functions he attends. There's nothing devious in that."

He had a point. Elena had plenty of opportunities to meet people. Besides, she travelled on her own most of the time; therefore, she could have been going up to the Gold Coast and seeing Geering there as well. "So what does this mean? Did we just stumble upon an affair or a motive for murder?"

"Look, there's nothing you can do except go to the police with this information. They ruled the whole thing as a suicide, but if they think there are suspicious circumstances they may reopen the case. Let me remind you, however, you refused to tell Smythe about the hairdressing appointment Linda Liu asked you to make. That's a very important piece of information the police should've had."

I seethed at the thought of Smythe and how he hadn't shared any information with me, so why should I tell him what I knew? I wasn't going to say anything to Dobbs about it, though. "Well, I can't go to the police now. They'll say I was withholding information."

Dobbs sighed resignedly. "I hate to say 'I told you so', but I told you so."

"Thank you. That's very helpful, Dobbs," I returned with sarcasm.

He ignored my tone. "My advice is you wait until I get back next Monday. I can talk to Smythe."

Perhaps this wasn't a bad idea. I wouldn't have to lose face by going to Smythe and, more importantly, I wouldn't get into trouble with the cops if Dobbs explained the whole thing. "Okay," I agreed. "I'm willing to go along with that. We'll talk when you get back."

"Meanwhile, no more snooping!" he warned me.

"Of course not," I replied; the voice of innocence.

"Yeah, yeah. I don't know why I waste my breath on you." Dobbs saw right through me. "Just try to stay out of trouble for once, Ferrari."

I promised I would and sent my regards to his family before I rang off. My energy levels had dissipated by now and I was ready for sleep. I would have to think about this whole situation later. I went to bed, and my last thought before I fell into deep slumber was whether I should tell David about his wife.

When I woke up I had just enough time to shower and have something to eat before my shift started. I still felt tired and couldn't focus at work; therefore, it was a good thing I could operate on automatic: room checks; duty manager's log; walking the premises; touching base with department heads to ensure all was okay; welcoming VIP guests and escorting them to their rooms; and the list went on.

During all this time I battled with myself as to whether I should tell David that his wife was cheating on him. What if he already knew? After all, they didn't exactly act like a married couple, so maybe they had a mutual understanding between them. This could also account for the fact that he had asked me out to dinner. Perhaps, they were giving the appearance of living in a marriage, albeit a bad one, but they each pursued a separate life.

By dinnertime I hadn't reached any decision in terms of what I should say to David. I telephoned him, however, regarding Friday evening and we made arrangements to meet at L'Incontro, an up-market Italian restaurant in North Sydney. After the call I went looking for Thorny, but she was on a day off so I headed for the staff restaurant to get some dinner. I sat at a corner table eating a burger and fries, and I must've been a thousand miles away because Chris joined me and I didn't even notice.

"Ground control to Major Mia," he said, waving a hand in front of my eyes.

I looked up. "Oh, sorry, Chris. I was miles away."

"That's obvious," he replied as he attacked his own burger and fries. "Hey, have I got news for you."

Oh, no! I didn't think I could handle any more surprises today. I was too afraid to ask, but curiosity got the better of me. "So what's up?"

"There's something I need to show you, but not here." He looked around the half-filled restaurant and kept his voice low. "Can you come up to the penthouse?"

My heart started beating fast. This couldn't be good. "Chris, I thought I told you to stay away from this."

He ignored my reprimand. "Trust me. When you see this you'll be glad I was on the case."

"What case?" I exclaimed in a rather loud voice and noticed several heads turning toward me. I lowered my voice by a few decibels and said in a harsh whisper, "What case? There is no case."

He gave me a mysterious smile. "Just come up to the penthouse in about an hour. You'll be singing a different tune then."

Although I pressed him for more information he refused to divulge anything further, and I had to promise I would meet him later. We finished our meals in silence and went our separate ways.

I was exhausted by the time I made my way to meet Chris at the penthouse. There were so many thoughts revolving around my head that I felt dizzy. I was one hundred percent sure I was now looking at a murder and not a suicide. Well, I'd always been fairly sure, but discovering Elena in Geering's arms pretty much confirmed it. The problem was whether I could prove it was murder; and if so, what then? I didn't want to endanger those around me, nor did I want to bring a bad name to the hotel. Plus if Elena was involved in all this it would destroy David and Chris. Nobody wanted a murderer in the family, not to mention what this would do to their feelings.

Chris opened the door even before I had a chance to knock on it. "Come on in," he invited me to enter.

I followed him to his desk and he handed me a piece of paper. "What the hell's this?" I asked as I took it.

"Read it."

I glanced at the paper and saw it was part of a business contract of some kind. I scanned through the legal jargon until my eyes came across the names of James Geering, Kwon Lee and none other than Hung Liu. I looked up and met the triumphant look in Chris's eyes.

"How did you get this?" I queried with trepidation.

"I hacked into Geering's computer," Chris remarked nonchalantly.

"You what?" My trepidation morphed into terror.

"Calm down, Mia. Have a seat. Can I get you a drink?" Chris went to the drinks cabinet and grabbed himself a Coke from the mini-bar fridge. I nodded dumbly and he grabbed another can for me.

I took the can with a shaky hand and scanned the document one more time. "How could you do this?"

"Well, I pressed the print button and a piece of paper …" He stopped talking and his grin dissolved when he saw the savage look I threw at him. He then sat opposite me on a sofa chair and popped the top of his Coke can while he explained, "I sent Geering a confirmation email for his extended reservation and added malware software that got me into his computer when he clicked on the attachment I—"

"No," I interrupted furiously. "I meant, how could you involve the hotel like this! You sent him an email from the reservations department? What were you thinking?"

Chris laughed. "Relax, will you? I didn't send an email from the *real* reservations department. I simply made one up and sent it from my computer. You see, all I had to do was—"

I put up a hand. "Stop it, Chris," I chided him. "I don't want to

85

know how you did it. I'm only concerned with your meddling in hotel business. This could come back to hurt the hotel's reputation, not to mention what you did is illegal!" My voice increased in loudness toward the end of the sentence.

"Murder is illegal," Chris argued. "Who cares about a bit of hacking in order to get proof."

I held the paper up in front of his face. "What proof is this anyway? It only says Geering, Kwon Lee, and Linda's father are partners in the restaurants they have in Asia."

"Yes, and now we know where the money to finance the projects came from. So much for property development—I reckon it's drug money. Wasn't Linda's father involved in money laundering?"

I sighed and leaned back in my chair. "There's no proof this is drug money. For all you know this could be a legit business partnership."

Chris shrugged. "Maybe yes and maybe no, but we have enough material to get the authorities to reopen the case."

This much was true, I thought. We also had enough here to get ourselves into a heap of trouble, both with the cops and the bad guys. How in heaven's name were we going to explain this bit of paper? We couldn't tell the cops we simply hacked into Geering's computer. The guy wasn't even under suspicion, for fuck's sake.

"You don't look very happy," Chris observed.

I wanted to pour my Coke over his head. "You must be kidding me. How can I be happy when you just admitted to committing a crime? Not only are you putting us in a difficult position, but if your father finds out he'll kill us." Especially if Elena is involved, I thought darkly.

CHAPTER 11

I telephoned Dobbs when I arrived home after my chat with Chris. It was four in the morning Hawaiian time and midnight in Sydney, but I just couldn't wait any longer to call. Despite our many exchanges about my getting involved in things that didn't concern me, I had great respect for Dobbs's opinion—this time, more than ever.

"Hel..lo." A groggy male voice answered the phone. I couldn't quite make out whether the voice belonged to Dobbs or his son-in-law and I felt bad about disturbing their sleep, but some things just couldn't wait.

"Dobbs?" I queried, feeling even more guilt about calling a second time in the past twenty-four hours.

"Mia?" It was Dobbs after all; and I breathed a sigh of relief. "What the hell is going on now?"

I knew he wasn't going to like the reason for my call, but this couldn't be helped. "I apologise for waking you at this hour, but I need your advice."

"My advice was to STAY AWAY FROM EVERYTHING!" He reminded me in a loud voice that made me wince.

"I know, I know. But, honestly, this time it wasn't my doing."

Dobbs sighed. "Okay, I know I'm going to regret asking this, but what's going on now that can't wait until a more civilised hour?"

I told him about Chris's findings, and it took me quite a while before I could get him to calm down and speak with me in a normal tone of voice. Not wanting to wake up baby Rose had not been a consideration for him, but the more I insisted that he should keep his voice down, so he didn't wake up the whole of Honolulu, the more it sank into his head. Eventually, his voice returned to normal. "There is only one thing to do," he finally said.

"What's that?" I asked with rising hope.

"You have to talk to Smythe."

"What?" Now, it was my turn to speak loudly. "No way!"

"Way!" Dobbs replied. "You couldn't leave well enough alone, so now you fix this."

I sighed with frustration. "But you said—"

"Never mind what I said. That was before you involved Chris in this mess. You have to tell Smythe now! This can't wait until I get back. God knows you and Chris have placed yourselves in danger."

My heart was in my mouth. I had also had a feeling we were in danger even though there was no real proof of this. Call it female intuition; but when Dobbs vocalised it, somehow it seemed more real and it hit home. "How do you mean?" I wanted to know what he thought.

"Look, I don't know much about hacking, but I can tell you if Geering or Kwon Lee know anything about computers they'll figure out Geering's laptop has been compromised. The software Chris used probably contained a type of Trojan program that can be activated at any time. It's more than likely the computer's security program will pick up on it."

I swallowed hard. "So you're saying these guys will be able to tell someone hacked into their computer, and maybe even trace who did it?"

"Well, like I said, it all depends on how good they are. So my suggestion is you'd better speak to Smythe as soon as possible."

"Shit!"

"You can say that again, Ferrari. And let this be a lesson to you."

"Hey! It wasn't my idea to hack into Geering's computer," I protested.

"No, it wasn't," he agreed, "but you know how Chris idolises you and always wants to help. Now, let me get some shuteye. Rose wakes up the whole household by six so I don't have much time."

"I'm sorry, Dobbs, but I didn't know who to turn to," I said, feeling contrite.

Dobbs's response was firm but kind. "Be careful, Mia."

We rang off and I went to get ready for bed. I would have to get in touch with Smythe in the morning and I wasn't looking forward to it, so it was important that I be well rested. I had a feeling I was going to need all my energy to explain my way out of this one.

I telephoned Smythe at five in the morning and almost laughed at the surprise in his voice when I suggested we meet at Bill's Café for breakfast. My shift was starting at seven so I suggested six. Thankfully, his shift was starting at the same time as mine. I must admit I was nervous as hell calling him, let alone so early in the morning. At least he sounded intrigued rather than annoyed, which was a good thing in itself. I wasn't looking forward to divulging the information I had, but it would have been far worse if he'd been angry with me for disturbing him. I vaguely wondered why angering him should bother me, but I really didn't have the time to analyse this.

I jumped in the shower instead and then dressed in my uniform of black suit, white shirt, and black tie. Without the long overcoat, I looked more like one of the main characters in *Men in Black* rather than the guy from *The Matrix*.

Bill's was very quiet at this time of morning. When I entered I espied a table with three uniformed cops—probably from the Kings Cross police; another table with a couple of hookers; and one with a family of tourists—Ma, Pa and two kids, all excitedly poring over a map of Sydney.

Smythe was waiting for me at a corner table away from the other patrons. He was drinking a cappuccino and studying the breakfast menu. He looked smart in a grey suit and a white open-necked shirt. His hair was still damp from the shower and he was freshly shaved. His blue-green eyes spotted me the moment I came in and followed my progress to the table, which made me feel rather self-conscious.

"Morning," I said when I reached him, taking a seat opposite and raising my hand for the waiter. I couldn't talk until I had a shot of caffeine. Meanwhile, I quickly studied the menu, and when my extra strong cappuccino arrived I ordered scrambled eggs on toast with a side serve of grilled Roma tomatoes. Smythe went with the ham and mushroom omelette.

"So, to what do I owe the honour of this meeting?" Smythe addressed me when the waiter walked off with our orders.

I took a large sip of my cappuccino and decided the best way was the direct one. "There's something you should know about the Linda Liu case," I started, holding up a hand when I saw he was about to speak. "No, let me finish; otherwise, I'm not going to get through this without leaving something out."

He sat back in his chair and regarded me with curiosity. At least he wasn't glaring at me. I had his full attention and told him everything I knew, starting with Linda Liu making the hair appointment on the day of her death. This almost had him trying to say something, but he let me continue. I then told him about the vanilla scent and the CCTV footage of Elena and Geering. He raised his eyebrows at that one, but still allowed me to go on. Then came the difficult part: Chris. I started by telling him Chris was one of these IT kids who thought searching information for the right cause was a civil duty, and this was where Smythe finally interrupted me.

"You mean he hacked into Geering's computer," he uttered, none too happy. His eyes pinned me with a look I didn't care to interpret.

"Well..." I cleared my throat. "I wouldn't call it hacking exactly."

"No?" he remarked sarcastically. "What would you call it?"

"Investigating," I replied, pleased with my quick answer.

Smythe, however, looked anything but pleased. He leaned toward me, and the look in his eyes was menacing. I didn't need interpretation this time. "Do you realise I could run both of you in for withholding information, obstructing an investigation, and hacking into someone's computer?"

Thankfully, my temper came to my rescue and I threw caution to the wind. Fuck Smythe and his high and mighty ways. "Listen, Smythe; if you cops had done your job properly in the first place I wouldn't be here now, telling you about what I was able to find out with the help of an eighteen-year-old boy!"

"Don't be a smartarse, Ferrari. I can arrest you both, and you could lose your job over this," he threatened.

I glared at him. "So do it! You're a typical cop, taking it out on one of the good guys; only because I was able to do what you guys should've been doing. Why don't you just do it, then, and let the bad guys get away with it?"

There was a moment's pause where we both threw daggers at each other with our eyes. Then Smythe burst into laughter. Trust him to take the wind out of my sails when I was ready to do battle.

"Okay, I'm not going to run you in. I don't want to be responsible for you losing your job," he assured me. "But, Mia, what you did was wrong, and you need to concede this. Besides, you could've placed yourself and the kid in danger."

Mia? He called me Mia? I needed another cappuccino and ordered one when the waiter came with our food. Smythe followed my example.

"I'll tell you what I'm going to do," he declared. "I'll reopen the case and run this by the feds." He saw the question in my eyes and added, "If there's a link to international drug money the feds need to be notified. At present, everything you told me is circumstantial so I'm going to have to dig deeper. You need to promise me, however, that you'll drop this—no more snooping for you."

I nodded, but of course I didn't mean it. This was my case. If it weren't for me, Linda Liu would be a suicide, which everyone had already forgotten; and I wasn't going to allow this to happen to the poor woman.

It was bad enough when men trampled on women while they were still alive; but it was worse when they did it to the memory of the dead. "Very well," I responded in a serious tone, "but I'd like to be kept informed."

Smythe gazed at me with incredulity. "Hey, you're lucky I didn't arrest you."

"And you're lucky I told you everything I found out," was my rejoinder.

He smiled reluctantly. "Fair enough. But I can't reveal anything confidential. You got that? I will, however, keep you informed of any progress."

Patronising bastard! "Fine," I said, thankful he couldn't read my thoughts.

Our coffees arrived and we sipped them quickly, mindful of the time. I was due at the hotel in fifteen minutes.

"One last thing." Smythe remarked. "Bear in mind this could all come to nothing. Linda Liu was taking a lot of drugs for her condition and it might well be this is, after all, a bona fide case of suicide."

"I know," I replied as I finished my coffee. But I knew better.

Smythe insisted on picking up the tab and I wasn't going to stop him. At least he was useful for something, I thought with cynicism.

"Thank you," I uttered begrudgingly. "You've been very understanding and I appreciate I still have a job." The words almost stuck in my throat. The last thing I wanted was to be beholden to him, but it couldn't be helped.

"Stay out of trouble, okay?" he replied with amusement in his eyes. He obviously didn't believe I would, and he was probably right. But I wasn't going to admit it to him—ever.

"Thank you for breakfast. I have to rush now or I'll be late." I bade him goodbye and left the café.

The streets were quiet while I walked back toward the hotel, which was a few blocks away, and I had the sudden, distinct feeling I was being watched. I stopped and turned, thinking it might be Smythe watching me from a distance, but I saw no one. I shrugged and glanced at my watch. I had five minutes to get to work so I picked up my pace, but something made me turn my head again—this time while still walking. Then I saw it. About a block away, an Asian face disappeared behind the corner of a building. It was a male face with long hair and a goatee.

CHAPTER 12

I decided to wear red for my dinner with David on Friday evening. He always saw me dressed in the hotel uniform and, while nicely tailored, it wasn't especially feminine. Moreover, I wasn't exactly the feminine type, either. I had always been more of a tomboy type, and I usually chose comfort over fashion. Having said this, my *comfort* had to be chic and cool, such as my black outfit with the long coat a-la-Matrix.

When it came to David, though, I wanted to look like a real woman because this was how he made me feel. He had always treated me like a lady, which is more than I could say for Nathan, who was so self-centred he only cared about one thing—himself.

I chose a knee-length, body-hugging, sleeveless red dress with a matching bolero jacket, and wore it with my only pair of black high-heeled shoes and a black evening bag with a spaghetti-thin shoulder strap.

I rarely wore jewellery, except a watch and tiny hoop earrings; and tonight was no exception, but the earrings I decided to wear this evening had special significance. They were the ones David had given me as a gift when we were in Venice. They consisted of small and daintily shaped Venetian carnival masks in 18-carat gold. It had taken me quite a while to decide if I should wear them. I'd debated in my mind as to whether they would send out the wrong signal. The last thing I wanted was to be perceived as coming on to him. This was simply a dinner between two friends and work colleagues. The earrings were so lovely, however, I couldn't resist so in the end I indulged myself.

I applied make-up very lightly plus a soft blush to my face along with black mascara, which accentuated the blue of my eyes. The last touch was bright red lipstick that matched the colour of my dress. I never wore eye shadow or anything heavy to emphasise my looks. In fact, I noted with satisfaction that the less make-up I wore, the younger I looked. Besides, I was blessed with smooth skin and hardly had any wrinkles for someone my age. My secret weapon—a diet high in olive oil. This was the secret of most Mediterranean women, especially Italian ones.

David was meeting me in the restaurant at my insistence. He had wanted to come by and pick me up from my place, but I thought it would be best if I met him instead. This would drive home the message that we were not out on a date, but simply two friends getting together for a meal.

I arrived to find him waiting for me at the bar. He was wearing smart-casual, tailored black pants and a matching jacket with a burgundy open-necked shirt. His wavy brown hair and green eyes complemented his tanned skin. Unlike me, he was olive-skinned and tanned easily; whereas if I went out in the sun for more than fifteen minutes I began to resemble a lobster; olive oil or not. I was, after all, descended from northern Italians, so in my family we had all been fair-skinned and susceptible to sunburn.

David's background was from Ireland, though he had been born in the United States. He had come out to Australia as a little boy but still had a soft American accent that, mixed with his deep-timbered voice, made him sound very sexy.

"You look beautiful." He greeted me with a peck on the cheek. I noticed his eyes go to my earrings, but he said nothing. I simply gave him a dazzling smile and accepted a glass of Pellegrino water from him. "I wanted to wait until you arrived before we ordered the wine," he added.

I sighed with delight. What a gentleman, I thought. "Thank you."

The maitre'd greeted us then, and offered to take our jackets. "It's rather cool this evening, but we have the heating on."

We handed over the jackets and David turned to me. "Would you like to sit in or out?"

The restaurant consisted of a formal dining area inside and an informal garden-like setting outside that was fully protected with clear Perspex sheeting and heating. "Outside would be nice," I suggested.

Our host nodded and showed us to a table in the garden area. It was quite lovely with vines and star jasmine growing in profusion all around the perimeter of the garden, which was enclosed with timber crisscross trellises. The setting reminded me of the Botticelli painting, *Primavera*. It was the epitome of spring—romantic but at the same time casual and therefore, more relaxed than the formal interior. We were seated at a corner table that, while cosy, was surrounded by the noise of other diners, and thus not conducive to true intimacy.

A sommelier came to enquire about our choice of wine and after a glance through the wine list, we settled on a pinot noir from the Piedmont region of Italy. Almost immediately, our table waiter came to tell us about the specials for the evening and rather than study the menu, we ended up choosing the same thing from the specials: *crema di pomodori al basilico*, a tomato and fresh basil soup to start and then *pollo al chianti*, chicken breast prepared with red wine, red pesto and grapes, served with a side of polenta and rocket salad with a piquant Italian dressing.

It was a simple meal but one that suited our palate for all things fresh and in season. We laughed when the waiter left to fill our order.

"We still have the same taste in food, I see," David remarked, and I knew he was referring to the short time in Venice where we went exploring the maze of narrow streets surrounding Piazza San Marco, which were filled with shops, cafés and quaint, intimate restaurants. This was a lifetime ago, but it seemed like only yesterday that we had been two young people who met on a holiday and fell in love within the space of a few days.

"I can cook most of this stuff myself, you know," I uttered in order to dispel the magic of the past, which was threatening to reach into my present.

"Yes." David nodded. "I know. But it's much nicer when someone else does it for you and you can relax."

We smiled at each other, and then the wine arrived. Thank God, I thought. We toasted to a lovely meal to come from the kitchen of L'Incontro while I was relieved that David seemed to have the same intention of keeping this on neutral ground.

"Thank you for looking after Chris during my absence," he added with another toast. "I don't know how you put up with his youthful energy, but thank you all the same."

I smiled and wondered how he would react if I told him that his son had hacked into someone's computer and we were now in potential danger; not only this, but his wife was having an affair with Geering right under her husband's nose.

These two thoughts revolved around my mind while we chatted about David's trip and I updated him on VIPs and functions coming up for the hotel. We continued talking through our delicious meal and I told him about Dobbs's granddaughter and how cute she was, as Dobbs had emailed me some photos of her. Then David told me he was thinking of expanding his hotels into the US market, starting with Hawaii and later moving to the west coast on the mainland.

By the time we finished off our meal with espressos and a slice of cassata gelato each, my head was hurting from my disturbing thoughts and I decided for now I should leave things alone. Telling him about Chris was out of the question; as for Elena's infidelity, this was none of my business. If the police informed David of the fact, then so be it.

We parted at the restaurant's car park with him pecking me on the cheek and I drove off feeling somewhat empty. What did I expect? David was still married, even though the marriage was not a good one, and I was still smarting from my break up with Nathan. The last thing I needed was to get involved with someone else.

The traffic started to slow down, even though it was past ten in the evening, and I wondered whether there was an accident up ahead. I switched on the radio in the hope of catching the traffic report. In the meantime, I drove in a stop-start fashion, heading toward the harbour tunnel. I looked around me to see if David had taken the same road as I had, but I didn't see him. If he was anywhere near he'd be behind me because he had waited until I was on my way before he drove off. I looked in the rear view mirror, trying to spot his navy blue BMW, and my heart stopped. Driving in a silver Mercedes a couple of cars behind mine was Kwon Lee.

I wasn't sure whether to ring Smythe or not. This could just be a coincidence, I told myself, and I was not really being followed. On the other hand, who was I kidding? Somehow, Kwon Lee and Geering were suspicious of me and now I was being pursued by a killer to see how much I knew. At least, I assumed Kwon Lee was a killer—he certainly looked like one with his creepy looks and that long pinky nail.

The traffic was still crawling and I was going nowhere fast. Not that I thought Kwon Lee was going to step out of his Merc and come to shoot me through the head in the middle of a traffic jam, where everybody would see him. But I didn't know what he intended by following me around. What worried me was that every person he saw me with was someone else I was placing in potential danger. I picked up my mobile and dialled Chris. Hopefully, his father was caught up in the traffic, as I was, and Chris could talk with me freely assuming he was home.

"So what's happening, Ferrari?" He answered on the second ring, obviously seeing my caller ID on his mobile screen.

"Are you at home alone?"

"Hey, aren't you taking things a bit too far? You don't have to keep an eye on me now Dad's back, you know," he teased.

"I'm not. Just answer my question."

He must've heard the urgency in my voice. "Yes, I'm home alone. What's the matter?"

"Tell me something; is it possible for someone to tell who hacked into their computer?"

"Sure it is, but it depends on how much they know about computers," he replied. "What's going on?"

"I'm being followed; that's what's going on!" I snapped.

"Geering?"

"Kwon Lee," I answered. "And this is the second time I've seen him tailing me. So I'm thinking he suspects me for hacking into the computer. But how could he know?"

Chris was quiet for a moment. Then he replied, "Well, it's almost impossible for them to know exactly who hacked into their computer."

I felt a glimmer of hope. "How's that?"

He sighed momentarily as if trying to simplify his explanation for my benefit. "Okay. In layman's terms, what I'm doing is going through the Wi-Fi service provided by the hotel for the guests; so there's no way for them to tell who actually got into their computer."

"You mean they can't tell it was a particular person?"

"That's right."

"How does that work?" I asked. I wanted to be absolutely sure.

"Too long and technical to go into, but let's just say that while they can trace this came from the hotel domain, they can't tell the exact computer that hacked into theirs; let alone, the person."

I didn't really want to know how this could or couldn't be found out. My understanding of computers went as far as using its applications. "All right," I uttered, feeling better. At least, they wouldn't be able to tell Chris was the hacker because they didn't about him. Let them think it was me instead. "So as far as they know it could be anyone in the hotel—even a guest."

"Right."

"Good."

"Did you want me to look up anything else in there?"

I felt my heart palpitating inside my chest. "No!" I shouted. "Chris, listen to me," I said in a serious tone. "You have to forget about all this, you hear? I don't want you to be in danger. Besides, Smythe knows about the hacking."

"He what!" Now it was his turn to shout.

"It's okay. Calm down." I tried to placate him. "He let it go this time, but he expressly warned me to stop snooping, and that goes for you, too."

"But why did you tell him?" Chris protested.

"Dobbs told me to. And if these guys can trace internet domains or whatever, it means they're good and we may be in danger." Then I added as an afterthought. "Oh, and whatever you do, don't tell your father."

"As if I would!"

Good. Chris understood exactly where I was coming from. I was almost tempted to tell him about Elena. But no, I could only discuss Elena with Dobbs. "I'll see you tomorrow then. I'm on afternoon shift."

"Okay. But, Mia, one question."

"What?"

"I'm certain these guys can't tell who compromised their computer; but even if they could, they can't trace it back to the actual person; then can only trace it to the hotel domain."

"Yes, and so?" I wondered what his point was.

"So why do you think they're following you?"

"That, my friend, is the sixty-four million dollar question," I replied as I felt the icy hand of fear around my heart.

CHAPTER 13

I really had no idea how Geering and Kwon Lee had made the connection that I was looking into their affairs. No one but Dobbs, Chris, and now, Smythe, knew what I was up to, and I was sure none of them would have blabbed to anybody; so I had no explanation as to why I was being followed.

It might have been a hunch Geering had due to my attentiveness toward him after his wife's passing or perhaps someone had overhead Dobbs and me talking; though, I didn't see how this was possible because we always took care when we discussed private matters. The only other possibility was that Richard may have let something slip when I borrowed the CCTV tapes. I didn't want to question him and arouse suspicion, but when Dobbs returned to work on Monday I would ask him to make some discreet enquiries.

When I took the tapes I'd had to sign them off in the security log, so anyone with access to the log could have found out I was viewing them. The date and time coverage of each tape would have been recorded there.

I glanced at the clock on the kitchen wall and saw it was only seven. It was Saturday morning, and I had six apartments to view before lunchtime. I had plenty of time, however, to have breakfast and shower before my first appointment at nine. Once I found a place I liked I could work out what furniture I would be taking with me.

Nathan and I had agreed to split the furniture fifty-fifty, with my having the first pick. I had already decided he could have the bedroom suite—too many memories there. More than likely I would take the lounge room furniture and a few other bits and pieces, but first I had to see what I could fit into a one-bedroom place. My current apartment had ample space plus a storage cage in the underground car park. I was going to miss this. At the same time, I looked forward to downsizing and adding a few touches of my own to obliterate the memory of my married life as much as possible.

Nine o'clock sharp found me standing outside a high-rise building on Macleay Street. The apartment I was about to view was on the eighth floor and had partial views of Sydney Harbour. The only problem with it was that it didn't offer a parking spot, which probably explained why the rent was reasonable.

I had thought about selling my car now that I was going to live close to work, but Sydney was a city where having a car was a must because the public transport wasn't renowned for its frequency or reliability.

By noon, I was exhausted but happy I had found one apartment that suited all my needs. Moreover, it had a parking spot, but alas, no water views. No matter. The parking was more important, and the Art Deco apartment was roomy and overlooked a lovingly landscaped garden. I put in an application and holding deposit immediately and the real estate agent advised he would let me know if the landlord approved me by Monday at the latest.

My shift at the hotel was starting at three, but I went in beforehand in order to have lunch with Chris. We decided to meet up at a small café around the corner from the hotel. We didn't want to run the risk of anyone eavesdropping. I recounted the events of Friday evening over coffee and Italian panini.

"The traffic was really slow going into the harbour tunnel, and Kwon Lee tailed me all the way to the eastern suburbs," I told him.

Chris frowned. "I hope you didn't go straight home."

"No, I didn't. But what does it matter? If they can find out their computer's been compromised, they can certainly find out where I live."

"True," he agreed. "So what happened then?"

"I pulled up into a service station to fill up the tank and took my sweet time about it. After a while, I saw him driving off. He probably thought I wasn't worth waiting for any more."

Chris looked thoughtful. "What I'd like to know is why he's following you."

"I thought about this already," I remarked, savouring my cappuccino.

"And?"

"Well, you pretty much ruled out the computer thing. There's no real proof as to who it was that hacked into their computer except it was done from the hotel. So my theory is someone overheard me and Dobbs discussing the case, or maybe they saw me borrow the tapes."

"What tapes?" Chris regarded me with curiosity.

Shit! I hadn't told him about the tapes because of Elena. "I just wanted to check the footage for the tenth floor to see if anyone went into Linda's room before she jumped," I quickly improvised.

"But I thought the police took those tapes."

"Yes, but I went back to footage covering a few hours prior," I replied, and added, "I found nothing."

Chris was a smart guy and if I kept talking about the tapes he would put two and two together and realise I could have been checking out who Geering was kissing. The last thing I wanted was for him to start asking questions, so I changed the subject. "Hey, I hope you didn't mention any of this to David."

He laughed. "Are you kidding me? I already told you I wouldn't."

"It's just that I don't want to bring disrepute to the hotel. Besides, if your dad finds out you're involved he'll have my hide."

"Your secret's safe with me," he reassured me.

"And you promise you won't hack into any other computers?"

He held a hand to his heart. "Cross my heart and hope to die."

I swallowed hard. I hoped no one else had to die. I went back to sipping my cappuccino in silence, and when we finished lunch we walked back to the hotel.

"I'll see you later," Chris said.

I made my way to the duty manager's office and signed in on the DM's log. Alex, the morning DM, was still around. "Hi, Mia," he greeted me, handing over the keys and pager. "We had a super busy breakfast so I didn't get to finish off a couple of the room checks. Do you mind?"

"No," I replied, "just give me the checklists."

Each duty manager was responsible for carrying out at least five random room checks. This was a way to ensure housekeeping turned over the rooms to the high standard required by Rourke Hotels. If something was found amiss we took it up with the executive housekeeper. Alex handed me the checklists.

"Thanks a million, darling. I owe you." He blew me a kiss in the air and waved farewell on his way out.

I smiled at his handsome face and retreating athletic form. Too bad he was gay—the real gorgeous ones always were. I shrugged and got on with checking his notes on the DM's log.

The hotel was quiet until the cocktail hour when in-house guests and business people gathered in the lounge around the piano to have a drink before dinner, discuss plans for the evening, or simply to enjoy the soft jazz played by our regular piano player, Martin.

On Friday and Saturday evenings we usually had a vocalist belting out the blues. Nola was an African-American from New Orleans who'd been with the hotel for close to five years. She had an Ella Fitzgerald type of voice that for some reason reminded me of hot chocolate. It was sultry and quite sexy.

As I crossed the lobby and passed the bar I thought how fortunate it was Linda Liu had not decided to jump on a night when Nola was singing. If so, we might have had more than one fatality. Luckily, Martin only played from six to eight, Sunday through to Thursday and was joined by Nola on Fridays and Saturdays, when they performed until late.

"Ms Ferrari," a male voice called out as I was walking past the lounge. I looked around and my blood turned cold. It was Geering, motioning for me to come over. He was sitting at a small marble-topped table having a drink with Kwon Lee.

I approached them with a cool and professional smile. "Good evening, Mr Geering," I greeted him and only slightly glanced in Kwon Lee's direction. After all, I wasn't supposed to know who he was. "How may I help you?"

Geering returned my smile, but I noticed it wasn't a warm one. In fact, it was more like a half smile. "Aside from wanting to thank you for looking after me so well, I thought I'd introduce you to my business partner, Mr Kwon Lee."

I then nodded at Kwon Lee, but made no attempt to shake his hand.

"Although Mr Lee is not a guest of this hotel you'll be seeing a lot of him," Geering continued, and I wondered whether he was making a veiled threat.

Lee didn't speak at all, and I gave a slight nod in his direction once again. "If there is anything I can help you with, please let me know." I directed this to Geering while I felt the Asian's gaze on me.

"Thank you, Ms Ferrari," Geering said. "We'll both remember that."

I managed a smile and walked away while I felt two pairs of eyes following me. I was in no doubt that I had just been warned off, and once again I wondered how they had become suspicious of me. I couldn't wait until Dobbs returned on Monday. I needed someone I could confide in. I fleetingly thought of Smythe, but telling him wouldn't help. Besides, I hadn't heard a peep out of him. Well, I wasn't holding my breath that he was going to keep me informed. Dobbs could handle him once he was back.

Toward the end of my shift I entered a couple of issues in the logbook for the night shift to take care of, and with a few minutes to spare I went on the internet and did a search on Geering's upcoming restaurant.

There were several articles from various news forums talking about *Capone's*, an obvious name for the gangsters and molls theme. Most of the information I read had to do with the entertainment Capone's was going to put on and certain acts that were coming to perform from overseas. There were a couple of photos from the Gold Coast Capone's theme restaurant and the article went on to describe the elaborate props that went into recreating the 1920s era.

I skimmed through a number of similar articles until one of them made me stop and re-read the paragraph about the props. It explained they were custom built in Hong Kong to maintain the consistency of the restaurants through the entire chain, and due to the delay with the Sydney building the props were currently warehoused in Alexandria along with all the restaurant equipment and furnishings. A warehouse! If there was any proof to be had about the link to drug money this could be it.

I picked up the telephone receiver with the full intention of calling Smythe, but then changed my mind and replaced it in its cradle. The police couldn't search the place unless they had a warrant, and in order to get one they would need to have enough of a motive to investigate. At present, all they had was what I had given them—a document linking Geering, Kwon Lee, and Hung Liu as partners in the restaurant business. The link to drug money was purely conjecture. Smythe would dismiss my theory and lecture me all over again for sticking my nose into police business.

This meant there was only one thing to do: I would have to go and take an unofficial look at it myself. Of course, I couldn't ask Dobbs to help me; he'd never go for it. Chris was also out of the question. I was sure he would jump at the chance to play detective, but it was far too dangerous. Not only this, but if we were caught by the cops we'd be arrested for breaking in; and if we were caught by Kwon Lee, I hated to think what would become of us.

I sighed with frustration and shut down the computer. There must be a way around this, but I needed time to think. In fact, I first needed to get the exact location of the place and go to take a look from the outside. If I went during the day I might be able to work out how to get in. Since Alexandria was full of warehouses no one would think it strange if I took a stroll around the place. If someone questioned me, I could always pretend I'd lost my way looking for some other warehouse. The main thing was to ensure I wasn't being followed when I went out there and that I wore some sort of disguise in case someone stopped me or my image was caught on camera.

"Mia." A male voice called and I jumped. It was the night manager. "What are you still doing here? It's past eleven."

"Just leaving, Jim," I said and grabbed my jacket, which was hanging on the back of my chair. "Nothing major to report. Have a good night." I smiled at him and handed over my pager and keys.

CHAPTER 14

Sunday was a busy day at work with a large luncheon function for a twenty-fifth wedding anniversary. I worked the morning shift and by the time I got home I was too exhausted to do anything but sleep.

Dobbs would be arriving on an evening flight from Hawaii, but he had rung prior to his departure to tell me not to worry about collecting him from the airport. He knew I was working hard and wanted me to get my rest. I insisted, but he wouldn't budge, and now I was grateful. I really needed to catch up on my sleep.

I awoke before dinner, had a long shower, and made myself a bowl of pasta with pesto for a meal. Then I settled down in front of the computer to do a little more research—this time on the possible drugs Linda Liu had been taking. There was still a chance I was running around in circles for nothing and that this truly had been a bona fide case of suicide. My intuition told me this was poppycock, but I had to cover all angles.

Smythe had refused to divulge the name of the drugs Linda Liu had been taking, and all I knew was that she had been on anti-depressants and some kind of insomnia medicine. I did a search on anti-depressants, and after reading up on side effects I discovered that any one of them could have been solely responsible for making Linda jump. This was rather ironic. Imagine taking anti-depressants, only to have them make you even more depressed to the point where you want to commit suicide. So what was the friggin' reason for taking the drugs in the first place? I asked myself in frustration. The sites I'd been reading did specify side effects like these were rare. Still, there was always a chance that the drugs alone would have made her jump out of desperation.

I realised I wasn't going to get anywhere with the anti-depressants research so I carried out a search on insomnia drugs instead. This turned out to be more interesting. There was a drug called zolpidem, sold under a whole lot of different trade names, which was used for the short-term effects of insomnia. The article was quite technical and obviously written for medical practitioners. Despite this, I could understand quite a lot of it, especially the part where it stated the drug was a rather controversial one as it had been found to have hypnotic effects on some patients.

Side effects were known to include hallucinations of varying intensity, delusions, and altered thought patterns as well as euphoria and/or dysphoria, a deep state of depression that often carried a heightened risk of suicide.

Great! I thought and slammed shut the lid of my laptop. Once again, what was the point of taking this drug when it could make you suicidal? No wonder the police ruled it as a straight case of suicide.

I sighed again with exasperation and decided to make coffee, which I drank while deep in thought, looking out the window of my apartment. For reasons I couldn't explain, I knew things didn't gel. There was still a niggling thought at the back of my mind that I couldn't quite figure out and it was driving me insane. All I knew was that it was important and connected with the possible side effects of this drug.

The telephone rang and I was jolted out of my trance-like state. It was close to ten. "Hello," I answered, wondering who could be calling this late in the evening.

"Honey, I'm home!" Dobbs said cheerfully at the other end of the line.

"Hey! Welcome home, Dobsy. How was the flight?" I was relieved he was back. We had so much to discuss.

"Too long," he complained, "but comfortable. I had no one sitting next to me so I stretched out and slept most of the way. And now I'm wide awake."

"Did Eileen return with you?"

"No, she's too happy being a new grandmother so she decided to stay on for the rest of the month. She'll be back in about two weeks."

I teased him. "Then, you're a bachelor for a little longer."

"That's right. Aah, sweet freedom," he joked back.

I remarked knowingly, "Sure. Sure. You know very well you're lost without Eileen."

"I know that, and you know that, but don't you dare tell her, girl, or she'll never leave me in peace." He snickered in a good-natured way.

"Hey, what time are you on tomorrow?" I changed the subject.

"I'm on at seven. Why?"

"I thought if you're not too tired we might do breakfast prior to starting our shifts. I'm on at seven, too."

"Count me in," he confirmed, "but I can't guarantee I'll be wide awake. I don't feel at all sleepy now."

"Serves you right for sleeping on the plane," I chastised him laughingly. "But don't worry; I'll make extra strong coffee, guaranteed to make your eyes will stay wide open all day."

"Does this mean you're making breakfast?"

"Yes. I don't want to run the risk of being overheard." I didn't want to tell him about Kwon Lee following me just yet. Dobbs was bound to worry, and then he definitely wouldn't get any sleep tonight. "I'll tell you all when you get here tomorrow. How's six o'clock?"

He agreed and we said our goodnights. I went to bed shortly thereafter with something still nagging at me, but as I couldn't tell what it was I figured getting some sleep would be best. I had an early start in the morning.

I tossed and turned, finding it difficult to fall asleep, but I can't say I was surprised after having drunk coffee so late in the evening. It must've been around two in the morning when I finally dropped off. And a little while later, I sat up in bed, wide awake, and knew what it was that had been bothering me all evening.

I went out to the lounge and switched on my laptop, going once again to the site regarding zolpidem. I glanced through the information and suddenly there it was: zolpidem had been found *to cause hypnotic effects in some patients.* I then remembered Thorny had mentioned something about her yoga class and how she enjoyed it because of a kind of self-hypnosis exercise they did, where they affirmed positive suggestions. I reasoned that if a person could affirm something positive to themselves they could just as easily affirm something negative.

It was feasible that under the effect of the drugs Linda Liu was taking someone could have suggested to her that she should take her own life. It made perfect sense. Geering told the police how Linda had been depressed due to the death of her father and that she would have been under severe stress because of the upcoming court case, where she was to testify. It was entirely possible, therefore, that with enough drugs and suggestions she could have been in the right state of mind to be convinced into taking her own life.

This was a wild theory, of course, but one worth noting, and I discussed it with Dobbs when he arrived at six.

Judging from the look in his eyes he hadn't slept any more than I had. After I let him in and gave him a big hug I went straight to the kitchen to make the extra strong coffee I promised him.

Dobbs brought me a set of Hawaiian glass coasters with embedded sand in various colours forming a beach scene. "Thank you, Dobsy," I said and pecked him on the cheek. "We'll use them right away for the coffee mugs."

He beamed at me and proceeded to set them on the dining table while I prepared scrambled eggs with grilled ham and Roma tomatoes. We mostly talked about baby Rose while I moved around the kitchen, but once we sat down to our meal I turned the conversation to what I found out regarding the drug. Dobbs listened carefully, without interruption, and only spoke when I finished.

"Well, it's certainly a possibility, but this could have worked both ways. Linda could have convinced herself to jump because of her depression or someone else could have talked her into it. Unfortunately, you can't prove anything."

I sighed, feeling helpless. "I know. All I have in this whole case is pure supposition."

"It certainly sounds that way, but tell me more," he prompted.

"Remember how Geering got his times mixed up, saying he headed for his suite at around quarter to ten; but then I saw him forty-five minutes later when they were taking away the body?"

"Yes. So?"

"So maybe he left the function a lot earlier and went to talk his wife into jumping. Once she did it, he stayed in the room for a while before he finally came out."

Dobbs had finished wolfing down his breakfast and now sipped his coffee. "But that doesn't explain why he waited a whole forty-five minutes before he came out and bumped into you. It doesn't make sense," he pointed out.

"Maybe he did it on purpose to make himself look like a devastated husband. You know, like someone in shock who couldn't think straight at the time. This would gain him sympathy in the eyes of the police."

"Well, it would certainly explain the time delay, especially if the cops believe he was in total shock. On the other hand, he could be telling the truth, and he got his times mixed up because of the way he was feeling. It's easy to lose track of time when something so tragic happens."

I nodded. "Granted. But this is only feasible if he's truly innocent."

"Well, if he's not he certainly put on a good act of looking distraught," Dobbs observed.

"You're right, of course." I sighed. I wasn't getting anywhere with this. "More coffee?"

"Please."

I refilled our mugs and brought out a couple of blueberry muffins. Dobbs did not refuse when I offered him one. "It's only a little reward because you managed to lose some weight," I declared with a smile. He had lost quite a few pounds from the look of him. "But don't you go putting it back on, okay?"

"I promise, Ferrari." He laughed and then attacked his muffin. "Mia," he remarked after a while, "perhaps this is as the police said— a clear-cut case of suicide—and you'll have to accept it."

"You could be right, but it still doesn't explain why Linda wanted to have her hair done."

"Maybe she was going through a mood swing," Dobbs suggested. "You did say this drug can have euphoric effects. So she could've been happy and planning to go to the function one minute, and then her mood changed and she felt depressed. If this was the case the last thing she'd remember would be the hair appointment she asked you to make. She simply wouldn't care about it."

"Of course, you're right. But when I get a hunch like this I just know there's more to it than meets the eye," I stated with conviction. "It's like when I knew Nathan was cheating on me. He was very careful to cover his tracks, but I just knew."

"Yes, but you can't go comparing Linda's case with someone you've lived with for years. Nathan's behaviour may have seemed different, because of what he was up to, and you simply picked up on it, no matter how subtle, because you lived with him for so long and knew him. Linda, on the other hand, was a complete stranger to you."

"Mmm. Perhaps." I refused to acknowledge Dobbs might be right.

"Ferrari, you're one stubborn broad," he remarked.

I smiled. "Good. Because I just know there's foul play here somewhere, and I'm going to get to the bottom of it come hell or high water."

"Okay. You know best, I guess," he conceded. "Now, tell me about your meeting with Smythe."

I frowned with distaste. "He's an arsehole!"

Dobbs laughed. "That's not what I asked. I know how you feel about him; but Mia, it was very decent of him to let you and young Chris off the hook. You withheld vital information in an investigation and Chris hacked into Geering's computer for God's sake!"

I smiled. "True. I must admit I don't understand why he let us off the hook. Could it be the man's human after all?"

"Stranger things have happened," Dobbs replied, tongue-in-cheek.

"Anyway, there's nothing to tell. He said he'd run it by the feds and let me know what happens as long as it's nothing confidential. That's his way of saying he won't discuss it with me."

"Well, I've got a poker game coming up on Friday. Perhaps, I can get something out of him." He grinned.

"Thank you," I said. "I was hoping you'd offer to do that."

"Hey, that's what friends are for. But you have to promise to stay out of this," he warned me.

That's when I gazed at him with a guilty look in my eyes.

Dobbs sighed. "Okay, Ferrari, what gives?"

I explained about Kwon Lee following me after I'd had breakfast with Smythe, and then again on the night I had dinner with David. I also told him about Geering's veiled threat when I saw him and Kwon Lee at the cocktail bar.

"How could they know I was up to something? Chris assured me it was pretty much impossible for them to track down the person who hacked into Geering's computer. They may be able to identify the hotel's ISP number, but we have hundreds of people using the Wi-Fi, and that's just the staff. Then there are guests, and even visitors; so it could've been anybody. I don't know why they think it's me."

"I can't answer that one; but maybe they have a hunch, just as you have about Linda. Who knows."

"Anyway," I went on thoughtfully. "There's also the matter of their warehouse."

The white in Dobbs's eyes grew larger. "Say what?"

I decided to confide in him. After all, there was no one else who could help me. "I read in a news article that they have their props made overseas and shipped into Australia. They're now stored, along with all their restaurant equipment, in a warehouse at Alexandria. I'm trying to locate exactly where this warehouse is."

"And why is that?" Dobbs asked in a careful voice.

"Because we need to go and have a look."

He frowned. "We, as in you and me?"

"Yes."

"You're crazy, Ferrari!" His tone was stern. "What part of 'stay out of it' didn't you understand?"

"But, Dobsy—" I started to say.

Dobbs stood up. "Don't you 'but Dobsy' me, missy. There ain't no way you're going to that warehouse. If you do, I'll tell Smythe!"

I stood to face him with daggers in my eyes. "You wouldn't!"

"Yes, I would," he stated forcefully. "Mia, I don't think you understand what you're getting yourself into. This isn't Magnum PI. It's real life. You could get hurt or worse."

"Okay, okay," I said and backed down. "Don't get your knickers in a knot."

Dobbs seemed pacified. "Well, we better get to work now."

"You go ahead. I'll stack the dishes in the dishwasher and I'll be right behind you."

Dobbs left after he threw me a warning look. I should have known better than to tell him. There was no way he was going to help me. He had left the force because of a near-fatal shooting and vowed never again to place himself in danger and risk making his wife a widow. So why would he help me now?

"Ferrari," I spoke aloud, "it looks like you're on your own with this one."

CHAPTER 15

I had asked Dobbs to take a peek in the security log to see if someone other than security personnel could have had access to the register and seen my signature for taking out the CCTV tapes, where I had discovered Elena Rourke in the arms of James Geering.

Dobbs met me for morning coffee at the staff restaurant. His eyes looked bloodshot.

"Man, you look as bad as I feel," I teased and got a glare out of him. He usually became grumpy when he had no sleep, and I didn't exactly feel like a million dollars, either.

"I had a look at the register," Dobbs reported, finishing his espresso and about to get up to go for another one.

I stood up. "I'll get it, Dobbs. You look like you're going to drop. Want to join me in a cappuccino this time?" He nodded, and I went to order our coffees.

When I returned, Dobbs added two sugars in his cup and continued talking. "As far as we can tell, no one other than the general manager saw the register. He had to approve an insurance claim that was made by a guest whose car got scratched in our car park."

"Well, it was worth a try. It'd be too much to hope the murderer would sign something off on the register, anyway," I remarked, feeling disappointed.

"By the way, Smythe called this morning," Dobbs announced.

"What does he want?" I was on alert.

"Nothing to get excited about, that's for sure. He actually asked for the tapes where you saw Elena with Geering."

"Isn't he going to subpoena them?"

"Yes, of course; but as a courtesy I'm letting him have them straight away," he replied.

"Did he say what's going to happen?" Surely Smythe must've told Dobbs something. I knew he didn't want to divulge things to me, but Dobbs was his poker buddy.

"He wants you to go in when you have time and make a statement about what you discovered on the tapes. It's just a formality."

I scowled. "Oh, so Mr High and Mighty doesn't want to give me any information whatsoever, but he needs my help now!"

Dobbs shook his head. "I will never understand this antagonistic attitude between you and Smythe. You really have to get over it, Ferrari," he chided me.

"I don't care what you think," I glowered. "He's an arrogant bastard!"

Dobbs laughed. "Arrogant or not, he can subpoena you if you don't cooperate. Besides, don't forget he let you off the hook."

"Yeah, yeah," I returned angrily. "How could I forget with you reminding me of it all the time?"

"I'll make you a deal," he uttered in mild amusement. "You cooperate, and I'll see what other information I can get out of him on Friday night."

I brightened at this. "Poker night!"

"You got it." He grinned.

My mobile phone vibrated just then and I took the call. It was the real estate agent coming back to me regarding my application.

"It's a go, Mia," he informed me. "When would you like the lease to commence?"

"Is two weeks okay?"

He agreed and we made a time for me to go to his office for the signing of the lease and to pay the security bond.

"Hey, you didn't tell me anything about your new place," Dobbs remarked when I finished the call.

"You were away, that's why. I managed to find a great Art Deco apartment in Potts Point. It's only got one bedroom, but it's large and the high ceilings are fantastic."

"Congratulations!"

"Yeah, well, I'll be saving money on petrol by walking to work now."

"Good for you. So when's the move?"

"I'll start packing immediately. I've got about five weeks left until I have to vacate my place, but the sooner I do it the better; don't you think?" I hated moving and frowned at the thought.

Dobbs must've read my mind. "Don't worry," he consoled me with a smile. "If you feed me I'll help you pack and move."

I wanted to kiss him but didn't think it would be appropriate in front of the staff at the restaurant. "Thank you. I really appreciate it; and I promise you a feast."

"Good. I'm counting on it." He stood up. "Now I'm off to do my rounds."

We walked out of the restaurant together and while Dobbs went to the security office to pick up a master key, I headed off to catch up on my emails. Once done, I carried out my room checks and later looked in on the kitchen. Thorny was in her office and, from what I could see through the glass window, she was telling off some poor chef.

It was close to lunchtime and the kitchen was buzzing with activity; therefore, I was surprised she was doing this when everyone could see what was going on. I was further surprised when after much hand-waving and hat-throwing, Thorny pointed at the door and the chef turned, let himself out of the office, and slammed the door shut behind him. He strode past me without seeing me and walked right out of the kitchen. I was stunned. The chef was Tony.

I opened Thorny's office door a crack and poked my head in. "Is it safe to come in?" I asked meekly.

Thorny sighed, picked up her chef's hat from the floor, and motioned me in. "God, you can't find good help anywhere these days."

I took a seat opposite her at the desk and watched as she shuffled through some papers. "The guy can't write a menu to save his life," she murmured, almost to herself.

"What happened?" I wondered how Thorny could be involved with someone at work and at the same time tell him off in that fashion. How could they possibly go on working together after this?

"Idiot Tony, that's what," Thorny spat out, still bristling. "I asked him to design a special menu for the Drummond wedding and he comes up with the most predictable, unoriginal menu ever! You'd think he was an apprentice chef instead of a senior one."

"So where did he go now? I saw him storming out."

"I sacked him," she stated in a dismissive tone.

"What? You can't do that! You have to go through HR. He'll take us to court for unfair dismissal."

"Let him try," she growled defensively. "I've issued him with several written warnings in the past for his substandard work, so I don't think he'll make any trouble."

"Okay, but what about the other thing?"

She gazed at me questioningly. "What other thing?"

She must've been so angry she'd forgotten about her fling with him. "You know—your personal involvement with him," I reminded her.

She glanced at me in confusion for a fleeting moment and then it dawned on her. "Oh, that," she said casually. "He was just a lay; and nothing to write home about, either." She threw the papers she had been shuffling in the bin and picked up a pen. "I better get to designing the menu now. The bride and her mother are coming by in one hour to discuss it with me and I have nothing to show them."

This was my signal to leave her alone and I took my departure, wondering how she could dismiss Tony so easily—both from work and from her bed. Thorny could be a puzzle sometimes. I had known her for about five years and during this time I'd seen her fall in and out of love with a number of men, but I had never seen her dismiss one so easily from her life. Perhaps, this was different because she worked with the guy and therefore didn't want to reveal her personal feelings for him, especially in front of the kitchen staff.

I went back to my computer, and with a little bit of time to spare before the end of my shift I ran a search to see if I could locate the warehouse used by Geering. I searched under "Capone's warehouse + Alexandria", but all that came up was a whole string of articles about Geering's restaurant in Sydney and the suburb of Alexandria. I then tried "Capone's warehouse" on its own; this didn't yield anything worthwhile, either. A search on James Geering revealed a whole bunch of articles about the man and his career in property development plus the theme restaurant concept including the ones in Asia. In desperation, I tried Kwon Lee, but nothing much came up other than the fact he was Geering's partner and ran the restaurants in Asia.

I gave up in the end and decided to make a start with the packing when I got home. The boys from the purchasing department had collected a number of carton boxes for me and had kindly helped to put them in the back of my little hatchback. My car was still at the loading dock so I went down there to thank the boys for the boxes and then drove home.

Once I arrived and changed from my work clothes, however, I lost the desire to pack and took a nap instead. I hadn't had much sleep the night before and I was really exhausted. When I woke up it was close to dinnertime and I fixed a quick plate of pasta with pieces of chipolata sausage laced in a tomato-based sauce. I suddenly thought of Dobbs, home alone. He loved chipolatas, with their piquant taste of herbs and onion, especially the ones I purchased from Giorgio's deli, which were made with finely minced beef.

I picked up the phone and dialled him. "What are you making for dinner?" I asked when he answered.

"Nothing yet. I didn't get a chance to go shopping so I was going to order a pizza."

"Why don't you come over? I've got chipolatas from Giorgio's," I said with a tone of enticement.

"I'm there, lady." Dobbs hung up, and I laughed. He loved my cooking and I liked having his company. After eighteen years of eating with someone it was difficult to go back to eating alone. I fleetingly thought of Nathan and decided I didn't miss him so much as I missed the idea of having someone to come home to.

Dobbs lived about ten minutes down the road from where I was, so I kept the sauce on low heat and added a touch of red wine to it while I cooked extra pasta. He arrived just as the pasta was ready and brought with him a bottle of cabernet sauvignon to go with the meal.

I prepared a mixed salad with homemade Italian dressing, and sliced some crusty ciabatta bread. Dobbs poured the wine and we sat down to eat.

"Thanks for the invite," he said. "I wasn't looking forward to pizza for one. This is much better."

I smiled. "Did it occur that I'm enticing you with my food so you can make a start on the packing?"

He laughed. "Ferrari, I wouldn't put anything past you; but I already told you I was going to help."

"I know. I'm only kidding. It's just that you love these sausages so much and I had plenty for two. Besides, if Eileen isn't home to look after you, I may as well do it."

"And I'm glad you're doing it," he replied cheerfully. "I hate cooking, and I'd probably end up eating junk until the wife gets home. Then, heaven help me." He rolled his eyes in supplication.

I grinned and helped myself to salad. "In that case, I better cook for you more often."

We ate in silence for a few minutes. Then, Dobbs spoke. "Smythe came by this afternoon to pick up those tapes."

I had a sip of wine and remained calm. I wasn't going to let Smythe spoil my dinner. "Good."

Dobbs seemed surprised that I didn't blow up at the mention of my archenemy. "I also found out a few little bits and pieces," he commented casually.

Now he had my full attention. "And?"

Before he went on, he helped himself to salad, took a bite of ciabatta bread and washed it down with a few sips of wine. I wanted to throw the bottle at him, but instead I waited patiently.

"And," he finally said, "it seems the feds came up with nothing. The business is legit. As for Elena, Smythe will want to question her. I told him she's overseas at present and he said he'll start by having a chat with David."

Oh, no! This was going to come as a huge shock. I had to warn him.

"What, nothing to say?" Dobbs was looking at me.

I faked a smile. "What do you want me to say? It's not going to be pleasant for David and Chris to find out Elena's been fooling around."

"It'll be hard on them, I agree; but let's face it, it's not like David and Elena have much of a marriage. She's always jetsetting off to some place or other," he observed.

"Yes, I know."

I changed the subject and told him about Thorny's dismissal of Tony, the chef, and we finished the rest of our meal talking shop. At the back of my mind I was already planning how I was going to warn David that Elena might be under suspicion. I couldn't let the poor man face this without being prepared.

Dobbs didn't know about my history with him. I had never told him because the subject had never come up. In any case, it wasn't like there was anything going on between me and David now.

CHAPTER 16

The following day was my day off and I caught up on my sleep as I was still quite tired. When I finally awoke I felt refreshed and ready to start packing. Dobbs was working the morning shift and I invited him over for dinner again. I vowed I was going to look after his diet until Eileen returned from Hawaii.

Today was also the day when I had made arrangements to sign the lease for the new place, and after lunch I made my way to the real estate office. I had only packed a few boxes with books and DVDs and thought if I made Dobbs a really nice dinner I could get him to work off some pounds afterwards by helping me pack some more.

As I drove toward Kings Cross I saw the hotel from a distance and decided now was as good a time as any to contact David and arrange a meeting with him. I had to warn him about the pending visit from the police regarding Elena. When I stopped at a red light I picked up my mobile and dialled his number.

"Mia." He answered on the second ring. "How are you?"

I had to put him on loudspeaker when the traffic got going again. "Hi David, do you have a moment?"

"Sure. Where are you?"

"I'm calling from the car," I replied, already feeling uncomfortable in anticipation of our meeting. "It's my day off, but I wondered if we could talk. There's something important I need to discuss with you."

"Of course," he said immediately. "Did you want to drop by the office?"

"If you don't mind I'd much rather meet you off-site." The last thing I wanted was for Dobbs to see me in the hotel on my day off. He would ask all sorts of questions and then accuse me of meddling.

"Okay," David agreed. "Is something the matter?"

"I'd rather we talk face to face. Can you make this afternoon?"

"Let me check my diary." He put me on hold for a moment.

I didn't know what he made of this call or the fact that I sounded dead serious, but he didn't attempt to find out. He simply took my word that I wanted to talk to him about something of importance. I liked this. Had it been any other male I would have been peppered with questions of all kinds. "How's three o'clock?" he said when he came back on the line.

"Perfect. Why don't we meet at Puccini's? It should be quiet at that time of day," I suggested.

David concurred and we rang off. I figured it should only take me about a half hour with the agent, so I had plenty of time to get home and tidy up before I met with David. Right now, I was wearing a pair of old jeans and a T-shirt. I wanted to make myself more presentable before I met with him.

I walked into Puccini's wearing black jeans and a red shirt, with my usual bright red lipstick to match and black sunglasses. David was at a corner table toward the back of the café. He was in full suit, having come straight from the office, but he'd taken off his jacket and loosened his tie. I thought he looked rather tired and I sighed. What I had to say to him wasn't going to make him feel any better.

"Thanks for meeting me." I smiled as I approached and took a seat opposite him, taking off my glasses.

A waiter came up immediately to take our order. I went for a cappuccino; David stuck to black coffee.

"So what is it that sounded so serious on the phone?" He spoke when the waiter walked off.

I sighed. "David, I don't know how to tell you this, but I thought you may want to hear it from a friend instead of the police."

His eyebrows rose. "The police? Is Chris in trouble?" There was concern in his voice.

"No, nothing like that," I reassured him. "It's to do with Elena."

"What about her?" His lips set in a firm line and I wondered why he put up with the woman; she seemed to bring trouble into his life every chance she had.

"There's really no easy way to say this," I continued, "so I'll just come right out with it—she's having an affair."

Green eyes gazed into mine steadily. "Is that all?" he remarked, not the least bit surprised. "But why the police involvement?"

So Elena had been unfaithful before. The man hadn't even reacted to it. I was about to explain the police involvement in the matter—which I was sure was going to elicit a different kind of response—when the waiter arrived with our coffees. David thanked him and the waiter turned and walked away.

I reached out across the table and placed my hand on his forearm. "The reason the police want to talk to you is because Elena is, or was, having a thing with James Geering. You see, there are questions about Linda Liu and whether she actually committed suicide."

David responded as I thought he would. He looked stunned. "How do you know this?" He managed to ask after a few moments.

I gave him a watered-down version of my involvement in the case and then told him about the tapes I had discovered. I didn't want to get into the whole thing with him lest he think I was interfering—which of course, I was.

"Look, I just thought I should warn you because the cops want to talk to you about Elena, plus they want me to give a statement about my findings on the tapes. It's all a formality and I'm sure it's the same thing with the questioning of Elena." I cleared my throat uneasily. "I mean, I'm sure she's not involved, but the police have to cover all angles."

David nodded. "Of course I'm happy to cooperate in any way I can, and I'm sure they'll want to talk to Elena at some point. I'll get her to come back early from Switzerland. I only hope it's as you say, and that it's just a fling and not something illegal."

"I'm so sorry, David. The last I thing I wanted was to tell you something so unpleasant, but I thought you should be prepared before the police call on you."

David covered my hand with his. I felt warm all of a sudden and slowly withdrew my hand on the pretext that I needed it to add another sugar to my coffee. Of course, I was fooling no one, least of all him, but he didn't remark on it. He simply smiled and I was surprised.

"You're probably wondering what kind of marriage I have," he remarked.

For once, I was at a loss for words. David had never spoken to me about his relationship with Elena.

"I've a confession to make," he said.

I cleared my throat again, this time feeling nervous. "You have?"

"We never spoke about this, you and me; but you need to know this goes all the way back to Venice."

He had my full attention, and since I didn't know what to say I let him go on.

"I was in love with you and wanted to marry you," he declared, "but you thought me too young at the time; and before I could convince you to give me a go, Nathan came along and swept you off your feet."

Now I found my voice. "David, I felt the same about you, but I couldn't see it working out for us. You were so young at the time, and I wanted you to experience life before you made such a huge decision about settling down. Oh, and Nathan never swept me off my feet—I want you to know that," I stated with sincerity. "At the time I mistakenly thought he was a safe bet. Of course, I didn't know I was marrying a psycho." I grinned, and this lightened the mood. It was getting too intense and I didn't want to go back to the *what if* scenarios with which I always tortured myself.

"Well," David continued, "I wanted to let you know the reason I went with Elena—it was on the rebound. And when I came to my senses, it was too late because she was already pregnant with Chris. I couldn't leave her then."

"It was the honourable thing to do," I reassured him. "Most guys would have dumped her. There is one thing I'm curious about though."

"What's that?"

"Chris is a young man now, and you didn't even seem surprised Elena is having an affair; so why stay married to her?"

He didn't answer straight away and I saw a number of emotions cross his face. Finally, he said, "I know this is going to sound lame, but you might say we fell into a kind of habit. At first we stayed together for the sake of Chris and later it just seemed natural to stay together. We formed a kind of silent agreement whereby we'd each have our separate lives."

I didn't reply and simply sipped my coffee. He was right. It was lame. I had always thought him a strong person and yet he had stayed with Elena for no good reason other than habit. I could understand at first when Chris was a young boy, but now … Well, it didn't make sense to me, but I didn't want to judge him. He chose a life of habit for his marriage just as I chose the security I thought Nathan represented. David and I had had our chance, I thought regretfully, and we let it slip away.

I noticed he was waiting for me to say something. "Look, it's really none of my business. I shouldn't have asked about your marriage. I'm sorry," I stated in a contrite voice.

He laughed suddenly. "No, you're not, Ferrari," he returned with a twinkle in his eye. "You may think I don't know very much about you, but I have eyes and ears; and I know you love a good mystery, too."

Dobbs! I thought; but perhaps Chris had let something slip. I hoped David had no idea just how much I knew. "David, one thing I ask of you," I added. "Don't tell the cops I warned you in advance."

He nodded. "Of course I'll keep this between us. You've done me a great service by warning me."

"I felt I should; and thanks for keeping quiet about it." If Smythe found out, he'd have my hide and kick my butt into jail for obstructing an investigation. Thinking of Smythe, I suddenly remembered I was supposed to drop by to make my statement about the tapes.

We finished our coffees and our chatter was mainly to do with the hotel. Before I left, I said, "David, thank you for being so open with me. I really appreciate it. I think this has brought us closer as friends."

"I'd like to think so, too," he replied.

"Don't think me bitter and cold, but right now I'm getting over a bad break up and I'm not always myself." I didn't want him to think his confession regarding Venice didn't mean anything to me.

He pecked me on the cheek. "Ferrari," he remarked, "whatever happens remember I'm here for you and that I'm a close friend—always have been and always will be, no matter what."

Our eyes met for an intimate moment and I saw in his the promise of something that might develop in the future. Thankfully, the waiter came by to clear up the table and the moment disappeared.

"May I get you anything else?" asked the waiter.

David shook his head and asked for the bill. I thanked him and excused myself. "I have to go and give my statement to the cops now."

"Try to stay out of trouble, Ferrari." David grinned.

"Have you been talking with Dobbs?" I made like I felt affronted.

"No, but I hear him calling you 'Ferrari' whenever he's exasperated with you."

I threw him a saucy smile. "Does this mean you're exasperated with me, too?" God, what was I doing flirting with him in this fashion? I had just told the man I was getting over a bad break up, for heaven's sake.

"It simply means it suits you. It's a good name," he answered.

"It's a good car," I returned.

"Get on with you." He made as if to shoo me out the door.

"Thank you," I said again, "and David, I'm sure everything will be cleared by the cops."

He smiled and I left. While I drove toward Kings Cross police station, I thought about our whole conversation but refused to go into the *what if* scenarios. I simply stuck to the official bits, meaning the police questioning David and later, Elena. I had told David I was sure Elena was not involved in anything illegal. However, after seeing her kissing Geering on the tape and knowing the kind of woman she was—one with a head full of power—it occurred to me this could be a crime of passion and suddenly I wasn't so sure Elena was incapable of something like this.

I didn't know anything at all about the woman, except that she had affairs and liked to throw her weight around as if she owned the world. This was not very reassuring and there was nothing to say she didn't have something to do with Linda Liu's death after all.

CHAPTER 17

Smythe wasn't around when I went in to give my statement to the police, and for this I was grateful. The man simply got on my nerves. Despite what Dobbs said about letting go of my resentment I still held Smythe responsible for my not getting into the police force. The fact that I could have re-applied at a later time, once the height restrictions had been abolished, was not the point. I still hated his chauvinistic attitude toward females.

Then there was Nathan, who had never wanted me to join the force in the first place. He used to tell me it was too dangerous for me, but in truth I knew he secretly felt it wasn't glamorous enough to have a wife who was a cop. Like a fool, I believed him about the danger bit, thinking he cared. All that really concerned him, though, was his own image. In the end, it was my own fault for listening to him and not re-applying. Even so, this didn't stop me from hating his guts—his and Smythe's. The two could have been twins for the way they felt about women.

I suspected they just couldn't handle a woman who knew her own mind. This went a long way to explain why Nathan had dumped me for a bimbo who probably thought she was nothing without a man, and why Smythe was divorced. Men!

After giving my statement, I was in a rush for time because I had to prepare dinner for Dobbs. I had every intention of getting him to pack at least ten boxes or more. Therefore, I had to provide him with some of my best dishes.

I made a quick stop at Giorgio's Deli for some fresh ingredients on the way home and then got busy in the kitchen. I worked long and hard, and by the time I was done I was proud to say the meal I prepared would have done justice to any five-star restaurant.

The entree consisted of *insalata verde con Gorgonzola* and *bruschetta casalinga*, homemade bruschetta. The insalata—or salad—was made with rocket and radicchio leaves, sprinkled with crispy, fried pancetta, walnuts, garlic, and crumbled Gorgonzola cheese, all dressed with extra virgin olive oil and balsamic vinegar. This was accompanied by the bruschetta bread, which was sliced and toasted ciabatta bread topped with chopped, sundried tomatoes, mozzarella, and dried oregano. I would slip it in the oven at the last minute so the mozzarella cheese would melt over the bread.

For mains, I had decided on a hearty beef stew with tomatoes, wine and peas, served with mashed potatoes to soak up the rich sauce. The side dishes to accompany the stew were vegetarian—stuffed porcini mushrooms with chopped, fresh parsley and garlic—to be finished off in the oven when Dobbs arrived along with roasted plum tomatoes brushed with extra virgin olive oil and served with ground black pepper and fresh oregano leaves. The whole feast would be rounded off with mini-cannoli and coffee.

I figured after this sumptuous meal Dobbs would have to work off the calories and pack a large number of boxes for me. It was true what they said about the way to a man's heart being through his stomach, and this didn't only apply to love; it applied to manipulation as well. I smiled in silent triumph and went to take a quick shower before Dobbs's arrival.

Dobbs was a happy man after dinner and he packed fifteen boxes with crockery, glassware and various other kitchen items; plus we made a start on my study and packed away files, stationery and books. We worked silently until about ten and then I rewarded him with the mini-cannoli and coffee. The poor man was exhausted, but the dessert and coffee picked him up.

"You working tomorrow?" He asked after finishing his last cannoli.

"Early shift," I replied. "You?"

"Same."

"I went to give my statement today," I informed him. "Thankfully, Smythe wasn't on duty."

Dobbs laughed. "Lucky for him. I'd hate to be your enemy, Ferrari."

I smiled. "Yes, I know. I can be extremely devious and wicked."

"And modest, too," he added with a grin, "but you are an

excellent cook, and this makes up for all your devious and wicked ways."

"Dobsy, you're not implying I cooked you a feast so you'd help me pack?" I teased.

He gave one of his deep belly laughs. "Girl, you do beat all. That's exactly what I'm implying."

"You know me too well."

"Let's just say I could see it coming," he parried and kept laughing.

We finished our coffee in this jovial mood; then Dobbs prepared to leave. "Superb dinner." He kissed me on the cheek.

"Dobbs, do you think Elena is capable of murder?" I asked suddenly.

He shrugged. "Who knows? I've lived long enough to learn that people are capable of anything when they want something badly enough."

I frowned. "I feel terrible for David and Chris. They're going to be so upset when all this comes out in the open."

"Can't be helped," Dobbs remarked. "And I hope it was only a fling and that she's not implicated in anything illegal."

I wanted to confide in him about having warned David, but I couldn't bring myself to do it. He would only get upset and tell me I was interfering too much. I knew I was, but I felt I owed it to David; and this was something I couldn't explain to Dobbs.

"Let me walk you out," I said. Once outside, I pecked him on the cheek. "Thank you for packing."

"Thank you for cooking," he replied and patted his tummy. "I think I'm going to gain all the weight I lost in Hawaii."

"I won't let that happen, Dobbs. Don't worry; I'll make sure you work like a dog to help me move." I grinned.

He let out a whoop of laughter and waved at me as he drove off.

The next morning I received a phone call from my lawyer asking if I was willing to move forward the settlement date for the sale of my home. He informed me that Nathan had agreed. Of course he had, I thought. The bastard wanted to get whatever equity he had left in the place, which wasn't much since most of it was mine.

Fuck it! Let him have his way. I wanted this whole thing over and done with so I could start my new life. Besides, I'd already signed the lease on the new place and I could move in any time after this week. I gave my consent and we set a date for two weeks' time. This brought forward my move and I rostered myself off for three days so I would have enough time to organise the whole thing.

No sooner had I fixed the roster that the phone rang again. I answered, "Mia Ferrari."

"Mia, do you have a moment?" It was David. His voice sent a rush of warmth through my body.

"Sure," I said, sounding as businesslike as possible.

"I'll meet you in the lobby café in ten minutes."

I beat him to the café and ordered a couple of cappuccinos while I waited. He joined me soon thereafter. "I wanted to let you know I received a call from Detective Sergeant Smythe."

I screwed my nose in distaste. "Just call him Smythe."

"You obviously don't like the guy." David remarked as the coffees arrived.

"Like him? He's an arrogant prick," I spat out. Then I saw the surprise in David's eyes so I explained, "Smythe and I go way back to when he was instrumental in the rejection of my application to enter the police force; so there's no love lost between us."

"I'm sorry to hear it," he sympathised. "But are you saying this guy can't be trusted?"

I sipped my coffee and thought about this for a moment. Smythe might have been an arsehole to me, but as far as I knew he was an okay cop. "No, I have no reason to believe he can't be trusted. Just put it down to my dislike of him, but don't let him browbeat you. You know how these cops are."

David smiled. "Thanks for the advance warning, but I think I can handle him."

"Oh, I didn't mean to imply you couldn't handle him. It's only that ..." I didn't really know what I wanted to say. "Never mind." Shut your mouth, Ferrari or else he'll think you're going soft on him.

"I got hold of Elena and asked her to get back to Sydney," David announced.

"Did you tell her why?" I hoped he had so it would teach her a lesson for being a cheating bitch. It wasn't only men who cheated after all.

"No, I told her I needed her to be here for the discussion on the Hawaii property."

I was surprised. "I didn't know Elena was involved in the

127

business. Most of us think she likes lording it over us." Oops! That came out before I was able to stop it.

David did not seem to mind and shook his head. "She's not involved in the business at all. The hotels belong to me, but she likes to think she's involved; and this time it suited me to let her believe it."

I smiled. "David, if I didn't know any better I'd say you're getting to be as sneaky as I am."

"You're not sneaky." He gazed at me with something like fondness in his eyes.

I felt the familiar warmth spreading through me again but needed to stay strong. Perhaps there was a future for David and me, only not now. Even if I were totally over the Nathan thing, there was still David's involvement with Elena. Sure, he'd said they had separate lives for a long time now, but this wasn't good enough for me. If I ever got involved with another man he would have to be totally and absolutely free. No ties. I wasn't going to be like these women who involved themselves with a guy simply because he said it was all over with their spouse, even though secretly they were still living with them. In other words, I wasn't going to be like Nathan's bimbo.

"I should be getting back," I stated, taking a peek at my watch and putting an end to a conversation that was threatening to become personal.

David finished his coffee. "Of course," he responded, looking a little surprised.

I hoped he hadn't expected me to enter into a flirtation with him simply because I had warned him about the police. "Thanks for letting me know about Smythe's call to you," I added as we stood up. "And remember not to say I warned you about the visit."

"Don't worry. And, Mia, thank *you* for tipping me off," he returned in his businesslike manner.

I liked it better this way. "You're welcome."

Our eyes met for a fleeting moment and I thought he was going to add something, but instead he turned and went on his way.

I was left feeling rather deflated. David had taken me into his confidence and I blew him off like he was coming on to me. I watched while he walked across the lobby and disappeared into one of the lifts. I didn't have time to think about this now, nor did I want to. David was out of bounds to me, which was how I liked it—at least for now.

When I turned to make my way back to my office I almost collided with Kwon Lee, who happened to be walking toward the café. My blood ran cold. I had almost forgotten he'd been following me. His creepy eyes looked into mine for a second and then with a nod of his head he walked on.

I went to my office and brought the DM's log up to date, checked emails, and handed in my room checklists to the front office manager, but all the while my thoughts revolved around Geering and Kwon Lee. It was entirely possible Elena had nothing to do with Linda's death; and perhaps it was something Linda knew about her husband and he had to shut her up. Why else was he now getting his business partner to follow me? This whole thing didn't make sense.

Nothing made sense anymore; but there was one thing I knew for certain—I had to get into that warehouse and see whether I could find any evidence to explain what in hell was going on.

CHAPTER 18

Dobbs decided to pull a double shift and called before I left the hotel to inform me he wouldn't be coming round for dinner. I laughed into the phone. "It's the packing that's got you worried, isn't it? I promise there isn't much left to do."

"You have some strange notions, Ferrari, but I'm sorry to disappoint you—it's not that. I'm just swamped with work," he said at the other end of the line.

"Okay, tomorrow night is open if you're interested."

"I'm there!" he replied, and we rang off.

In fact, I was rather relieved I didn't have to cook this evening. I was tired and the only thing I felt like doing was ordering pizza and watching a DVD. There was simply too much going on in my life at present and I wanted a bit of peace and relaxation.

It was difficult to cope with so much change all at once. Not only was I having to get used to living on my own again; I also had to move from what had been my home. On top of this, I was getting nowhere with the Linda Liu investigation; plus David was back on the scene.

Well, it wasn't so much that he was back on the scene, but more like there was now potential for him to re-enter my life. We were friends already, but not in the way I was friends with Dobbs. There would always be a kind of sexual tension between David and me; so we were more like intimate friends.

I showered when I got home and pottered around the place trying to decide what furniture to take with me and what to discard. Before I knew it, it was past six and I wasn't surprised at the rumblings in my protesting stomach. I was famished. Lunch at work had consisted of a quick sandwich in between room checks and attending a couple of meetings; therefore, an early dinner was just what I needed along with a nice, long movie like Lawrence of Arabia to put me to sleep. Just as well I hadn't packed all my DVDs as yet.

I decided to order in and was reading through the pizza menu from a local place down the road when the doorbell chimed. Not now! I want food! "Yes?" I queried through the security intercom.

"Mia, it's me," said a young male voice.

"Me? Who's me?" I replied, hoping this wasn't a ruse by Kwon Lee to gain entrance to my building or worse still, a couple of Mormons coming to talk about "God's chilluns".

"It's Chris." The voice cut into my thoughts.

"Chris! Come through." Surprised, I buzzed him in. Chris had never come to my place before. We always saw each other at the hotel. How odd that he should come to my home. Then my heart skipped a few beats. What if something had happened to David?

When I opened the door, however, and saw Chris's smiling face, I expelled a sigh of relief and let him in. He didn't look distraught at all, so whatever it was it couldn't be bad.

"Sorry for intruding in on you." He greeted me with a peck on the cheek. "I should've called first."

I motioned him into the lounge room. "Have a seat and excuse the mess. I've been packing."

He parked his tall frame in one of the sofa chairs. "Dobbs told me he's been helping you pack. When do you move?"

"In a couple of weeks." I felt my tummy rumbling again. "Hey, I was just about to order pizza. Want to join me?" I simply had to eat or I would faint.

Chris nodded. "That'll be great, thanks. I'll have anything with pepperoni on it."

I went to the phone and ordered two large pizzas, one with pepperoni and the other with ham, mushrooms and olives. "I only have Coke to drink," I announced after I placed the order.

"Perfect." Chris looked pleased. "My favourite drink."

I took a seat on the sofa opposite him and curled my legs under me. "So what's going on? Don't tell me your dad kicked you out and you've decided to move in here."

He laughed. "Not quite. I just wanted to see you face to face to thank you for what you did for Dad. He told me the whole thing this afternoon."

I went on alert all of a sudden and wondered what he meant by "the whole thing". Chris must've guessed what was on my mind because he explained, "If you're wondering about Elena, I've always known she cheats on Dad."

"Oh." I nodded, like it was the most natural thing to do. What else could I say to the boy?

"I know Dad filled you in on their 'special arrangement'," Chris added, sounding rather cynical.

I shook my head, feeling confused. "I'm sorry. I'm not quite sure what you're getting at."

He sighed in exasperation. "I mean Elena's lifestyle—the travel, the spending of Dad's money, the many men in her life. Need I go on?" He noticed me gazing intently at him. "I'm not exasperated with you, Mia," he assured me. "Don't get me wrong. I'm simply fed up with Elena."

"Well, this is between your parents. I mean, I know they live separate lives and all, but Elena's still your mother."

Chris replied with bitterness in his voice. "My mother? I never had a mother—at least not since I can remember."

I frowned. "But—"

"I know you're confused," he interrupted. "What I meant to say is that Elena was never there for me. It was always nannies when I was little and then on to boarding school while I was growing up. She barely spent any time with me, and if it weren't for Dad I'd never see her again."

My heart went out to him. I had always thought of Chris as the son I could have had. He was a smart and respectful young man, and I enjoyed his company immensely. How could Elena throw it all away? Some people just didn't appreciate what they had.

"I'm so sorry, Chris," I commiserated. "David never mentioned anything to me about your relationship with your mother."

"Don't call her my mother. She's just someone who had a baby. A real mother is defined by what comes afterwards."

He was dead right. Almost anyone could bring a child into the world, but it was what happened afterwards that was important. Elena was a case in point. She'd had the baby, but then lost interest in the bringing up of this lovely young man. I assumed David was responsible for everything Chris had become.

Chris stood and came across to where I was sitting. I moved

over on the two-seater to make room for him; even so, he was a bit too close for comfort. I realised this was now a vulnerable boy sitting next to me and not the confident young man I usually dealt with.

He turned to me and continued talking. "I've always known about her affairs—more than Dad knows." There was pain in his eyes when he admitted this. "The worst part was that no matter what I said to Dad, he wouldn't leave her." He paused, as if gathering his thoughts, and then added, "I told Dad he should fight for you, Mia. You should've been my mother; not Elena. You guys really stuffed up, you know? You went off and married that good for nothing Nathan, and Dad went on the rebound and married the ice queen."

My mouth dropped open to form the figure O.

Chris smiled when he saw the look on my face. "I know all about Venice. Dad told me some time ago."

"I ... I don't know what to say," I murmured when I was able to find my voice.

"Don't say anything," Chris said. "What I'm trying to tell you is since I've known you you've treated me as a son more than Elena ever did. I always wanted you as my mother. Besides ..." He went silent for a moment as if searching for words. "Besides, you're cool," he declared finally.

I laughed. I had been called many things in my life, but never *cool*. "I'll take that as a compliment then."

"It was meant to be one," Chris stated. "I guess you oldies can't relate to what it means to be cool," he observed as a matter of fact.

"Hey!" I protested and shoved him back with my hands on his shoulders. "Speak for *other* oldies, mate! This chick," I stated, pointing a thumb at myself, "is as cool as a cucumber."

Chris laughed. "See? I knew you'd understand; and I didn't mean to call you an oldie. You're all right, Mia Ferrari."

I felt my cheeks grow warm. "Well ... I mean ..."

"Hey, I'm sure you can take a compliment from a younger man. After all, Dad's younger than you by ten years."

"Yes, but you could be my son," I pointed out. "And I'm not a cradle snatcher."

We laughed together. This was the kind of banter I could see having with a real son; if I'd ever had one.

Chris's face was serious once more. "This is difficult for me to say because I don't know how you're going to react. But I want you to know that as far as I'm concerned I've always considered you to be a kind of mum to me. I used to fantasise you were my mother when I was younger and hung out in the hotel with you during school holidays. Now, I see you as a role model."

I grinned. "First of all, I'm relieved you fantasised about being my son and not anything else. That's a real relief," I emphasised, and he smiled. "Second, I'm not much of a role model for you. Look at me; I almost got us arrested by Smythe."

"Yes, but you managed to get us out of it, too," he responded with a grin of his own.

Just then, the doorbell chimed. "That's probably the pizza," he announced. "I'll get it."

He went for the door and I stood and followed. "Hey, it's my treat."

"No, no. It's mine," he insisted and buzzed the pizza man into the building.

"Thank you. You're sweet." I went to get plates, paper napkins and glasses.

We ate at the dining table and Chris almost consumed the whole bottle of Coke by himself. I had to get another one out of the fridge. "Too much sugar, Chris," I chided.

He gave me a cheesy smile. "Now I should warn you that this is the only part I don't like about having a mother. Don't nag," he said in jest.

"Okay, mister, I won't nag; but when you get fat and ugly and full of pimples don't come crying to me that girls won't go out with you."

He threw me a wicked look and winked. "No one's complained so far."

We finished our meal with general chatter and Chris cleared up the table while I made coffee.

"So how're things with the case, anyway?" He asked when I came back to the sofa with a tray holding coffee cups, milk jug and sugar bowl. I had also sliced some oranges into wedges to refresh our palates after the pizza.

"Well, your dad obviously told you about Elena being on the tape with Geering."

"Yes, that was a good move on your part. Even the police didn't think of it."

"It was a coincidence really. I was trying to work out what time Geering had left the function and was hoping the tapes would show him taking the lift up to his suite, but I couldn't find anything. Then I remembered your telling me about having seen Geering with some woman."

Chris nodded. "Little did I know it would turn out to be Elena. So what happens next?"

I shrugged. "The police will question her when she's back in Sydney. In any case, it's all circumstantial evidence at the moment. Geering's not a bad-looking guy, and though not a nice thing to do, it's not illegal for someone to have an affair. So this doesn't necessarily mean Elena's involved in any kind of foul play."

Chris sat forward in his chair, his imagination obviously taking flight. "Yes, but she may know something," he pointed out. "She might even be the motive for Geering committing the crime."

I waved my hands in front of his face. "Wait! Wait a minute." I looked at him questioningly. "What makes you think Geering did anything?"

He leaned back in his chair with an orange wedge poised near his mouth. "C'mon, Mia! I was the one who hacked into his computer, remember? Geering was in cahoots with Linda's father; and the father was connected to the drug underworld. It only takes two and two to put this together." He then sucked on the orange wedge while his eyes gazed at me with satisfaction.

"It's not that simple, Chris." I hated to deflate his enthusiasm. "Hung Liu was a partner in the restaurants, but there's no proof that connects Geering, or even Kwon Lee, to the drug cartel. As far as the cops know Hung Liu was the only one involved in the drug activities. As for Elena, she may or may not know anything. My guess is she doesn't."

Chris looked pensive for a moment. "But you don't know for sure, do you? About the drug thing, I mean."

"No one knows for sure. The police checked out all the information I gave them and couldn't find anything suspicious. So far, it's all supposition."

We were both silent for a while as we finished the coffee and orange wedges. "So," Chris finally said, "if Elena doesn't know anything, we're back to square one."

"So it would seem," I replied with frustration.

"Something's nagging at you." Chris threw me a knowing look. "I can tell by the determined gaze in your eyes."

"Of course there is," I admitted. "After all, why would Kwon Lee be following—" I stopped cold, but it was too late.

"There *is* something going on." Chris jumped out of his seat and came to sit next to me again. "You're holding something back."

I regarded him, so young, so full of enthusiasm, *so willing to help me.* What kind of a mother figure did I make that I was about to endanger my pseudo-son by asking him not only to locate the warehouse, but to help me break into it?

CHAPTER 19

"**B**loody oath, I'll help you!" Chris's eyes shone bright with excitement when I told him about my little espionage project.

"I'm bad, Chris," I confessed. "I shouldn't be asking you to do this."

"Hey, don't worry. Honestly. We'll be fine." He tried to put me at ease. "Besides, this is the most fun I've had in a long time."

"It's not going to be much fun if we both end up in jail," I pointed out dryly. I could just imagine the pleasure Smythe would derive from throwing us both in jail to rot, until we were bailed out by David. Well, I assumed David would come to my rescue. I knew he'd definitely come to his son's. But when he found out I had instigated the whole thing he'd probably leave me to fend for myself. "Perhaps this isn't such a good idea," I uttered, about to change my mind.

Chris would not back down, however; not after I had opened my big mouth. "Mia, we can't give up now. Remember, we're doing this for a good cause. Somebody ought to help that poor woman who jumped, or was made to jump, I should say."

When he put it like that I couldn't refuse. "Very well," I caved in. "But we do this my way. If you so much as slightly deviate from my instructions, you're out," I warned him.

"Okay, Mum," he said in jest, but at the same time threw me a fond smile. "You know, Dad's so blind."

"What about?"

"About you," he answered, suddenly shy. "He should sweep you off your feet and marry you."

I felt a blush rush to my cheeks. "Thank you, but that's not possible."

"Why not? Don't you love him still?" he asked with the directness of the young.

"It's complicated," I responded with a serious look in my eyes. "Don't forget I spent eighteen years with Nathan and I'm only just getting into 'single mode' again." I shook my head dismissively. "Look, let's not talk about this anymore; it makes me uncomfortable. Besides, you should go home. It's getting late and we both need to get some sleep."

Chris shrugged and stood up. "You're right. Let's leave the mushy stuff for later. First, we have a job to do."

I rolled my eyes. "Hey, this isn't a game, you know. It's real. Are you sure you want to help me out?" I still regretted having asked him for assistance, mainly because I feared for his safety.

"Try and stop me," he responded with determination. "I'm off to do some searching for that warehouse right now."

"You're not going to hack into Geering's computer again, I hope." I heard the anxiety in my voice.

Chris patted me on the shoulder to reassure me and said in a rather smug way, "The less you know, the better."

Oh, God, I thought, what have I unleashed? But it was too late. Chris hugged and kissed me goodnight and was out the door before I could stop him.

"That was really low, Ferrari," I talked to myself as I got ready for bed. "This could all blow up sky high." The funny thing was that I wasn't too concerned about my own safety. It was Chris I worried about. Despite this, when I closed my eyes I fell asleep within moments.

The telephone rang and brought me out of a dream I was having about Smythe cuffing me and shoving me into a dirty jail cell that smelled of cat urine. I felt groggy as I picked up the receiver and saw the time on my clock radio.

"It's friggin' two in the morning," I growled into the phone. "God help you if you're a telemarketer from India." There was laughter at the other end of the line and I sat up in bed, switching on the bedside lamp. "Chris, is that you?"

"Who else did you think it would be? A telemarketer from India! Where do you come up with these things?" He laughed again. "Boy, they must really love you over there."

"Cut the crap and tell me why you're calling so late," I snapped.

"Okay, okay," he said to pacify me. "I've got the location of the warehouse."

My bad mood forgotten, I was instantly wide awake. "You have?"

"You betcha! So the question is when shall we do a drive-by? We need to check it out before we decide how to get in."

"I'm doing the day shift today, so how about we go straight after? Are you working?" I tried to think what I had on after work. Only Dobbs coming over for dinner, but I had plenty of time before I had to cook for him.

"I've got the day off. Let's meet in the car park when you're finished," he suggested.

I suddenly thought of Kwon Lee. What if he was still following me? "No," I said. "We need to take your car in case I'm being followed. I'll leave the hotel and drive to the shopping centre at Edgecliff. Then, I'll leave my car in the underground car park and meet you somewhere inside."

"And after that?"

I yawned. "Let me think about the details later and I'll call you, okay? I need my beauty sleep."

I switched off the light and lay back down on the bed; but unfortunately, sleep would not come. My mind was filled with thoughts of how I was going to throw Kwon Lee off the scent—and when I finally figured it out it was dawn. Damn! I had to get up in an hour. As it happened, I slept right through the alarm and made it into work a half hour late.

"Ferrari, you've been burning the midnight oil again." Dobbs greeted me as I bumped into him doing his rounds in the lobby. "Your eyes are positively re—"

"Shut up, Dobbs," I cut in. "I need a favour."

He sniffed. "If you're going to talk to me in that manner, you're in no position to ask me for anything."

I sighed impatiently and protested, "Hey, I'm cooking for you while Eileen's away, aren't I?"

"And I'm packing for you," was the rejoinder.

I nodded. "Okay. I'll buy you a cappuccino and a muffin." It was almost ten-thirty so we were due for a coffee break.

Dobbs smiled at the sound of this. "You've got a deal, lady. So what can I do for you?"

We talked while we made our way to the hotel's café. "I need to step out for about half an hour or so. Can you look after my pager and cover any calls?"

"Is that all? Yeah, I'll cover for you, Ferrari," he replied and eyed me suspiciously for a moment. "But what are you up to?"

"Well ... I have to drop by my doctor's." This was the first thing that came to mind.

His gaze turned from suspicion to concern. "You okay, girl?"

"Yes, yes. Just have to pick up some test results, but all is well," I added when I saw he looked even more concerned. "Women's tests, you know? Routine stuff. Now, let's go for that coffee."

I wasn't sure whether he believed me, but he seemed to accept it. After our coffee break I handed him my pager and took off for the Elizabethan Theatre Trust, which was located a few blocks down the road from the hotel. I took care that no one was following, but even if they were they would assume I was running an errand for a guest.

The hotel was hosting a charity costume ball on Saturday evening and quite a number of the invited guests had been enquiring about fancy dress rentals. The Elizabethan Theatre Trust was the nearest place that rented out costumes from productions held in the past, and this was what gave me the idea of how to evade Kwon Lee.

I rented a black wig in the style of Cleopatra and quickly returned to the hotel with my goods in a plastic bag. Then I went to see Chris in the penthouse.

"Hey," he said as he opened the door, "just in time for lunch."

"Is David around? I don't want to be seen here."

"No, he's at a business luncheon in the city. I ordered a burger and fries from room service. Want to share?"

"No, thanks. I have to rush off, but I'll have a glass of Coke if you've got it." I needed the caffeine to lift my flagging energy and I was too hot after my walk down the road to have another coffee.

Chris handed me a full glass of Coke and I drank half of it before I spoke again. "Okay, here's how it's going to play out. I'll meet you outside the French pastry shop at Edgecliff. I'll be wearing a black wig and different clothes from the ones I'll have on when I park in the shopping centre."

"You're going to change in the ladies' toilet." Chris was quick on the uptake.

"Exactly. So if Kwon Lee is following he'll be looking for me and not a black-haired woman. By the time he realises I pulled a switch, we'll be long gone."

Chris gazed at me with admiration in his eyes. "Good call!"

"I'll meet you there at three-thirty. Don't be late." I drank the rest of my Coke and left.

At exactly three twenty-five that afternoon I walked out of the ladies' toilet at the shopping centre, wearing my black wig with heavier make-up than usual on my face, including purplish eye shadow and dark rose lipstick. I accessorised with dangly silver earrings and bangles, and my get-up consisted of old jeans with a tear at the knee, a white Indian cotton shirt and an embroidered green vest I had picked up in Thailand years ago. Kwon Lee would be looking for a blonde woman with short hair, dressed in the hotel's black uniform.

"Wow!" Chris exclaimed when I met him at our appointed place. "You look really cute as a hippie." He winked at me.

"Shut up and let's go," I muttered.

We made our way to the lift, which would take us to the car park. "What level did you park on?" I asked.

"The rooftop."

"Good," I said as the lift arrived. We entered and hit the button for the roof level. "He'll never know where I've gone, so he's probably watching my car right now."

"That's if he even followed you," Chris pointed out. "We don't know this for sure."

"No, we don't, but it pays to take precautions."

Once we arrived at Chris's car, an old green Mitsubishi Lancer, we climbed in and made Alexandria within fifteen minutes. Chris turned off from the main drag and negotiated a number of smaller streets until we came to a long road flanked with warehouses on either side.

"This is some kind of an industrial park area," Chris explained, "but it's an old one."

I looked around and saw that the warehouses were rather shabby, not like the new and shiny ones that were sprouting up all over western Sydney. The suburb of Alexandria was now being redeveloped as a residential area with trendy apartments for those who wanted to live close to the city, but some parts of the place were still run down; this was one of them.

Chris slowed the car and turned into a driveway where there was a sign that read: Joynton Avenue Business Park. Directly under this were about six company names and unit numbers, signifying in which warehouse they were to be found. Geering's warehouse was not under the name of Capone's as I had thought. "So where is it?" I asked Chris while he kept driving slowly around the warehouses and searching for the unit numbers.

"We're after Unit 5. The name is JGKL Supplies."

So they ended up using their name initials, I thought. No wonder I couldn't find them on the net. I knew Chris had probably hacked into Geering's computer again to get this bit of information. I frowned but remained silent. Ahead of us was Unit 5, an even shabbier warehouse than the rest, if that were possible.

The warehouse doors were locked and the place looked deserted. Chris stopped the car, but we remained inside. "The places here are only used for storage these days," he informed me. "These businesses don't run their offices out of the warehouses as they used to do in the past."

"How do you know this?"

"Because once I knew the name of this particular industrial park, I checked up on the head office and branches for each of the businesses listed here, and they're all located off-site. They only use this area for storage."

I regarded him with pride in my eyes. "I'm impressed."

His face coloured under my praise, but he said nothing. I gazed at the building in front of us and then looked around to make sure we were truly alone.

"It looks almost too easy," I said finally.

"How's that?"

"See toward the back of the warehouse, on the left side?" I pointed in the direction to which I was referring. "The steel ladder there." Chris nodded, and I explained, "That's a fire escape ladder that leads onto an escape hatch on the roof."

"How do you know?"

"I've hung around enough warehouses that belonged to hotel suppliers in my time. I used to do some work for the purchasing manager before I became a duty manager. Anyway, suppliers always want to show you around their place and impress you with their goods."

"I didn't know this," Chris remarked.

"We're talking years ago," I replied, clearing my throat a little. "When I was younger things were done differently. Nowadays, equipment and supplies come direct from China or some such place. We don't get to see where things are stored anymore nor do we care. We simply contact the distributor and they deliver direct to our doorstep."

Chris smirked. "Oh, so you're talking like 1938 or something— prior to the war?"

I mock-slapped him over the head. "Don't be a smartarse! I'm not *that* old."

"Sorry, you know I don't mean it." He gave me a naughty smile.

"Pay attention!" I snapped. "Now, all we need is a pair of bolt cutters." Chris looked at me with a question in his eyes so I explained further. "Most of these hatches are locked with a padlock."

"Well, that rather defeats the purpose, doesn't it?"

"What do you mean?"

"You said they use this as an escape hatch in case of fire," Chris stated. "So if they lock it, how are the poor devils supposed to get out?"

"They don't use them anymore. They've got fire exit doors everywhere. A fire inspector might use it to inspect the roof and make sure it's still fire-worthy and that it meets safety standards."

"Won't the hatch be alarmed?"

"Good question," I replied, "but nine out of ten times they don't bother. The warehouse doors are usually alarmed. In any case, this is a risk we'll have to take. For all intents and purposes this is a storage facility in a really shabby place, so I don't think any high-profile burglars are going to waste their time here just to steal tables and chairs."

"You have a good point."

"Okay, let's get going. I'm nervous parking here. You know, they could come at any time to check on their goods or to store more stuff."

Chris started the engine. "Have you seen enough?"

"Yes," I answered. "The only thing I want to check is the gate on the way out. It's probably chained shut at night, which would be easy enough to break through. I doubt very much they would have guard dogs here, not unless these businesses are storing something really valuable."

"From what I could tell when I did the search," Chris said as we drove past the gate, which did have a chain and padlock hanging from it, "most of the goods stored here are paper goods and second-hand office furniture. I don't imagine anyone would store high-priced goods in this dumpy place."

I took a good look at the gate when we drove out and saw a smallish sign informing the public that the place was guarded by McCoy Security. There were no warning signs of guard dogs on the premises, which was a legal requirement if the place used dogs.

"They've got a security service doing rounds. You may want to check out who McCoy Security is. I've never heard of them. If they're a small outfit, chances are they'll send a guard to lock the gates at night and do a drive-by once every blue moon."

"Got it." Chris nodded. "So when do we break in?"

CHAPTER 20

"Friday night," I replied. "Friday is Dobbs's poker evening with his cop buddies so he won't miss me. I'm cooking dinner for him until his wife gets back, you see."

"That's nice of you," Chris remarked on our way back to Edgecliff.

"Yeah, well. He's helping me with the move."

"Hey, I'll help you, too, Mia. I don't want Dobbs straining his back. Just let me know when the big day is."

"Thanks. That's nice of you," I replied. "Anyway, back to Friday night. I have some bolt cutters Nathan left behind. Let me know if you find out anything about the security company."

"Will do."

Chris dropped me off at the shopping centre and I went in to change back into my uniform. If Kwon Lee was still hanging around where my car was parked he would simply see me with a couple of plastic bags that held my other clothes, and he would assume I'd been shopping.

I arranged to have the day off on Friday, seeing as I was going to have to work all weekend, and this would give me a chance to be rested and relaxed for our little adventure. Dobbs dropped by for dinner and some final packing on Thursday evening and I prepared homemade gnocchi.

"I'm going to miss your cooking, girl," he remarked while we sat out on the terrace sipping coffee after our meal.

"Eileen's coming back?"

He nodded. "Next week."

"Well, it's a good thing you've been doing all this packing for me. You look very fit and healthy."

Dobbs laughed. "Hey, stop buttering me up, Ferrari. I've already said I'd help you pack and move."

"No, Dobbs, I mean it," I assured him. "You managed to keep

your weight down. You've done well."

Dobbs looked pleased with himself. "In that case, I'm a hot guy again!"

I winked at him and he gazed at me contentedly. I could see he had missed having his wife around and was happy she was finally coming back. This made me think fleetingly of the fact that I had no one waiting for me anymore.

A feeling of depression threatened to rear its ugly head within me, but I pushed it away with my willpower and thought about Friday night. I'd heard it said that when you're down and out you should help others because it will make you feel better. I was helping Linda Liu. It was too bad she had died, but if I could clear up the mystery of her death this would at least bring the truth out in the open and whoever committed the crime would be punished.

Chris telephoned me late in the evening to let me know that McCoy Security was no more. "They must've gone bust or something," he informed me.

"So I wonder who locks the gate at night," I commented.

"Maybe no one does. After all, it's easy enough to break through that gate, so why bother?"

"True," I agreed, thinking ahead to Friday night while I sent a silent prayer for our safety.

I asked Chris to leave his car in the underground car park where I lived, and wearing my trusty wig again and a khaki jacket with old jeans I drove off in his car and met him a few blocks down the road, where I had told him to wait for me. He jumped in and we drove off.

"There's no way Kwon Lee can follow you tonight," Chris observed. "He certainly wouldn't be looking for this car in your car park."

I nodded. "Especially since I got you to park the car in a totally different spot from mine," I replied, keeping my eyes on the road. It was around nine in the evening and there was very little traffic on the way.

"We'll be there soon so you better repeat back to me what we discussed over the phone the other day." I had laid down some ground rules for tonight in order to keep Chris safe and had extracted a promise from him that no matter what happened he was not to come into the warehouse.

"I think you're being overcautious," Chris protested, "but if it'll make you feel any better: I'm to stay in the car at all times, and the car will be parked out on the road. If I see anything suspicious I'm to text your mobile and let you know; and if you're not out of there within five minutes after I text you, I'm to call the cops. Under no circumstances, however, am I to go into the warehouse to look for you."

"Good," I said. "It pays to be cautious, so don't knock it."

"There's always the element of the unexpected," he argued. "What if something happens that neither of us has foreseen?"

"Then, I guess, you run like hell," I replied. "If anything happens to me it's my own fault, but I couldn't live with myself if I placed you in any danger. In fact, I should never have permitted you to come along. Now that we've seen the layout I could've gone by myself."

Chris puffed up his chest. "I would never let a lady go anywhere near danger."

I was touched by his sense of chivalry. "It's nice to know, but don't forget this was my idea."

We arrived at our location and I parked the car across the road, a few metres down from the gate, which to our relief was hanging open. "So much for security," I remarked.

"Let's hope they don't have a drive-by service," Chris said.

"I doubt it," I replied while I peeled off my wig and reached in the backseat for a black cap to cover my blonde hair. I also took off my khaki jacket and old jeans to reveal black ski pants and a long-sleeved black top underneath.

Chris watched with amusement. "You look like a cat burglar."

I grinned. "Well, in essence, that's what I am. After all, I'm breaking into the place. Only difference is there are no jewels here."

"Where are the bolt cutters?" he asked.

"In the trunk," I told him and checked my mobile phone to make sure it was on vibrate mode only. "Okay," I turned to Chris, "this is it. Wish me luck."

He reached across the seat impulsively and gave me a big hug. "Be careful."

"I will."

I took a deep breath and opened the car door to get out; then shut it gently behind me. I went to the boot of the car, unlocked it, and retrieved the bolt cutters, which were packed in a small backpack. Then I came back to where Chris was sitting and handed him the keys through the open window. "You have a clear view of the warehouse from here, so don't worry about a thing."

"Be careful," he said again.

I nodded and took off at a slow run toward the open gate. I didn't stop to look around me and kept going until I reached the back of the warehouse where the fire escape ladder was located. I then secured the backpack straps over my shoulders and started to climb the ladder slowly. It was imperative I didn't slip on one of the thin rungs and fall off.

Luckily, I made it to the top without mishap and took a few steps along the narrow iron walkway, which led to the escape hatch. I could already see the hatch door was held shut by an average-looking padlock and knew I wouldn't have any trouble cutting through it. When I reached the hatch I knelt before it and the bolt cutters made easy work of the padlock. I carefully put the cutters away before I lifted the door.

This was the only tricky part. If the hatch was alarmed I would have to abort the whole thing and make a run back to the car. I took a deep breath to calm myself and carefully placed both hands on the small door. No guts, no glory, I thought, and then I lifted it. Surprisingly, the door gave way easily and I was able to open it fully. There was no alarm, much to my relief.

Before I climbed in I took out a small flashlight from the backpack and shone its ray of light inside the actual opening so I could locate the ladder that would take me into the warehouse. I took one look around the outside to ensure no one but Chris was present; then I placed the flashlight between my teeth and started the slow climb down the ladder toward the warehouse floor.

The flashlight didn't cast too much light, which was a good thing as I didn't want it to show through any windows. Even so, once I was at floor level, I kept the flashlight pointed downward so all I could see was a small circle of light around my feet. Enough light reflected off the floor, however, to enable me to see what I was doing.

The warehouse was packed with wooden crates, restaurant tables and chairs, and what looked like stage props symbolic of the 1920s era. I was standing close to a car with bullet holes sprayed across its windscreen. The car looked real and I wondered whether it was an original 1920s vehicle or simply a metal shell made out to look like a car.

I walked by the crates, which lined most of the walls, and noticed that some of them were open, so I stuck my hand inside. In some, I felt plates and crockery protected by bubble wrap and packing pellets; in others, there were cooking utensils, pots and pans, and a whole myriad of kitchen equipment. I kept walking, keeping close to the walls of the warehouse so I wouldn't lose my way in the semi-darkness.

There seemed to be nothing here other than what the news article had stated—restaurant equipment and props. Of course in the dark, and without knowing where to look, there could be something hidden at the bottom of a crate or underneath one of the car props, and I had espied several of these by now. In order to find anything, though, I would have to have proper lighting and some muscle to help me shift the crates about. I shook my head, wondering why I'd made such a stupid decision as to come here. What was I hoping to find?

I sighed at the waste of time this had been and thought it best to get out and forget about the whole thing. I was fairly sure I wasn't going to find anything of value to help me with the case; but when I turned to go back the way I came, I bumped into someone.

The flashlight fell to the floor and my hands came up against a hard chest encased in what seemed to be a suit. It took all of my willpower not to scream out. My legs grew weak, and I waited for a blow to my head or the sound of a gun before everything went black and I fell to the floor like a dead duck. Nothing happened. No arms came around to squeeze the life out of me, no guns went off, and no one hit me.

I glanced at the circle of light on the floor emitted by the flashlight and saw a pair of black shoes and the bottom of black-cuffed trouser pants. I then moved away from my would be assailant and realised I had bumped into a life-sized dummy holding a machine gun and dressed in a 1920s suit with a black hat sporting a white band. I almost laughed aloud as I bent to retrieve the flashlight to shine it on the figure in front of me. The gangster face looking back seemed almost real. I reached out to touch it and felt the semi-hard surface that passed for skin. It was obviously some sort of rubber over what felt like plaster. When I knocked on the dummy's chest it sounded hollow.

I started to walk toward the fire ladder and came across a few more dummies of gangsters and dancing girls in fabulous dresses. Some wore skintight leotard type costumes with feathers and strings of pearls; others wore the typical 1920s fringed dresses with sequined headbands and a single feather. They looked fantastic, and I had no doubt the theme restaurant concept was going to be a real success for Geering.

A sudden click from somewhere behind me made me turn quickly and I saw a light shining in what looked like a glass enclosed office in the distance. "Shit!" I whispered. Someone was in the warehouse; so why hadn't I heard them come in? I quickly switched off my flashlight and waited, not knowing what I should do. If I waited until whoever was here left I could be stuck for hours and Chris would surely call the cops. If I tried to leave, however, I would run the risk of being caught.

Shit! Shit! Shit! This was one situation Chris and I hadn't figured on. We had never considered that someone might already be inside the warehouse. I wondered why they didn't hear me come in. The hatch door had made some noise when I opened it.

I moved closer to the light, making sure I kept close to the crates so no one could see me. When I went as far as I dared, I craned my neck over a crate and was able to get a view of the office enclosure. It was small and contained a desk, chair, a couple of filing cabinets, and what looked like an old sofa. The light that had been clicked on came from an old-fashioned desk lamp.

I managed to move closer to see who had switched on the lamp, and then I froze. Sitting on the sofa and stretching his arms up in the air as if he'd just woken from a nap was Kwon Lee. Oh, fuck! I was in real trouble and had to get out of here, pronto.

I tried to work out why I hadn't seen a car parked outside the warehouse; then I realised the car could have been on the other side of the building, away from the road. I hadn't checked that side on my way in. I had simply assumed there was no one about because everything had been dark when Chris and I arrived.

Chris! I must warn him. But how? Then I remembered the mobile. Thank God! I crouched down behind a crate and took it out of my pocket to text him. *"Kwon Lee here in office. Think he was taking nap. Light just went on."* I hit the send button and waited. A few seconds later my phone vibrated. I checked Chris's reply. It was one single word: *"FUCK!"*

Very helpful, I thought with sarcasm. I texted him back. *"Will try to sneak out. If not back within 10 mins, call Smythe."* I hit the send button and knew that calling Smythe was the most sensible thing to do. Chris wouldn't have to explain the whole story to him like he would if he had to tell the tale to cops who were not involved in the case. Besides, Dobbs would be with Smythe and he'd hopefully keep him from chucking me and Chris in jail for breaking and entering.

I put away the phone and started to go back the way I came, nice and slow. Once I moved away from the light cast by the office lamp I couldn't see very much at all, but there was no way I could risk switching on my flashlight. I had to feel my way out of the place.

Then it happened. One moment I was walking alongside the crates, nice and quiet; the next, I tripped on something lying on the floor and crashed into what seemed to be a dummy. I fell down with the dummy smashing to pieces under me.

The warehouse lights went on, almost blinding me, and when my eyes became accustomed to the light I saw a broken female dummy next to me with a whole bunch of small rectangular plastic bags spread all around her, filled with what looked like some kind of white powder.

My legs didn't seem to want to respond, but I somehow managed to hoist myself to my feet by getting a hold of one of the crates. I had to get the hell out of here before the running footsteps I'd heard caught up with me.

I noticed the crates around me were all in rows, forming aisles like in a supermarket, and my brain told me that within seconds Kwon Lee was going to get to my aisle and find me.

The only chance I had was to run out of one of the actual fire doors. This would set off the alarm and alert the fire brigade. Meanwhile, with luck, I would make it back to the car before Kwon Lee took a shot at me. Then, when the fire brigade arrived, they would call the cops as soon as they found the drug packets on the floor. Because of one thing I was sure—those packets did not contain baking powder in them.

I espied the door nearest me and made a run for it, but before I could reach it a body jumped me from behind and we both went hurtling down to the floor.

CHAPTER 21

The wind was knocked out of me and for a couple of seconds I thought I was going to pass out. Thankfully, I went into self-preservation mode and the tae kwon do training I'd had years ago came to my rescue without my having to think about it. It was just instinct, plus I was fighting for my life.

I found the strength to shake the body off my own and in a millisecond I realised the body was now lying face up, like mine. I took the opportunity to attack. My elbow came down right into the solar plexus, knocking the wind out of my assailant and giving me time to stand up. Of course I was not surprised it was Kwon Lee who had attacked me; he was obviously here on his own, for which I was grateful. Right now, he lay in a fetal position with his arms crossed over his chest.

From what I could see he had no gun; therefore, I kicked him in the ribs while he was still down, and he let out a loud groan. I turned and ran, but I never made it to the door. Somehow, he found his feet and reached me with lightning speed. I turned just in time to see him deliver a hook kick to my face, but I was faster than him and my forearm came up to block his leg.

He had barely enough time to give me a look of surprise when I raised my own leg in a waist-high snap kick and made contact with his balls. He dropped to the ground like a sack of potatoes and lay there with both hands covering his groin. Served him right, the sneaky bastard. He wasn't going to be shagging anyone for a long time to come!

I acted quickly and ripped off a dress from one of the female dummies, which I then tore into strips. Kwon Lee was already trying to get up and I delivered one last kick to the side of his head, knocking him out cold. I then proceeded to tie his hands behind his back and both his ankles together. There was no time to look for rope or twine in the warehouse so the strips I tore from the dress would have to do.

When I had him secured I took out my mobile and rang Chris.

"What happened? Are you all right?" he exclaimed anxiously.

"The bastard attacked me, but I'm okay. I knocked him out and tied him up." It was then I felt my legs turn to rubber and had to sit on the floor.

"Oh my God! You sure you're okay? Smythe and Dobbs are on their way," Chris informed me.

I knew this meant trouble for me, but I had found something of value to the cops so Smythe would have to take this into consideration. "Chris, get in here. It's safe to come in now and I need you to help me keep an eye on this guy while I check something."

"I'm there." He rang off and within two minutes he was standing outside the front door of the warehouse, which I opened from the inside. Surprisingly, no alarm went off and I figured Kwon Lee must've deactivated it when he had come to the warehouse earlier.

Chris engulfed me in a bear hug. I winced, already feeling sore in muscles I didn't know existed. "Let go," I protested gently. "I'm fine; just a little sore."

He pulled away but still kept a hand on each of my shoulders while he examined me. "Good God, woman, you've got a purple bruise beginning to show on your cheekbone, some blood on your lip … What did the bastard do to you? I'll pulverise him."

I smiled, but it hurt to stretch my bottom lip. "It's okay, honest. I must've bruised my face when we hit the ground. He came up from behind and threw himself on top, bringing us both crashing down. Good thing he was alone; I don't think I could've handled more than one opponent."

Chris's look turned to one of hero worship when I told him how I defended myself. "Wow!" Was all he could say as he followed me to where I'd left Kwon Lee, who was still out cold. "He's not dead, is he?" Chris asked rather casually.

I eyed him with concern. He didn't seem at all worried that I'd just knocked out a person, albeit an evil one, but a person nonetheless. "No. He's out cold. Listen, I need you to search his pockets and see whether he's got any weapons on him; and then find something stronger to tie him up with. Meanwhile, I need to check on something."

Chris didn't even ask what I was going to look for; he simply nodded, excited at the prospect of being allowed to take part in the apprehension of one of the bad guys.

I figured we had less than ten minutes before Smythe and Dobbs arrived so I went back to the smashed dummy with the little plastic bags around it. I felt a sense of the surreal when I picked up one of the packets, ripped open a corner and tasted a little bit of the powder with the tip of my pinky finger. I was Serpico and Dirty Harry all rolled into one.

I had never tasted heroin before, but I did know it had a bitter taste to it. Since the props had been imported from Asia I assumed the stuff came from the Golden Triangle. It was obvious Kwon Lee and Geering had good contacts in customs; otherwise, this stuff would have been found straight away. And now it would fall to Smythe and his guys to work out who was being bribed to turn a blind eye when shipments came in.

There were at least thirty dummies I could see around the warehouse and I wondered if they were all filled with drugs. Unfortunately, I didn't get the chance to find out because just then I heard a police siren and moments later Smythe burst into the warehouse with a couple of uniforms in tow, all holding guns up in the air. Dobbs stood outside, waiting for the signal that it was safe to come in.

When Smythe saw me he lowered his weapon and so did the uniforms. "You can come in, fellows," I called out. "We've secured the area."

There was murder in Smythe's eyes. "We? What do you mean by 'we', Ferrari?" His voice was loud; his tone angry. "I hope you know you're going in for breaking and entering."

Chris joined me then, with Dobbs coming in behind him looking worried. "Mia, you okay?" Dobbs eyed me with concern.

I sneered at Smythe. "At least someone cares enough to find out whether I'm okay first." I then turned to Dobbs. "I'm fine. Kwon Lee attacked me, but I knocked him out."

Smythe looked like he was going to burst. "What? Am I going to have to add assault to your charge sheet as well?"

I lost it then. "Oh, shut the fuck up, Smythe!" I yelled at him and saw the uniforms behind him wearing smirks on their faces. They were obviously enjoying the show.

Smythe seemed as though he had turned to stone—he simply glared at me and tightened the grip on his Glock. I hoped he wasn't going to shoot me. "Look, just get over it, okay?" I stated in a normal tone of voice.

Smythe finally found his tongue. "Listen, Ferrari, you seem to forget you're not a cop. You're not authorised to break and enter or knock someone out. My God, woman, this isn't Starsky and Hutch!" He gazed at Chris as he said this last bit. "As for you, I can only assume you're Rourke's son, the computer hacker. I was lenient with you last time, but you have a lot of explaining to do, plus you're going down for accessory after the fact."

Chris said nothing. He was too stunned to speak. Dobbs looked alarmed. The uniforms were still smirking. And I wanted to grab Smythe's gun and shoot the idiot through the head with it.

"Are you done now?" I remarked sarcastically.

The surprise on Smythe's face was almost comical. He was beyond words again, so he simply nodded.

I took a deep breath for patience and knew I had centre stage. "Okay, Smythe, let me explain this whole thing to you so you can come off your high police horse." I waited for a smart comment, but nothing came forth so I continued. "First of all, Chris has nothing to do with this. He simply let me borrow his car and right up until you guys showed up, he was sitting outside and had no idea what was going on in here. Secondly, it might interest you to know that Mr Kwon Lee has been smuggling a shitload of heroin inside prop dummies. He attacked me when he saw what I discovered."

I motioned for the group to follow me to where the plastic bags lay scattered on the floor, and I picked up the one I had sampled earlier. "I'm not an expert on drugs, but I'm sure this is heroin." I shoved the bag under Smythe's nose and waited until he took it from me and tasted the stuff.

He nodded. "It's heroin, all right," he concurred. "But you still broke in here."

God, men were stupid sometimes! Couldn't he see I had single-handedly discovered a drug smuggling operation, even if it was by chance? I decided to tell him a little white lie to get Chris and me out of trouble. "I asked Chris to locate this warehouse because I had reason to believe something illegal was going on. When I discovered the drugs, I simply made a citizen's arrest."

Smythe looked floored. "You expect me to believe this bullshit? You've just been snooping as you always do. I warned you about this, Ferrari, and told you that next time—"

"Hey, cut her some slack, man," Dobbs spoke up—finally. "She's just busted a drug operation, and this might also be the motive for Linda Liu's murder."

Smythe looked pensive for a moment before turning to one of his lackeys and asking him to call for an ambulance. Then he told the other cop to put in a call to the station and get some more uniforms to the site. "It's going to be a long night, gentlemen … and lady," he added, turning to me. His eyes held a hint of reluctant admiration. I felt myself blush and quickly turned away.

"Someone might want to check on Kwon Lee," I suggested. "He should be coming round sooner or later."

"I'll do it," Dobbs volunteered and went off with Chris, who offered to show him where Kwon Lee was.

"The paramedics will check you for any injuries," Smythe offered grudgingly. "Your face looks quite bruised."

This was obviously his way of calling a truce and I decided to be gracious. After all, he was doing his job. "Thank you."

"I'd better go and put in a call to the feds. They need to be notified when we have a narcotics bust," he explained.

I nodded and watched him go. I felt exhausted all of a sudden and wondered where I could get a coffee. Smythe was right. It was going to be a long night.

Dobbs and Chris rejoined me after a couple of minutes. "Kwon Lee's just beginning to come around," Dobbs reported and then asked, "How's Smythe?"

"I think he's cooled down." I smiled and then winced; my lip still hurt. "There's a sofa in the small office. I need to lie down for a while."

The boys escorted me to the office while Dobbs scolded like a mother hen. "You do beat all, girl. What if Kwon Lee had a gun?"

"But he didn't," Chris announced, "not even a knife. Mia, you were great! Wait until I tell Dad."

I turned on him. "No, Chris. You can't tell him! At least, don't tell him I got you involved."

"Well, let's not worry about that just yet," Dobbs put in. "We'll see what Smythe has to say first, and we can only hope this whole thing is reported as a police find so you guys will be off the hook."

I looked at Dobbs with incredulity. "You mean they'll stage it so it looks like they found the drugs, and they'll take all the credit?"

"What do you want, Ferrari, anonymity or public exposure with Chris involved right alongside of you?"

He had a point. "Okay, if Smythe can swing it, we'll play along. We can be the 'quiet achievers' like in the BP ad," I smirked.

Chris laughed at my remark, but Dobbs frowned. "You were lucky tonight. This could've turned out very differently."

I sobered up and had to acknowledge what he said was right. If Kwon Lee had been carrying a gun, I would be the one lying on the floor now, most probably dead. As for Chris, he would've been implicated in all sorts of trouble like being an accessory to breaking and entering, among other things.

We entered the office and I stretched out on the soft leather sofa. It was an old one, but comfortable. "Hey, guys, see if we can order pizza and get some cappuccinos going. You heard what Smythe said—it's going to be a long night."

Chris grinned while Dobbs's jaw dropped open.

CHAPTER 22

The paramedics checked me out and pronounced me as "A little bruised, but she'll survive". Kwon Lee was just as lucky, except he was bruised more intensely and his balls would be sore for a long time to come. He was taken away to hospital for observation for the concussion, but not before Smythe booked him for assault and turned him over to the feds. Two cops went into the ambulance with him to keep him under guard.

When the pizzas and coffee arrived I felt more energised and gave Smythe a step by step account of the evening's events. Dobbs put to him that it would be a good idea if Chris and I were kept out of it.

"I don't like it, Dobbs," Smythe remarked. Then added almost reluctantly, "But under the circumstances, it's probably for the best."

I wasn't sure whether he was doing this for Chris and me or for himself. In any case, I didn't care. The less we were involved officially, the better. "Thank you," I replied, almost gagging at the thought of having to be civil to a cop.

"So let me clarify this," Smythe stated as he quickly went over his notes, thankfully unaware of my thoughts about him. "You really came out here not because you suspected drugs, but because you thought you might find something that would link Geering to Linda Liu's alleged suicide."

Now that Smythe had agreed to leave us out of it, he deserved the truth. "That's correct," I confirmed. "I mean, the thought crossed my mind Geering and Kwon Lee might be involved in drug smuggling, but I didn't have any real information pointing to this. It was mere supposition." I picked up another slice of pepperoni pizza and munched into it. "I thought coming here would reveal something about Linda Liu, but it didn't; that is, unless we make the assumption that she found out about the operation and this is why they had to get rid of her."

"Too circumstantial," Chris remarked, and earned himself a look of irritation from Smythe.

"We don't have any proof at all that Linda was murdered, you know this already," Smythe declared. "But now we can question Geering and Kwon Lee further and see what transpires."

"What about a potential connection between them and Linda's father? We know he was involved in the restaurants," I pointed out.

"The feds looked into it already and came up with nothing. The restaurants are a legit operation."

"Perhaps funded with drug money," Chris chimed in.

I threw him a warning look to stay quiet. He mouthed the word "sorry" and helped himself to another slice of pizza.

"We'll ask the feds to check again," Smythe advised. "But we still can't find any proof that Linda was murdered. We have tens of witnesses who saw her jump and we have the video footage as well. Linda jumped of her own accord. There's no question about it."

I thought about the insomnia drug zolpidem, but this, too, was a supposition. Even if Linda was taking it, there was no proof she jumped because someone had suggested it to her. She could just as well have jumped because of the effect of the drug or simply because she'd had enough and wanted to end it all. I sighed, feeling frustrated. I was afraid we would never get to the bottom of this.

"I want to be there when you question Geering and Kwon Lee," I uttered all of a sudden.

Smythe shook his head vehemently. "No way, Ferrari. You're lucky we're keeping you out of it."

Damn! "Okay," I gave in, knowing there was no changing Smythe's mind on this one. But I added, "Still, seeing as Chris and I gave you guys all this info I think we deserve to know what comes out at the questioning."

Smythe laughed. "I'll say this much for you, you're one pushy chick."

Dobbs joined in the laughter and I wanted to slap his head. "That's what I keep telling her," he remarked, winking at me, "only, I call her a pushy broad."

I threw daggers at him. "Shut up, Dobbs." He simply grinned

and I ignored him, turning to Smythe instead. "Hey, c'mon. Under the circumstances, I think I'm entitled to know what happens."

"Under the circumstances, you're lucky I didn't arrest you," Smythe parried.

I pursed my lips. It was obvious I was going to have to utilise Dobbs to extract the information from Smythe. I was sure the men exchanged information between them, especially on poker night.

"When do you pick up Geering?" Dobbs asked.

"Right after we finish here," Smythe answered and then turned to me with a cocked eyebrow. "What, nothing to say, Ferrari?"

I stuck out my tongue at him like a petulant child. "If you're done with me I'd like to go home. I'm very tired, you know."

He went over his notes once more while I waited for his response, and I really felt like kicking him in the balls to give him a taste of what Kwon Lee had experienced. After a few minutes he addressed Chris and me. "Okay, you two can go."

I stood and walked out of the office without so much as a nod of farewell. Chris followed after me.

"Man, you're on a death wish," he remarked once we were out in the cool night air.

"What are you talking about?"

"That Smythe guy; he's a real arsehole. I was scared shitless of him."

I laughed. "He's all bark but no bite. You just need to learn how to handle him."

"He could've thrown us in jail, you know."

I raised my brows at him. "I'd like to see him try."

We got in the car and Chris drove me back home. It was past midnight and all I wanted was a nice hot shower and bed. "If your father gets wind of this, tell him to discuss it with me, Chris. I'll take full responsibility. I don't want you to get into trouble—got that?" I said when I climbed out of the car.

"Dad's cool," Chris replied. "But if something comes out regarding my involvement I'll definitely ask him to talk to you. Goodnight."

I waved at him as he drove off and then turned to go inside my building.

The next day, I was on the late shift. I tried to cover the dark purple bruise on my cheek with make-up and did a good job of it, but it was still noticeable and there was slight swelling around the cheekbone. I was thankful at least I wasn't sporting a black eye. Even so, I received a number of questions from my workmates, who wanted to know what had happened. I told them I tripped and hit the side of my face when I landed on the pavement. This was as close as I could get to the truth.

"Good God," Thorny exclaimed when I walked into the kitchen to have my customary coffee with her in the early hours prior to the evening preparations. "What in heaven's name happened to you?"

I told her the same thing I'd told everyone else. She made me an espresso and brought me a chocolate custard cannoli, and we sat down in her office. "That must've hurt," she remarked. "Well, at least you did a good job of covering it up. Mind you, tonight's the costume ball, so you could paint on some more bruising to your face, wear a ripped up suit, and go as one of the many residents of Kings Cross." She laughed at her own wit.

I made a face at her. "Very funny."

"So why didn't you take the night off?"

"No one would swap with me," I replied. "Besides, I wanted to work the ball."

She shrugged as if she didn't care one way or the other. "What for? It's going to be bedlam with over three hundred guests in the ballroom."

"I'm good at bedlam," I said in jest. "It's okay, really. I'm fine except for this stupid bruise. Besides, I have a few days off coming up next week because of the move, so I thought I should work tonight."

"That's right, you're moving soon," Thorny commented. "How's it all going?"

"Pretty much all packed up now. Chris and Dobbs will help with the move; and I'm renting a van." I glanced at my watch; it was coming up to four in the afternoon. "Well, I'd better go and start my rounds. Thanks for the coffee and sweets."

She smiled. "Hey, what are chefs for?"

"You got that right." I winked at her, and then said, "Incidentally, did you end up replacing Tony?"

A momentary frown marred her pretty face, but it was gone almost immediately. I wondered whether she was mourning for the broken relationship or the loss of her fling—I wasn't sure which. "I found someone already. He starts next week."

I didn't know if I should offer some words of comfort, but thought the better of it. Thorny wasn't given to great displays of emotion—her temper tantrums, however, were something altogether different. "I'll catch you later." I gave her a smile before I left the kitchen.

As I walked across the lobby I wondered whether Geering had been taken away. I hadn't had a chance to catch up with Dobbs as yet, but I did find out what happened from David. He had seen me walking past Reception and motioned for me to join him for a moment. "God, what happened to your face?"

I told him the same lie I told everybody else.

"It looks painful," he observed. "Why don't you take the night off? I'll get someone to cover for you."

"I'm okay, honestly. It looks worse than it is," I reassured him. "Did you want to see me about something?" I was hoping it wasn't about Chris, but I needn't have worried.

"Smythe came to see me this morning. They arrested James Geering in the early hours for drug smuggling."

"Yes," I told him, "I read the security log." I hadn't actually read the logbook, but I imagined it had been recorded there, and I didn't want to seem like I knew nothing about it.

"Who would have thought?" David shook his head in wonder.

"Did you get to talk to Smythe about Elena?" I ventured to ask.

He didn't seem to mind. "Yes. I actually told him I wasn't surprised about the affair seeing as we live separate lives, but as to her involvement in the Linda Liu case …"

"No, I'm sure this has nothing to do with Elena," I assured him, hoping she wasn't "in the know" about the drugs. This was the last thing we needed.

"Anyway," David went on, "she's flying back next week, and Smythe will pop in to question her."

"How's Chris?" I asked. I figured I may as well find out because David hadn't mentioned him at all.

"He's fine. I had to tell him about his mother's involvement with Geering, but he didn't seem surprised, either. He's a strong boy," he stated with pride in his voice.

"He's a young man now, David, and it's a good thing he takes after his father," I remarked.

He smiled but didn't reply, and I wondered what he was thinking. Perhaps, he would have liked it if Chris had been my son. I quickly shoved the thought away. "Well, if there's nothing else I'd best get going. Big night ahead of us."

"Yes. Take care, Mia," David spoke warmly. "No more tripping, okay?"

I grinned. "Trust me; I'll pay more attention next time." I left him standing at the reception area and went in search of Dobbs. I caught up with him in the staff restaurant.

I greeted him. "Hey, early dinner?"

"We're going to have our hands full at the ball tonight so I thought I'd eat now," he replied.

I took a seat opposite. "Tell me what happened after I left you guys last night."

"I had to listen as Smythe carried on about what a pain in the ass you are," Dobbs reported with a smile, which I returned, "and when he was done, I left. Man, you really rub him the wrong way."

"Well, who does he think he is?" I made an effort to keep my voice down even though I wanted to yell. "I give him all this information; I bust up a drug ring; and what do I get from him? Zilch."

Dobbs's eyes held a look of incredulity as he regarded me. "Ferrari, you're crazy. He's the police. He doesn't owe you anything. Besides, he did you and Chris a big favour by leaving you out of it."

"Hey, whose side are you on, anyway?" He was starting to get on my nerves. Trust these bloody men to stick together.

"It's not about sides," Dobbs argued. "Fair is fair."

"Fair is fair," I mimicked him. "Dobbs, wake up and smell the coffee! If it weren't for my snooping, the bad guys would still be out there smuggling their drugs."

Dobbs sighed. "You're right, of course." His concession pacified me momentarily. "But you have to remember you're not in the police force. They have a way about doing things in the force and you should've gone to Smythe with the information you had."

"I did go to Smythe! He obviously didn't dig deep enough."

"Don't forget you stumbled across the drugs by coincidence, girl," he pointed out. "It's not like you knew these guys had illegal booty in the warehouse."

I hated it when Dobbs was right, but I had to be fair. "Okay.

Let's drop it. I'll try and be nicer to your *poker buddy* next time I see him."

"See? There you go again." He threw me an accusing look.

"What do you mean?" I asked, the picture of innocence.

He waved a dismissive hand at me. "What's the point of arguing with you? You'll always be nasty to him."

"Okay, Dobbs. I promise I'll be nicer next time." I couldn't believe this whole conversation. You'd think Smythe was a frail old woman—mind you; even a frail old woman would have more brains than him. "Now, I have a favour to ask."

Dobbs smiled knowingly. "When haven't you got a favour to ask if it relates to Smythe?"

I shot him a look of irritation. "How can you tell I'm going to ask about him?"

"Let's just say it's a feeling I have," he returned with a grin.

I ignored his smug tone. "I need you to find out as much as you can about the questioning session with Geering and Kwon Lee."

"Why do you need to know this?"

"Just in case they let slip some clue about Linda Liu." I cast him a pleading look. "So will you do this for me?"

He took his time in answering, but I waited patiently. Finally, he sighed with resignation and smiled. "Oh, okay. But only if what I find pertains to Linda."

"Of course," I replied. "I'm not interested in the drug thing anymore. That's pretty much over and done with."

He regarded me with doubt in his eyes. "Yeah, well—you just behave yourself."

"Will do," I stated. "By the way, David told me they took Geering away early this morning."

Dobbs nodded. "Yes. I had to meet Smythe at five and witness the arrest on behalf of the hotel."

"Did you go right into the room with them?"

"Of course. I had to let them in, didn't I? He looked upset.

"What's wrong?"

"You need to ask?" Dobbs went on grumpily, "I barely had any sleep, and then I start my day with a drug bust. Not very pleasant."

I smiled. "Well, it must've been less pleasant for Geering and his little sidekick. Irrespective of whether they knocked off Linda or not, they got what they deserved."

"Yes, that they did," Dobbs agreed.

I got up to go. "So remember to pass on anything you learn from Smythe, okay?"

He rolled his eyes. "How could I forget?"

CHAPTER 23

I planned a kind of farewell dinner for Dobbs seeing as Eileen was returning from Hawaii in the next couple of days. We had grown used to the routine of dining together when we were both off in the evenings, and I marvelled at how easy it was to form a habit.

I had enjoyed cooking for my work colleague and dear friend and knew I was going to miss our dinners and banter. Once again, I was going back to being single in a singles' world where once a woman was over the age of forty she had a better chance of being killed by a terrorist than getting married. I had heard this in *Sleepless in Seattle*, one of my favourite movies. Well, now I was going to be sleepless in friggin' Sydney.

The sad part was society pretty much supported the view that women over forty were too old and no longer attractive, whereas men were said to improve with age. Look at the likes of Richard Gere and Sean Connery. They were like one hundred and fifty years old, but still looked damned good. The other sad thing was that women were made to believe they could only find self-validation if they had a man in their lives. I mean, what crapola was this? Why should a woman be made to feel inferior simply because she didn't have a man? Perhaps this explained why bimbos like the one who ran off with my husband were co-conspirators in the break up of a marriage. These women had such low self-esteem that their only salvation was to be with a man—even one that was married. So they entered into an affair with him and then set the trap shut.

Men, of course, were gullible fools on the one hand and bastards on the other. In fact, they were such fools they needed a new woman to bolster their flagging egos, especially their middle-aged, flagging egos. And they were bastards because they actually cheated on their wives or partners and ran off to *find themselves* with a bimbo.

My only consolation in all of this was if Nathan had dumped me for a tart after eighteen years of marriage, what hope did she have that he'd treat her any better? If his psychopathic mind justified his decision to dump me—a wife who had been faithful to him and supported him through thick and thin—I was sure this witch had it coming to her a lot faster. After all, men didn't respect whores.

Thank God I had friends like Dobbs and a pseudo-son in Chris. In terms of female friendship I only had Thorny. We weren't very close, though, as she was rather guarded with her emotions and didn't share very much, but at least she was someone to have coffee with. I used to have other female friends, but they were all married, and since Nathan and I had split up most of them had ceased to keep in touch. They either felt uncomfortable or I had become a pariah in their eyes overnight.

Stop wallowing in self-pity, Ferrari! Time to go shopping for tonight's dinner, I said to myself as I headed for Giorgio's after work. I didn't have a menu in mind for the main course, but I definitely had fresh figs and prosciutto planned for the entree.

I found a parking spot right outside Giorgio's and went in to get my groceries. "Ciao, Giorgio!" I called out to the rotund, little man.

"Ah, Signorina Ferrari! Che piacere," Giorgio replied. *What a pleasure*, he'd said. At least to men like Giorgio, who were short, fat, and pushing seventy, I was still a Signorina, a Miss; not a Madam. Oh well, it was good for the ego even if it came from an old man.

I picked up half a dozen figs and ordered 200g of prosciutto, and while Giorgio was slicing it for me, I espied some homemade pasta. "How fresh is that, Giorgio?" I asked the little man, pointing to a platter with three-coloured tagliatelle.

"Made this morning per la mia moglie," he replied. His wife had made it, so I knew it would be good. Giorgio's wife did not use a pasta-making machine; she made all the pasta by hand.

"Okay, I'll have half a kilo of the tagliatelle, thanks." I planned to make pasta primavera—pasta with spring vegetables—and I would add my own touch to it by chopping up some nice porcini mushrooms in the sauce.

I was busy planning the rest of the menu when a hand landed on my shoulder and made me jump. I turned to look straight into the blue-green eyes of Phil Smythe.

"Sorry to startle you," he said. "I thought it might be you."

God, was that a smile coming from him? Incredible! "Hello, Smythe," I greeted him with a dry voice. "What brings you here? Shopping or simply following me to make sure I don't go snooping for drugs anymore?"

He gave me a charming smile, which put me on guard. He must be up to something for him to be civil. "I shop here often," he replied. "I told you before I love cooking Italian food."

I remembered, and I had to admit it was rather civilised of him. I had always pictured him as someone who ate greasy food and doughnuts. "That's nice." I forced a smile to my face and wondered how much longer Giorgio was going to be with the prosciutto and my pasta.

"Hey, got time for a coffee?" Smythe asked, almost flooring me. He couldn't possibly be asking me to coffee just to be sociable.

"Why, what's wrong?" I eyed him suspiciously. He laughed then, and for the first time I noticed he had a deep and attractive laugh. He should laugh more often, I thought. Oh, shit! Wake up, Ferrari. You must be desperate to go digging at the bottom of the barrel for someone like Smythe. It didn't matter he had that Tom Selleck look I liked so much; the guy was uncouth as far as I was concerned.

"Nothing's wrong," he answered. "I'm going to have a coffee before I go home and thought you'd like to join me."

"And I thought you couldn't stand my company," I threw at him.

"That's only when you go sticking your nose into police business," he stated and made it sound like he was paying me a compliment.

How in hell did he do that? He's telling me off, but at the same time he's paying me a compliment. So what he's saying is if I don't stick my nose into his business he wants to see me socially. Oh, fuck! "I … I …" I was stuck for words.

He smiled charmingly. "C'mon, Ferrari. It's better than drinking alone, right?"

Okay, this was more like the Smythe I was used to. "Well, if you put it that way, I agree." I accepted with my own charming smile, and at the back of my mind thought I might be able to get something out of him. I was sure by now they would've questioned Geering and his sidekick.

Smythe waited until Giorgio finished serving me and we then walked up the road to Puccini's for cappuccinos and biscotti.

"So how are things at the hotel?" he asked.

"Okay, I guess." I hated chitchat with someone I didn't know that well or liked. Besides, I was dying to ask about Geering and Kwon Lee. "How are things at the station?"

"You know, forever cleaning up the streets of the Cross to keep them safe for tourists," he replied with half a smile.

He knew what I was trying to do and I wanted to wring his neck. "How're your poker nights going?" I had to talk about something. "Dobbs tells me how much he enjoys them."

"Well, it keeps him in touch with the boys in blue, as you know. I think he misses the days when he was in the force."

"Yes, I believe he does," I agreed. "But it was his decision to leave."

"The guy was in a near-fatal shooting," Smythe informed me as if I didn't already know.

"Yes, I'm aware of that. He didn't want to make Eileen a widow so he made the decision to leave," I commented. "She's a lucky woman, Eileen."

"How's that?"

"She's got a great husband who'll do anything for her." I couldn't hide the hurt in my voice, but I didn't care. Smythe knew my marriage had broken up recently.

"I know what you mean," he commiserated with me, which was surprising seeing as he had been divorced for some years.

"Do you miss being married?" When I had lunch with him some time ago he'd said something about wanting to have kids.

"I do at times," he admitted, "but it's tough finding someone who's going to put up with shift work plus the danger police work can expose you to."

I was intrigued. "Is that what happened?"

"You mean why my marriage broke up?"

"Yes."

He sighed. "It's a long story, but no, it wasn't that. She was having an affair with a mate of mine from the force." This time there was bitterness in his voice.

I was surprised that after so long Smythe still felt for someone who'd betrayed him. Worse still, I hoped it didn't take this many years to get over a betrayal. The last thing I wanted was to think about Nathan and his cheating ways for years to come. "I'm so sorry to hear it," I said sincerely. "My ex was cheating on me, too."

His brows rose in surprise. "What a loser," he replied.

"What's that supposed to mean?" I was starting to believe Smythe had a thing for me, and I didn't feel comfortable with it.

He cleared his throat as if he'd realised he unintentionally revealed something. "Oh, simply that cheaters are real losers. They don't have the guts to confront themselves and solve whatever issues are bothering them in a relationship. They think it's easier to jump ship and on to someone else's bones instead—like that's going to fix everything."

I regarded him with interest. "It's exactly what I think."

"So we finally agree on something," he remarked and finished his coffee.

I glanced at my watch; it was time I got a move on if I wanted to make a start on dinner, but first I had to ask—even if Smythe told me to bugger off. "Listen, I'm not trying to be nosey, but I want to know if you have any reason to believe Linda's death was more than a suicide. I imagine you've questioned the scumbags."

He looked as if he was going to fob me off with some smartarse remark, but he seemed to think the better of it and replied, "The guys were grilled by us and later by the feds. They confessed to the drug smuggling and swore it was a sideline to finance the restaurants. They said there was no link to Linda's father or to her."

I sighed in disappointment. I had hoped some clue would have come to the fore and that I could pick up from where I'd left off. "Okay, thanks." I went to reach for my wallet.

Smythe waved a hand at me. "My treat."

"Thank you." I stood up, preparing to leave.

"Mia, for what it's worth, Geering actually broke down and swore he loved his wife and had nothing to do with her jumping to her death. He truly believes it was suicide."

I sat back down for a moment. "He loved his wife, you say? Is this why he was cheating on her?" I couldn't keep the sarcasm out of my voice.

"I know. I know. He admitted to the womanising. In fact, he brought it up before any of us mentioned it."

This is surprising, I thought. "That's a new one. He probably said it to make it look like he had nothing to hide. Maybe it was done in order to throw you off the scent."

Smythe nodded. "Perhaps you're right, but at the end of the day we still have the witnesses and the video showing Linda jumped without any help."

I was tempted again to share my theory with him regarding the zolpidem and the suggestive hypnosis, but there was no point. If I didn't have proof the police were not going to waste time on something that so far was simply my intuition.

"Well, I have to go now." I stood up again and picked up my shopping bag.

Smythe stayed behind to wait for the bill. "Take care."

I nodded and walked away with the feel of his eyes on my back.

CHAPTER 24

The day of the move arrived and Chris picked up the truck for me at seven in the morning. He offered to do this, and I was rather relieved seeing as I'd never driven a truck in my life.

Dobbs came direct to my place and started taking apart my bed in preparation for loading it on the truck. When Chris came in I was in the kitchen making a hardy breakfast to sustain us through the long day.

"Mmm! Something smells wonderful," Chris poked his head into the kitchen.

"I have to feed you boys. You're going to need all your strength. I'm almost done here so why don't you tell Dobbs to leave the bed for now and I'll join you at the table."

Chris nodded. "You got it." He then yelled at the top of his lungs, "Dobbs, tucker's ready."

I shook my head at him. "I could've done that myself," I chided, and shooed him out of the kitchen.

I brewed the coffee and waited until the toast was ready before I took the dishes out to the table. I'd made a large omelette with Italian sausage to be served with a side of grilled tomatoes and sautéed mushrooms. The boys' eyes lit up when they saw the food.

"This looks great," Chris exclaimed. "I'm starving."

Dobbs didn't have to say anything. A look at the delight in his eyes said it all.

"Eat up then," I ordered while I started pouring the coffee. They needed no prompting to dig in.

"So when does the apartment settle?" Dobbs asked in between bites of toast laden with butter.

"Well, remember the buyer wanted a quick settlement? Anyway, when he found out I intended moving out of my place early he decided to settle by tomorrow." I had a sip of coffee and started eating.

"That's great," said Chris, almost finished with his breakfast and eyeing mine.

I grinned. "God, you are a ravenous beast. Good thing I made more. I had a feeling there'd be requests for seconds." I got up and went to the kitchen to get a second helping for him.

"So what are you going to do with your money, Mia? It would be prudent to buy a property," Dobbs called out.

I came back to join them with a new plate for Chris and placed it in front of him. He smiled his thanks and tucked in. "I don't think I want to get bogged down with another property just now. I need time to think about things. Besides, I may have other plans."

"You mean travel?" Chris asked before he shoved another forkful into his mouth.

"Not so much travel, but I have something in mind I'd like to buy." I didn't tell them what it was.

"So what is it?" Dobbs asked.

"You'll just have to wait and see," I replied in a mysterious tone. "Any more omelette for you, Dobbs?"

"You need to ask?" He gave me a wide grin.

I smiled and went back to the kitchen. When I came back out I topped up everybody's coffee and we finished our meal with general chitchat.

Then, Chris dropped the bombshell. "The police came for Elena yesterday evening."

Dobbs and I turned to him, looking stunned. "And when were you thinking of telling us?" I rebuked him.

He shrugged. "I wanted us to enjoy our breakfast first."

"When did she get back?" David had informed me he was going to call Elena so she would come back early from her trip, but he didn't update me after this—not that he was obligated to do so.

"Yesterday morning," Chris replied. "And then, there was a huge row between Dad and Elena. God, it was so loud it woke me up, and I can usually sleep through a cyclone."

I observed with a cocked eyebrow, "You don't seem to be very upset by all this."

He gazed directly into my eyes with a look that was mature and yet a little unsure. "Why should I be?" His voice held a tone of bravado, and I knew he was doing his best not to give in to his feelings. My heart went out to him.

"I know you and Elena aren't close, but there's nothing wrong with getting upset over this. After all, she is your mother," I pointed out gently.

Dobbs nodded in agreement but didn't say anything. He was too busy finishing off the last of his toast.

"Do you want to tell us what the row was about?" I asked tentatively. I didn't want to upset him even though he was putting a brave face on the whole thing.

"Well, once Dad told her the truth as to why he'd asked her to come back early, she flipped. She denied anything going on between her and Geering. Then Dad told her Smythe informed him that Geering spilled the beans about their affair, and that the police would get it out of her, so she may as well tell the truth."

I poured us all more coffee and after a few sips, Chris kept talking. "This worked because she was afraid she'd be wrongly convicted for something she didn't do—meaning the drugs—so she admitted she had a thing with Geering but had no knowledge of anything illegal. She also said Geering was two-timing her with someone else; and that's why she decided to go off to Switzerland."

This was a bit of a revelation. I never really believed Elena was involved in the drug operation, so as far as I was concerned she was only guilty of infidelity. I had never imagined, however, that Geering was also two-timing his lover.

"Anyway," Chris went on, "after a bit of a screaming match Elena confessed she believed Geering when he told her he wanted to leave his wife and marry her. When Elena found out about this other lover, though, she told him to drop dead and took off for Europe."

"Wow," Dobbs remarked. "This keeps getting more and more complicated. I wonder who the other lover is."

"Yes, that's the million dollar question," I replied thoughtfully. "But we may never find out. In the meantime, Elena couldn't have had anything to do with Linda Liu's death—not if Geering promised to leave his wife for her."

"How long has this been going on? Maybe Elena got sick of waiting," Dobbs remarked.

"Guys, Elena might be a lot of things, but she's no murderer,"

Chris uttered.

"I agree," I stated. "I still think Linda didn't commit suicide and that some kind of foul play is involved, but I don't think Elena did it. Meanwhile, Geering confessed to the police he was cheating behind Linda's back even though he claimed he still loved her. Yet, everything keeps pointing back to him."

Dobbs grinned with sarcasm. "It was very cooperative of him, volunteering information like that."

I nodded. "Exactly what I thought." I had told Dobbs upon his arrival at my place about my run-in with Smythe and the information he'd revealed regarding Geering. "Well, he's either telling the truth or trying to confuse the cops as much as possible so he can get away with it."

"Or there's a third party involved," Chris interjected.

I gazed at him with agreement. "It's definitely a possibility, but this third party, if there is one, had to have a motive to get rid of Linda. Now, we know it's not the drugs because according to Geering, Linda had no knowledge of what was going on. So it's got to be something to do with her testifying regarding her father's activities or the motive is a more personal one."

"Such as?" Dobbs asked.

"Jealousy."

I had two pairs of eyes looking at me intently, and I went on to explain, "What if this third party Geering's been seeing was told the same thing as Elena? Then, the third party finds out he's not only a cheat but a liar, on top of which he not only intended to stay on with Linda, but he had yet another lover on the side."

Dobbs rolled his eyes. "Man, it sounds like this guy had a whole harem going." He and Chris laughed.

"Hear me out, you guys." I cast them a serious look. "This other lover decides with Linda out of the way Geering will fulfill his promise, so she does away with Linda."

Dobbs frowned. "Girl, you've had too much coffee and your imagination is running wild. We still have no proof Linda was murdered in the first place."

I threw him a look of annoyance. "I know this! First, we have to find the elusive lover."

Dobbs waved his hands up in the air as if dismissing the whole thing. "I think we're wasting our time."

"Do you think the elusive lover knew about Elena, too?" This came from Chris.

"Now there's an excellent observation," I said admiringly. "You should become a cop, Chris."

He shook his head. "No, thanks. Computers are my life."

"To answer your question," I stated, "I think if this person knew Elena was the other lover, Elena wouldn't be alive today."

There was a momentary silence from both men; then Chris remarked, "Good thing she went off to Switzerland."

"Exactly," I replied.

"Of course, none of this matters now," Dobbs declared. "Geering's ass is in jail for drug smuggling, so whether he had two or two hundred lovers is irrelevant."

I felt frustrated. "I don't know why this is, but although none of us has been able to find any proof about Linda's death, I still think she was murdered."

Dobbs stood up. "Well, while you think about it why don't we start on this move? If we keep dissecting this thing we're never going to get any work done."

"True," I agreed and began to clear the table while the boys made a start on loading the truck. This whole thing would have to wait.

Two days passed in unpacking and settling into the new place. Once finished, I was absolutely exhausted, but happy that all had been done and I could now return to work.

My lawyer transferred the money from the proceeds of the sale, which was my part of the equity, to my bank account. I viewed my bank balance with both joy and sadness—joy at the fact that I had been able to save the legacy my father had left me and sadness because despite all this, the money represented the break up of a marriage and the loss of my matrimonial home. It was a bittersweet reminder of the dissolution of eighteen years with a significant other with whom I believed I was going to spend the rest of my life.

All this was gone now, and I felt like a small boat that had come loose from its mooring, bobbing up and down in an ocean full of traitorous and frightening currents. So the last thing I wanted at present was to do something sensible like buy another property, as Dobbs had suggested. Instead, I decided on the best medicine for a broken heart—retail therapy.

I had another day off before I had to go back to work and I spent it productively. I then contacted Dobbs and Chris, who were doing an afternoon shift at the hotel, and invited them for a thank you drink for helping me move. We agreed to meet in the hotel car park when they finished work at eleven.

At precisely five minutes past eleven I roared into the car park, and when the boys saw me their jaws dropped wide open.

Mia Ferrari, I thought with glee, had decided this whole marriage break up needed huge retail therapy. So huge, in fact, that she made an impulse purchase and pulled up in a bright red Ferrari Spider 360 looking her usual cool self and wearing black leather.

Dobbs's eyes seemed to pop out of his head while Chris simply let out a wolf whistle and gave me a big smile. I lapped up the admiration in their eyes and felt like a million dollars.

CHAPTER 25

"**A**ll right!" Chris exclaimed, running his hands over the car as if he were caressing a woman. "This is beautiful!"

I couldn't help but feel proud of my new baby, except the feeling was marred by Dobbs's frown.

"Girl, have you taken leave of your senses?" he berated me.

"Aw, c'mon Dobbs, this is my divorce present to myself. A girl's got to have something nice to get her through the tough times," I protested.

"But not this expensive," Dobbs returned with disapproval. "I bet you went and spent all your money."

"As a matter of fact, I didn't," I explained. "I purchased it privately off a friend of a contact of mine. He gave me a good price for it; so I still have money left."

Dobbs lifted his eyebrows in doubt. "Not that much, I'm willing to bet."

I started to feel irritated with him. "Hey! I thought you'd be happy for me."

"I'm happy for you, Mia," Chris remarked and jumped in next to me. "Will you take me for a spin?"

I smiled at his exuberance and felt a little better. I couldn't blame Dobbs for being conservative. He expected me to buy a smaller place to live in and save any money that was left over for a rainy day. But I wasn't ready to throw in the towel just yet. Financial security was high on my list, but it was amazing how liberating being dumped could be sometimes. It was as if a hurricane had swept through my life and taken everything away from me; and now I had to start all over. I had a blank canvas to fill and I wasn't going to fill it with humdrum security.

I had learned the hard way about the fickleness of security from my experience with Nathan. I married him because I thought he was going to be steadfast and more reliable than David. I was sure he was going to provide the security I had craved at the time; and look what happened! So now I was simply going to enjoy my life and live in the present. As far as I was concerned, the future could take care of itself.

"Dobbs, don't worry about me. I'm a survivor. Now, are we going to have that drink or not?" I didn't want to spoil the moment by getting into an argument with my friend.

Dobbs sighed. "Yes, of course," he replied. "And Mia, I know I sound like an old fuddy-duddy, but on the other hand I'd be totally unfeeling if I didn't tell you I'm in love with your Ferrari."

His smile was all I needed. "Well, let's go for that drink then." I smiled at him.

"Hey, we can't all fit in here. There are only two seats," Chris stated.

"I didn't mean with the car, silly," I uttered. "We're going up the road to Bill's." Chris looked disappointed and I took pity on him. "Tell you what, after drinks I'll take you for a spin. Dobbs'll have to go home to his wife so he won't mind." I grinned at Dobbs. Eileen was back and he was only allowed to hang out with us for about an hour; then he had to go home. Ah, domesticity, I thought, and suddenly I didn't miss it one bit.

We left Bill's at around midnight and I took Chris for a spin around the city, across the Harbour Bridge and into North Sydney. Then I took the Pacific Highway, did a loop over the Gladesville Bridge and Victoria Road, passed inner-city suburbs such as Drummoyne and Balmain, turned onto the Anzac Bridge, which took us back to the city, and finally onto William Street, which led us back to the hotel. The night was rather balmy and I left the roof down. The feeling of freedom I experienced was worth every cent I had spent on this wonderful car. Chris was totally enthralled with it, too, and when I pulled up outside the hotel he turned to me.

"Hey, let me drive it for a few minutes."

"Dream on, baby." I shook my head. "Now, scoot. I have an early shift and it's already gone one."

Chris kissed me on the cheek. "Thanks, Mia. That was great. Next time we'll have to go faster."

I laughed. "Yeah, and get ourselves arrested, right? C'mon, off you go."

He got out of the car, came round to my side, and leaned over so the valet who was standing a few feet away eyeing us wouldn't hear. "I thought you might like to know that Elena's leaving my dad."

"What?" I exclaimed; but I wasn't really all that surprised—not after what had transpired.

Chris took a moment to speak again and I knew he was fighting tears. He might put on a show like he didn't care about Elena, but good or not she was still his mother. "She's leaving in the morning," he said, and then he ran inside the hotel.

I put the car into gear and purred away with the valet gazing after me. He was looking at a Ferrari driving a Ferrari. I liked that. As I drove home, only a few blocks away, I thought of poor Chris and the effect his mother's departure would have on him. He was on the brink of becoming a man, but he was still a boy who needed a mother.

I parked the car in the security car park of my building and went up to my Art Deco apartment. It was smaller and older than where I had lived, but it had character and style. I loved the high ceilings and the large timber-framed windows, which let in so much light. I'd only been here a few days, but it already felt like home. My home. It didn't matter I was renting; it was still my place.

Thoughts of David popped into my head while I got ready for bed, but I was too tired to think about him and his reaction to Elena's departure. In my opinion, I believed it was a good thing. Despite the fact that he and Elena had had their little arrangement to live separate lives, this couldn't have been very satisfying for either one of them.

I fell asleep as soon as my head hit the pillow and must've dreamed about David because a few hours later I woke up to the sound of the alarm clock and his face was still on my mind.

I dragged my body out of bed and jumped into the shower, hoping it would wake me up fully; but it was only after two espressos that my eyes truly opened. I then dressed for work and arrived ten minutes later by foot.

It was great to be able to walk to work. I didn't have to do battle with the traffic and my Ferrari was sleeping safe and sound at home. *Mia*, as I decided to christen the car, was my pleasure machine. She and I were destined to have many adventures together, but driving to work was not going to be one of them. I had ordered special number plates for the car that would simply read: Mia.

No, I didn't name the car after myself. Ironically, in the Italian language, a car was referred to in the feminine tense; hence "my car" in Italian would be *la mia machina*. So I christened the car Mia, meaning *my* or *mine*. I thought this was rather clever and also very symbolic. My car, my freedom, my life.

The hotel lobby was crowded with guests checking out and group arrivals waiting in the café area for their rooms to be allocated. Meanwhile, they enjoyed complimentary tea, coffee, and pastries. The porters were running around with luggage trolleys, either packing them sky high with the suitcases of arrivals or wheeling out luggage to waiting taxis and limos bound for the airport. It was a typical busy morning at the hotel.

I was about to make my way to the back office when I saw Elena coming out of the lift accompanied by a porter and a large trolley jam-packed with numerous suitcases.

She wore a silver-white, close-fitting pantsuit, and white, impossibly high heels. Her blonde hair hung down her back and framed her beautiful model's face. She stopped for a moment and gave instructions to the porter who in turn proceeded with the trolley to a waiting limo parked outside the front door.

My heart jolted as I realised this was my only opportunity to talk to her before she left. I hadn't heard anything from Smythe about her questioning and from the little Dobbs and Chris had told me, I felt if anyone could supply a clue as to what happened with Linda, it was Elena.

Perhaps I was barking up the wrong tree, but even so I wanted to leave no stone unturned. And although I had never liked the ice queen, for the sake of Linda Liu I decided to approach her.

I swallowed hard and walked up to her while she was rummaging through her handbag, and just as I reached her she pulled out a pair of Chanel sunglasses and put them on.

"Mrs Rourke," I greeted her. "I'm Mia Ferrari."

Elena peeked at me from the top of her glasses and her steely blue eyes gave away nothing of what she may be feeling. "I know who you are," she replied in a not-too-friendly tone. "What do you want?"

Elena was taller than I, and her high-heeled shoes made her

tower over me even more, but I wasn't intimidated. "I heard you're leaving," I stated, deciding to get to the point. People like Elena were known to have little patience for others. "I was wondering if you would be kind enough to give me a few minutes of your time."

Elena took off her sunglasses and eyed me up and down in a derisive manner. "Why should I give you any time?"

I wondered if there was a way to appeal to her, so I told her the truth. "It's to do with Linda Liu's death, Mrs Rourke. I have reason to believe her death was not a suicide."

She regarded me with surprise in her eyes. "Tell me how this is any of your business in the first place," her voice was hard.

I looked at her square in the eyes. She may have a steely glance, but so did I when I wanted to. "I might not be the police, but I'm a woman trying to help another woman who obviously couldn't help herself."

Elena smiled sardonically, revealing perfect teeth. "And who are you, Wonder Woman?"

I returned her smile, but mine held warmth in it. "Let's just say I believe in the sisterhood."

This seemed to intrigue her because she didn't answer straight away but regarded me thoughtfully. She then glanced at her watch and back at me. "Okay," she said, "I'll give you five minutes."

"I appreciate it, Mrs Rourke."

Elena turned on me. "And for God's sake, don't call me that. I'm Elena."

"Very well, Elena." I was beginning to respect her.

We made our way to a small function room on the mezzanine level where we could talk without all the noise around us. I switched on the lights and we sat at opposite ends of one of the trestle tables, facing each other. Elena waited for me to speak, and again I decided to be direct.

"Mrs ... I mean, Elena," I began, "on the day Linda died she asked me to make an appointment with the hotel's hairdresser. She had every intention of attending the function that night. I don't believe someone planning to commit suicide would make a hair appointment."

I noted a reluctant look of admiration in Elena's eyes as she regarded me. "Well, it's refreshing to finally come across someone with a brain," she stated. "You probably know the police questioned me." I nodded, and she went on. "They thought I might be involved in the drug dealings with James, but this was never the case."

"I know that," I acknowledged.

Elena ran her long, manicured fingers through her hair. "By the way, I know about your history with David," she added in a matter-of-fact tone. I was shocked but remained silent. I didn't know David had discussed me with her. Elena continued talking. "Look, David and I should never have married. He was on the rebound from you and we had a fling. Only I happened to fall pregnant with Chris and David wanted to do the right thing. But that's neither here nor there," she remarked. "I'm not trying to justify my actions to you. So let's just say I had a number of affairs, as I'm sure David did, too." She paused thoughtfully for a few moments. "Or maybe he didn't; I wouldn't know. All I know is he's married to his hotel empire."

"I know it's none of my business, but why leave then? You're free to come and go," I ventured to say.

At first, I thought she was going to refuse to answer, but then she replied, "I've had enough of this life of deceit and I deserve better. Whatever you may think, I don't enjoy having flings, and James promised me a real marriage. He had every intention of divorcing Linda, or at least that's what he had me believe." Her tone was cynical and I could relate to her. It was like Nathan promising he'd be with me for the rest of my life and then dumping me for some bimbo.

"So you're going to start a new life."

"Yes, and after this last experience it's going to be a single one—at least, for the time being." This time her smile was more genuine.

"I know you talked to the police and nothing came of it, but is there anything you can think of that may point to the fact James Geering would have killed his wife?"

Elena took a moment to think about my question. "No," she said finally. "The reason I know this is because the night of the VIP dinner I went to his room to console him. He was devastated by Linda's death."

"Oh." I was surprised and made a mental note that this might explain Geering's time lapse on the night and why he took so long to come out of his room to notify the police. Then I thought of the time I went to check with him about the CEO dinner. "You were there when I came in to ask him about the CEO dinner," I stated.

"You wore the vanilla perfume."

She nodded. "Yes. I was hiding in his bedroom when you came knocking on the door."

This cleared up one mystery, I thought. "Elena," I queried, "do you remember how long you spent in Geering's room on the night Linda jumped?"

Elena didn't even blink at this question. "Not exactly. James was in shock and called me from the room to tell me what had happened. As you know, I was at the function with David so I couldn't very well leave for too long, but I went to see him briefly to provide emotional support."

This made sense. "But why didn't he mention this to the police later? He gave them the right time as to when he went down to the room, but he didn't account for the time he spent in there."

Elena glanced at her watch. "Look, I have a flight to catch," she informed me. "All I can tell you is, I don't know. Maybe he didn't want to tell them he was with me as this would have raised a whole bunch of other questions." She stood up, and I walked with her.

"One last question, if you please," I said.

Elena grinned. "You're quite the determined little thing I heard about," she remarked.

"Oh?"

"Chris worships you," she declared, but didn't seem to resent the fact. "Keep an eye on him, will you? I was never the maternal type, but I do love him."

My heart warmed to her and I realised she wasn't the ice queen all of us seemed to think. She was a feeling human being with her own set of problems, just like the rest of us; only, she didn't want to appear vulnerable. I felt a sense of kinship with her all of a sudden and regretted I had been as bad as the others in judging her.

"So what's your last question?" Elena prompted while we waited for the lift.

"Well, with Linda Liu dead the way was clear for James Geering to marry you, so what happened?"

Elena frowned. "He was two-timing me with another woman. James never had any intentions of divorcing Linda for anyone. When I realised this I left him and went off to Switzerland."

"I don't suppose you know—" The lift arrived and the doors slid open. We stepped inside and Elena punched the button for the lobby.

Turning to me, she said, "No, I don't know who the other woman is, and I don't care. I don't think he meant to marry her, either; if that's what you're thinking. Besides, even if he did, it's too late now because the bastard is in jail. Well-deserved as it turns out."

The lift doors slid open at the lobby and we exited. "Thank you, Elena," I said sincerely. "You've been able to clear up a couple of unanswered questions. I don't know if I'll ever be able to uncover what happened to Linda, but it's good to know you're also part of the sisterhood."

Elena looked like she was going to say something else, but then she seemed to think the better of it and simply left with a casual wave.

CHAPTER 26

I bumped into David the following morning while I was doing my rounds. He looked glad to see me and smiled. I returned his smile and felt that warm feeling I had come to associate with him every time he looked at me.

"I saw Elena leave yesterday," I remarked when we stopped to talk for a minute in the lobby. "I'm sorry."

He shook his head. "Don't be. It should've happened a long time ago. I thought Chris was enough to keep us together, but I was wrong. Elena and I were a mistake."

I nodded and wanted to say Nathan and I had also been a mistake, but I didn't want to think about him anymore. My new life started the day I moved into my apartment at Potts Point and when I purchased Mia, my lovely Ferrari.

"I sometimes think it's better to be on one's own," I said, thinking of my own situation. "You probably heard that a person can feel lonelier in a bad relationship than if they're on their own."

He cast me a thoughtful look. "Yes. You're right."

"Well, then." I smiled and made to move on.

David stopped me by placing a hand on my forearm. "By the way, Chris told me about your new car. He's been driving me crazy about it and thinks I should buy him one."

I laughed. "Young men love fast cars."

"And so, it seems, do you," he replied with a glint in his eye.

"Hey, I'm Italian, remember? Ferrari's are as much in our blood as pasta, Vespas and soccer."

"You're a real case, Mia Ferrari." His eyes held a look of fondness in them, which reminded me of that time so long ago in Venice. I had to get out of here.

"I'm a bad case right now because I'm falling behind in my room checks," I stated, glancing at my watch and steering away from personal topics.

David seemed to remember himself and suddenly he was all business. "I didn't mean to keep you. Are you on tomorrow? We have the function for the Real Estate Institute."

"Yes. I'm on in the evening. I'll probably see you then." I nodded briefly and walked off.

David was in a vulnerable place right now with his own marriage break up and the whole thing of Elena's involvement with James Geering. It had been all over the news recently; one of the reasons why Elena had decided to go back to Switzerland, where she had family.

When I finished my rounds I caught up with Dobbs in the staff restaurant.

"So how are you enjoying the Ferrari, Ms Ferrari?" He grinned at his little joke.

"Just fine, Dobbs, and the name is Mia," I corrected him.

"I know your name's Mia," he replied, looking confused.

"I meant the car. Remember, I told you that *mia* in Italian means *mine?*"

He nodded when understanding dawned on him. "Oh yes, you did explain. Frankly, I think you should've called it Magnum PI." He sniffed with faint disapproval.

I searched his eyes to see if there was envy written in them, but I couldn't see any. Dobbs was obviously concerned for me because I had gone and done something crazy.

"Hey, don't worry about me, okay?" I reassured him. "I'm happy with my purchase. It's been very liberating for me."

"Yeah, liberating you of a huge chunk of money," he quipped.

"Stop it already!" I scolded. "Why can't you just be happy for me?"

"Because you're throwing away money that could go toward buying yourself a place to live."

"You sound like my father, and while I appreciate your sentiments I think I'm old enough to make my own decisions." I smiled when I said this so it wouldn't come out sounding harsh, but I wanted to put a stop to it once and for all; therefore, I changed the subject. "Now, tell me if there's any news regarding Geering and

Kwon Lee."

Dobbs sighed resignedly. "Very well. I had a drink with Smythe the other day and he told me they've been turned over to the feds. After all, it was a major drug bust and part of an international smuggling operation that the feds were already working on. So as far as Smythe is concerned, his part in all this is over."

I frowned. "So they've given up on Linda Liu?"

"They have no proof—and neither do you, Mia. You tried your best." He tried to comfort me. "At least you were instrumental in busting up a drug operation. Just think of the countless people you saved from buying drugs."

"They'll only go and buy from someone else," I argued.

"Okay, but it's one less drug smuggler on the planet."

I smiled. "At least you have a positive outlook on this." I then told him about my encounter with Elena and he listened with interest.

"So the ice queen is a bit of a kindred spirit after all," he observed.

"I wouldn't go that far; but yes, she turned out to be quite decent in the end. In any case, she didn't give me anything to work with, but at least we now know what Geering was doing during those forty-five minutes I couldn't account for."

"It was a good thing she was able to shed some light on that," Dobbs pointed out.

"She was also in the room the day I went to see if Geering was attending the dinner function," I added. "But something's still nagging at me. I can't quite put my finger on it."

Dobbs stood up. "I have to get back to work now," he announced, "but, Mia, don't go tearing yourself apart over this. You tried your best, which is more than I can say for the cops. If it weren't for you—and young Chris—those two scumbags would still be carrying on with their drugs, and Elena might have been placed in danger."

I sighed thoughtfully. "You're right, of course. If she'd stayed with Geering she might have found out about the drugs and they might've had to snuff her."

"You have such a way with words," Dobbs teased, and I stuck out my tongue at him.

That evening, I took Mia out for a drive to clear my head. It was fine out and I left the top down. The air was cool but just what I needed to energise me. I drove to the northern beaches and stopped off at Newport Beach, where I consumed a burger for dinner while I sat on the sand watching the waves roll in. It was still dusk and there were a few brave surfers out there, not at all concerned with the possibility of sharks. Of course, it was only spring and the water was still too cool for the creatures.

I tried to clear my mind so whatever was nagging at me would come to the fore. This happened to me at times when I was searching for the solution to a problem. If I sat quietly, gazing into the distance, sometimes the answer just popped into my head. This time, however, nothing came to mind except the picture of poor Linda Liu spread out on top of the baby grand.

After an hour or so I gave up and decided to drive home. It was quite chilly by now and I wanted to get into something warm and make myself a cup of coffee. I stood and started to make my way to the car.

"Hey, baby, nice wheels," a male voice called out from behind me. "Want to give me a ride?"

I turned to see a lone surfer who'd just come out of the water. He was in his twenties, tall with an athletic figure, and extremely good looking. "Thank you, *baby*!" I replied with emphasis on the last word. "But I'm not into cradle snatching."

The surfer let out an attractive laugh. "C'mon, you can't be more than thirty," he said, all charm.

I winked at him. "Come back in ten years and maybe I'll take you on," I retorted with a saucy grin as I turned back to the car.

"It's a pity," was his response.

"So it is," I threw over my shoulder, climbed in the car, and drove off with a wave of the hand and a smile on my lips. I wondered if he would have tried to pick me up if he hadn't seen my Ferrari.

The following day I slept in and at around mid-morning I drove to Giorgio's to pick up some groceries. I was working that evening but had the next day off, and I had invited Dobbs and Eileen for a 'congratulations on the baby' lunch. I planned to make the typical Italian repast of antipasto followed by pasta with meatballs, and accompanied by crusty Italian bread plus a mixed salad dressed with plenty of olive oil and balsamic vinegar.

Once the groceries were done, I picked up a cappuccino on the go from Puccini's, and on my way to the car I almost collided with someone.

"Mia, how are you?"

I looked up and found myself face-to-face with Tony, the sous chef Thorny had sacked. "Tony." I smiled in greeting. "I didn't know you lived in these parts."

"I do now," he replied cheerfully. "Getting the sack from Rourke's was the best thing that could've happened to me. I landed a fantastic job at Pruniers, and I love it."

Pruniers was a premiere restaurant in Woollahra. "Good for you. Congratulations are in order. Say, can I buy you a coffee?"

"Why not? Thanks."

We didn't go into Puccini's but walked farther down the road to Rosetti's. I ordered an espresso and for Tony, a cappuccino.

"I'm sorry you had to leave so abruptly," I said when we sat down at a table. I hadn't known him very well, but I had heard he was a good chef, which was rather baffling as Thorny told me his performance was substandard.

Tony frowned at my mention of what happened. "Well, I'm glad I got out of there. That woman is a real bitch, and if truth be told she's not such a great chef herself." His tone was bitter.

I couldn't blame him seeing as he had been sacked for his performance, despite his fling with Thorny. At the same time, I didn't think he should be so critical of her. As far as I knew, Thorny was a good chef and, though Tony's pride had been wounded, he shouldn't go around bad-mouthing her professional skills.

The guy was rather attractive with his dark, sultry looks. Surely he was over Thorny by now and onto some other woman, so there was no need to gossip about her. "Tony." I gave him a grave look. "You know I'm a friend of Thorny's; besides, I can never agree with you about her being substandard in performance. Rourke's only employs top of the range personnel—you being one of them. So frankly I'm still a little puzzled as to why she dismissed you, but I assume there was a good reason."

Tony's eyes flashed fire when he replied, "I see she lied to you, too. She did the same thing to human resources. She told them my standard was below average, but this was never the case. She liked my work well enough until I caught her kissing that guy they arrested— the one whose picture was all over the papers recently. From then on, she did her best to get rid of me; and was successful in doing so without any questions being asked."

My jaw dropped open and I did my best to close it before I dribbled into my coffee. "Say what?"

"You mean you didn't know?" Tony queried like I was an idiot.

I shook my head.

"She was carrying on with the Geering guy, and I had the misfortune to catch them kissing in the cooler once. After this, she changed toward me and started picking on everything I did. Then, in the space of a couple of weeks, she issued me with a few written warnings and later sacked me."

Tony had worked himself up into a bit of a frazzle and I offered to buy him another coffee, which he accepted.

Meanwhile, I had the most awful feeling at the pit of my stomach and knew that everything was about to come together. "Tony," I spoke in a calm tone, though I felt anything but calm, "are you saying you and Thorny never had a fling?"

The look he gave me was all the response I needed. "Is that what she told you?"

I nodded, momentarily at a loss for words.

"I'm engaged to be married, for God's sake, and everyone knows it! Why would she tell you we had a fling?"

Why indeed? I asked myself, and then I froze. The vanilla perfume! That's what had been bugging me all along. Elena wasn't the only one who wore it. Thorny was the other woman! The third party—and now I had confirmation from Tony.

Suddenly, the awful thought crossed my mind that while Elena might simply dump Geering because he was two-timing her, someone like Thorny, who had such a volatile temper, would be more likely to stick a knife into his heart. More awful still, what if Geering had promised her the same thing as he had to Elena?

Elena went off to Switzerland when she realised Geering had no intention of divorcing Linda, but what would Thorny do?

I refused to think she would be capable of doing away with another human being so she could get the man she loved, but images of her terrorising her staff kept flashing into my mind. I concluded that although I'd known Thorny for a long time, you never really knew people, and anything was possible. I prayed I was wrong.

CHAPTER 27

My shift ended at eleven that evening and I hadn't been able to focus on anything. Luckily, we did not have any problems and even the few functions we had on had gone smoothly. I spent most of my time doing rounds and room checks, and thinking about the information I'd learned from Tony.

The vanilla perfume Thorny sometimes wore meant nothing, except that she and Elena had the same taste in fragrance. I'd already had it from Elena herself that she was the one who had been in Geering's room the day I went to enquire about his attendance to the dinner function. Later, I smelled the perfume on Elena when she was in the lobby by the Concierge desk.

For all I knew, Geering could have been carrying on with ten women who wore the same perfume; but Tony's news had come as a real shock. It confirmed Thorny was definitely involved with Geering. Even so, there was no proof she'd had anything to do with Linda's death. I briefly wondered whether I should alert Smythe of this latest development, but decided that unless I had some real proof there was no point in involving him.

On a personal note, I felt betrayed by Thorny. I had always trusted and thought highly of her, and all this time she had been carrying on with Geering and hadn't mentioned a word. I guess I couldn't blame her, especially when Linda died and the whole thing became public. I didn't think Thorny would have liked to become involved in the investigation simply because she'd had a fling with Geering, but why lie about Tony? She obviously hadn't told anyone else about it. She had simply fabricated the lie for my benefit.

Perhaps, she found out I was investigating the situation and became worried I would make her a suspect. By pretending she was having a fling with Tony, she knew I would never suspect anything. Of course, when Tony caught her in Geering's arms, she then had to get rid of him. She couldn't afford to have him blabbing around the kitchen. Therefore, she had gone into damage control mode and managed him out as soon as was humanly possible.

I logged off my computer and handed the keys over to the night manager. I felt bone-tired and needed to sleep, but I was suddenly overcome by the temptation to go searching through Thorny's office. If I was going to find some sort of link to the Linda Liu case, this would be my last attempt before I gave up. Besides, this was the perfect opportunity to go snooping as only the graveyard shift was on duty and the kitchen would be dead quiet, except for one of the junior chefs catering for room service.

As a duty manager, it wouldn't look strange to anyone that I was in Thorny's office. I constantly popped in and out of offices. Sometimes I needed to fetch a checklist or a document to address an issue or deal with a guest query, so it would be easy to come up with an excuse if anyone questioned me.

I wasn't sure what I hoped to find, but I didn't want to leave any loose ends before I finally let go of the whole thing. Thorny was the last link in the case, and if I didn't follow up on this I would never rest.

I told the night manager I had forgotten to take care of something and took back my keys from him before I made my way to the kitchen. Upon entering I noticed the lights were on, but the junior chef was probably taking a break because the whole place was deserted. Even better.

Thorny's office was locked; but I had a master key and let myself in. I switched on her desk lamp and started rummaging through her desk while keeping an eye on the kitchen door in case the junior chef returned. I found nothing unusual.

Her desktop was piled with cookery books, menus, a large amount of flyers from food and wine distributors, and some empty coffee cups, which had never made it to the dishwasher. The desk drawers were unlocked and revealed more flyers, menus and a whole lot of stationery items plus a couple of chef hats and aprons.

I wondered if I was wasting my time doing this, but something drove me on. So I turned to the bookshelves, which lined one wall of the office. They were filled with books and piles of papers amongst more chef hats and aprons. I stuck my hands behind the books and papers to see if anything was hidden there, but I came out with nothing.

I then stopped and glanced at my watch; it was a little past midnight. I sighed, a feeling of fatigue coming over me. The junior chef hadn't yet returned and I figured he was off somewhere, grabbing a nap. Smart boy. I only hoped he didn't get into trouble for sleeping on the job.

I craved for a strong coffee to keep me alert, but now was not the time. I had to finish searching the office before anything else. I turned to a filing cabinet in one corner of the room and tried the drawers. Locked. I hadn't noticed any keys in the desk drawers so I assumed Thorny took the keys home. So this was it. I couldn't very well break into the cabinet. The only thing to do was return when Thorny was on duty and hope she was too busy to notice me slip into her office and search through her files.

I yawned and decided it was time to go home. One quick look at the kitchen revealed it was still deserted. I turned to switch off the desk lamp, and as I did so my keys flew off the key chain, which was attached to the waistband of my suit pants. The rattling sound of them landing on the floor startled me. As opposed to the administration offices, the kitchen office did not have carpet, but an easy-to-mop painted cement floor. The keys ended up just behind the filing cabinet with the broken chain peeking out. The chain clasp was still attached to my waistband.

"Shit!" I murmured and bent down to retrieve the keys. I pulled on the key chain, but it seemed to be caught on something behind the cabinet. I stuck my hand in between the back of the cabinet and the wall in order to free the chain and felt a small hook that was attached to the back of the cabinet with something dangling from it. One of the key rings had become caught on the hook, so first I freed up the keys and put them in my pocket; then, I stuck my hand back in to retrieve whatever was dangling from the hook. I drew out a small velvet pouch with drawstrings like those often used for jewellery.

I quickly cast my eyes toward the kitchen, to ensure it was still empty, before turning my attention back to the pouch, which I now held in my hand. It felt light, and as I opened it to pour the contents out, a small plastic bottle with a label fell onto my open palm. I

leaned over the desk, holding the bottle close to the light of the lamp to read the label, and froze.

At that very moment, a heavy weight landed on my back, sending me sprawling over the top of the desk, knocking books, papers, and the lamp to the floor. The plastic bottle in my hand flew off in some unknown direction at the same time as I felt a searing pain tearing at my shoulder.

I thought I was going to black out, but the adrenaline in my body pumped energy into my muscles. I pushed upward with my hands on the desk to dislodge whatever was on top of me.

I heard something crash on top of the fallen lamp and the office was cast into semi-darkness; but I was able to see the pure hatred in Thorny's eyes as she jumped back on her feet, holding a meat cleaver high up in one hand and about to plunge it into my chest.

I blocked her descending arm with my forearm, knocking the cleaver out of her hand and sending it flying to the other side of the room, where it landed on the floor with a loud clatter. Thorny screamed with animal rage and came at me with her bare hands. She pushed me onto the desk again. This time, I landed on my back and felt the excruciating pain down my spine; I ignored it and raised one foot, just as she lunged at me, and made contact with her chest. I pushed with all my strength and sent her reeling back across the office to crash-land against the bookshelves.

She was winded for a moment and I took the opportunity to push myself off the desk and kick her in the face, breaking her nose in the process. The fight went out of her then, and she grabbed at her nose, which was bleeding copiously.

"You fucking bitch!" she yelled with hate. "You had to spoil everything!"

Her voice sounded like some unleashed demon from hell and not the person I thought I knew. I ignored her tirade of insults and grabbed an apron I espied lying on the floor. As I ripped it in half, I kicked Thorny in the ribs, ensuring she stayed down. She screamed in pain but made no attempt to get back up. I bound her ankles together with the ripped apron and with the other half I tied her wrists in front of her so she could still go on holding her nose. I then picked up the meat cleaver and held onto it in case she tried to make a grab for it.

The pain in my back was subsiding, but my shoulder was

throbbing and I felt something wet soaking through my suit jacket. I touched the area around my shoulder blade and felt the large rip in the material of the suit; and my hand came away soaked with blood. The cleaver had ripped my shoulder open. Thorny was still cursing like a possessed entity when I picked up the phone and dialled security.

"Get an ambulance," I barked when Nat, the security officer, picked up. "We have a couple of injuries in the kitchen; and get the police to track down Detective Sergeant Smythe." I hung up before Nat could ask any questions and turned to Thorny, who was still swearing. "Shut the fuck up!" I yelled at her.

My reaction seemed to shock her into silence and she finally stopped her tirade of curses and just lay there, propped up against the bookshelves and holding onto her bleeding nose. The eyes glaring at me were not hers. I was sure it was pure evil staring back at me, and I felt my blood run cold.

"You killed her, didn't you?" I accused her. "You wanted her out of the way so Geering would marry you."

At first, I thought she wasn't going to reply, but then she laughed like some demented banshee and smiled coldly. "He was a weakling!" she spat out with loathing. "So I had to make up his mind for him."

Her face took on the look of someone not of this world, and I had a fleeting image in my mind of the girl in *The Exorcist*. I shivered and wished the ambulance and Smythe would hurry and get here; but at the same time, I wanted to know exactly what had happened.

"You drugged Linda with zolpidem!" I exclaimed, but Thorny did not reply. She just kept regarding me with that freaky, malevolent look. "Somehow, you gave her enough of the drug so you could suggest she jump." I was guessing, of course, but I had nothing to lose.

A shrill laugh from Thorny made me squirm with dread. I wanted out of the room, but I also wanted to hear what she had to say.

"She was a stupid druggie, anyway," Thorny declared, her voice hoarse from all the screaming. "She was on anti-depressants and zolpidem, not a good combination. Let's just say I simply helped her a little." A haughty smile played around her lips, like she was visualising how well she had executed her plan, and how much she had enjoyed it.

I shivered again. "You were in the room when she jumped, weren't you?" Again, I was guessing, but it made sense. Thorny nodded, and I went on. "You went in there to tell her about your affair with her husband, and when she became upset you slipped her some extra zolpidem in a drink. Then, you suggested life wasn't worth living and that Geering was going to leave her. So you told her she may as well jump."

"You're right, my clever and nosey friend," Thorny answered with contempt in her voice. "Linda was so drugged up that a little extra zolpidem made her open to suggestion. She was on a real downer and all I had to do was offer her an alcoholic drink spiked with the drug. She drank it all down like a good girl. Then, I talked her into jumping, and simply waited inside the room until it was safe to come out without being caught on camera. It was so easy." Another shrill laugh from her brought home just how deranged she really was. "But even after she jumped, that bastard wouldn't marry me. He was already involved with Elena."

So she *had* known about Elena. It was just as well Elena had taken off for Switzerland, I thought, otherwise we might have had two deaths instead of one. After being attacked with a meat cleaver, I had no doubt Thorny was capable of committing multiple homicide.

"Geering couldn't keep his dick in his pants long enough," Thorny went on bitterly. "When I found out, I wanted to kill him; but you beat me to it," she grinned maliciously. "With all your snooping, you stumbled upon his illegal activities and had him put away. You saved me the job of having to put him out." She almost seemed disappointed by this.

"But why use Tony?" This was something I really had to know. "Why make it look like you were having a fling with him?"

She sneered at me. "Because, you stupid bitch, you were getting too close to the truth, and I had to throw you off the scent. I couldn't be connected to Geering in any way; otherwise, they may have suspected me of killing his idiot wife—not that it would've been so easy to prove!"

I shook my head in disbelief. How could someone who performed her duties so diligently; someone who was my friend, end up being a psycho like this? Then I thought of Ted Bundy and other murderers. They were sociopaths—they could function in normal society, hold down a job, and act all friendly and charming around people in order to gain their trust; but inside, they were rotten to the core. Something was missing; something crucial—like a soul.

The telephone rang and made me jump. "Ferrari," I answered abruptly. It was Nat.

"Mia, the ambulance is here, and Smythe is on his way down to the kitchen with Dobbs. I thought Dobbs should be present, too."

"You did good, Nat," I said in a softer tone and hung up. I turned back to Thorny. "One other thing." She waited for me to go on, the mad look still in her eyes; and yet, she was still the person I had called my friend. "How did you know I was investigating this?"

"You're not the only *investigator* around here," she jeered with contempt. "You and Dobbs were always together, yapping in secret. So I figured you were looking into this whole thing involving Geering. I know your nature; you're the kind who can't let go. You just have to check out every little thing, don't you? So to test my theory I invented the story about being caught on camera with Tony to give you something to think about. If you weren't nosing around the case, you wouldn't have had any interest in the tapes from the mezzanine cameras. Later, I saw your signature on the security log from when you went to get the CCTV tapes. I knew you'd be onto it immediately, and I was right. I told Geering and he had that Chinese idiot follow you around to see what you were up to. We wanted you to stop sticking your nose into our business. It's a shame the fuckwit didn't kill you."

So Elena getting caught on camera with Geering had just been a coincidence. Thorny had had no idea of this; she had only been testing out her theory that I was on the case because she wanted me out of the way. She had wanted me dead. I was speechless; and somehow she read in my eyes the questions I wanted to ask.

"Yes," she said, "I've always hated you. You and Rourke. You must've spread your legs for him hundreds of times because you have him eating out of your hands. Anyone can see he'll do anything for you and no one else had a chance with him, not even Elena." Her face took on a gruesome look that was filled with pure envy. It seemed to me she hated whatever she couldn't have. She had probably set her sights on David and when this didn't work, she turned to Geering. The look in her eyes told me the only aphrodisiac for this woman was the power that huge wealth could bring. I felt sick to the stomach.

"The drugs—" I started to say even though I couldn't stand another minute in her evil presence.

"I knew about the drugs, but Geering didn't know I killed his wife. What a fool! All he wanted was to find out if you knew about his smuggling activities." Her hateful gaze made me squirm. I could say no more while I imagined the pain of the poor woman who hadn't had a chance against this deranged creature who was now lying on the floor.

Just then, Smythe walked in with a couple of uniforms, followed by Dobbs and the paramedics. Dobbs switched on the office light and I blinked from the bright glare. I saw deep concern in the sea of faces around me, but my eyes were too busy looking for the proof I needed to give Smythe—the small bottle that had brought about Linda Liu's death.

Entry from Mia's Case Book

Case No 1 - Linda Liu

I am so glad Linda Liu did not die in vain. Sometimes we have to persevere if we want to make something happen. Dobbs thinks I'm a real pain in the arse and like a dog with a bone, but I don't care. Persistence enabled me to help someone who couldn't help herself.

I don't even have to try to imagine what agonies Linda must have suffered when she found out her husband was having affairs. I totally relate to how she must have felt because my own husband did the same thing to me. The only difference being I am strong and blessed to have good friends around me like Dobbs, Chris, and even David. Perhaps, Linda was not so lucky, and she had no one to whom she could turn.

It is very sad when the actions of one person create such ripples in the pond of life. So much so, that not just one person, but many, are hurt. In the case of Linda Liu, she lost her life because her self-centred and selfish husband had an affair with a psycho who wanted Linda out of the way. His actions also affected his lover Elena, for she lost the man whom she thought was *the one*. It affected me because I lost someone I thought was a friend—someone who almost succeeded in killing me. And, finally, it affected Thorny because I truly believe Geering's inability to fulfill his promise to her pushed her over the edge. People don't seem to realise when they commit an act that it's not just one person they hurt, but many—sometimes thousands.

Thorny is now in a mental institution, awaiting the hearing for the crime she committed. She will probably spend the rest of her life in a mental facility: alone, unloved, and unhinged.

After I was given a dressing-down by Smythe for interfering yet again, I caught a faint glimmer of admiration in his eyes for solving a case that no one had suspected was a murder. With my testimony and the bottle of zolpidem I found in Thorny's office, it was an open and shut case.

Dobbs didn't leave my side until I had fully recovered from the fifteen stitches I had to have for my shoulder wound. In fact, he and Eileen ended up cooking the celebratory Italian lunch I had planned as a "congratulations" for their granddaughter. It was heavenly to be waited on for once.

David was horrified when he heard about my run-in with Thorny. He gave me a week off to recuperate, but not before he made me promise to stop snooping. I promised, but I had my fingers crossed behind my back.

Chris came to visit me every day during the week I had off and the little rascal talked me into letting him drive me around in "la *mia* machina". My car. My Ferrari.

The End

About the Author

Sylvia Massara is a multi-genre author based in Sydney, Australia. She loves to dabble in wacky love affairs, drama, murder, sci-fi (or anything else that takes her fancy) over good coffee.

Born in Argentina from Italian and Spanish descent (with a bit of Swiss thrown in) and transplanted to Australia at age 10, Sylvia describes herself as a bit of a "moggie" cat by way of mixed pedigree. She is also a citizen of the world as she has travelled widely throughout most of her life and she's the proud owner of three passports.

From a creative perspective, Sylvia has been writing since her early teens and her work consists of novels, screenplays and freelance writing. She has also dabbled in acting on and off, songwriting and even had her own band during her teens/early 20s where she performed at various venues.

As with most authors, Sylvia draws on her varied experience from the often puzzling tapestry of life. A few years ago Sylvia resigned from the human race because she discovered the animal kingdom was a much nicer place to be.

Currently, Sylvia lives with her cat, Mia; and always vicariously through the many characters in her head. Occasionally, Sylvia ventures into the world of humans, and she cherishes genuine friendships as they are a rare find.

Sylvia has recently released her 7th novel, The Stranger, a sci-fi apocalyptic romance with moralistic issues that involve the fight of love vs evil in the cosmos.

Please visit the author's website to keep up with her latest novels or to contact her at: www.sylviamassara.com

About Massara's Novels

The Mia Ferrari Mystery Series

<u>Playing With The Bad Boys</u>

A woman plunges ten floors down an atrium and lands on a baby grand piano in the luxurious Rourke Hotel Sydney. The police rule this as a straight case of suicide; but 48-year-old hotel duty manager and wannabe investigator, Mia Ferrari, thinks otherwise.

As Mia sets out to unravel the mysterious death and prove the cops wrong, especially her archenemy, Detective Sergeant Phil Smythe; she comes up against an unsavoury cast of characters who will do anything to shut her up. But with a little help from her friends, Mia will not stop until she unearths the truth.

Mia Ferrari is a "wiseass", older chick with determination and an attitude, and she never takes "no" for an answer.

<u>The Gay Mardi Gras Murders</u>

Mia Ferrari, smartarse, older chick, super sleuth, is back in her 2nd murder mystery, and this time, she is up to her neck in drag queens, a rare diamond with a curse and murder most foul against the backdrop of Sydney's world famous Gay Mardi Gras.

A female impersonator is found dismembered in her hotel suite bathtub, and a rare diamond worth twenty million dollars is gone. The Gay Mardi Gras is fast approaching and Mia Ferrari, senior duty manager of the exclusive Rourke International Hotel Sydney, has to juggle a bunch of drag queens, a number of fabulously handsome gay men, a transsexual with a dark mystery, a young cop with sex on his mind, a close friend from the UK who is having marital problems and a mounting body count.

As Mia pits her investigative skills against her archenemy, Detective Sergeant Phil Smythe, to solve the case, she not only becomes embroiled in the life of the people around her, but it looks like she is the next target for a serial killer with a grudge against gay men.

The South Pacific Murders

It's a well-known fact that wherever Mia Ferrari goes trouble always follows, and going on a holiday cruise to Hawaii is no different.

A killer is on the loose onboard ship. A number of doctors from a medical convention are being murdered one by one. The captain of the cruise liner asks Mia and her travelling companions to take over the investigation while the ship is in the middle of the Pacific Ocean toward its final destination. A secret sex club and horse racing bets are the only clues that can uncover the identity of the killer, but will Mia be able to solve the mystery before the killer strikes again?

Join Mia and her friends, plus her sexy detective archenemy, on a cruise to murder, mayhem, and sizzling hot sex.

Science fiction romance

The Stranger

The Stranger is a sci-fi apocalyptic romance with moralistic issues involving the fight between love and evil and its repercussions.

Rhys is on a mission on Earth in order to determine Earth's destiny, but his judgement is in danger of becoming clouded when he meets and falls in love with Carla, a human. The balance of life on Earth depends upon Rhys's recommendation to the League of Galaxies. But how will Rhys choose between his mission and his love for an Earthling? Rhys is forced to weigh up the collective evil on Earth and its causal effect on the greater good of other life in the universe against the love he has for one woman.

This is not simply a tale of love between two beings but a story of the unconditional and sublime love, which is the force that drives the cosmos.

The Stranger was dedicated to the Loving Memory of David Bowie.

Romance

Like Casablanca

What does internet dating and Casablanca have in common? Nothing, unless you go to Rick's Cafe and find out what antiques dealer and dating blogger, Cat Ryan, is up to.

Cat's doing research for her internet dating blog gig, and the place she chooses to meet her many dates is at Rick's Cafe in Sydney. But what of its disturbingly handsome owner, Rick Blake?

Cat wonders what he thinks, seeing her with a different male all the time. What's more, why does this bother Cat so much? It's not like she wants any involvement after her recent break up with Josh, her cheating ex. Besides, it looks like Rick is trying to get back together with his ex-wife, Denise. So Cat decides to play it safe, but her heart has different ideas.

The Other Boyfriend

Sarah Jamison is on a mission to find a boyfriend for Moira, who is her lover's partner. And Sarah's best friend, Monica, comes to the rescue with the perfect solution. Enter the enigmatic Mike Connor.

Monica is sure that Mike will sweep Moira off her feet, leaving the way open for Sarah to be with her true love, Jeffrey.

Sarah hates Mike on sight despite the fact that her body tells her otherwise. He is a romance novel "hero-type" who is smug and full of himself. But the only way to accomplish her mission is for her to work with Mike so she can be together with the man she loves.

Jeffrey has promised her that the minute he can end his platonic relationship with Moira, he will be with Sarah for good; but he is having trouble letting go of the wretched woman, and Sarah feels her time is running out. She is terrified of the pending big "M" (menopause), and seeing as she's just turned forty, and her hormones are driving her to do insane and desperate things, she is sure that it is not too far off into the future!

So here she is, building a multi-level marketing business in Taiwan, and struggling with it all: a stranger in a foreign country, away from her mother and friends back in London; a reluctant lover; a drop-dead gorgeous man who might have ulterior motives for helping her, and finally, a business that seems to be dwindling.

Sarah is doing it all in the name of love and the last chance to have a family, and if this means scheming and working with the devil himself, then she will do it! What she doesn't take into account is the fact that instead of getting closer to her goal, Sarah's feelings take a turn, and she finds herself increasingly thinking about the very man she despises the most – "the other boyfriend".

Contemporary fiction - drama

The Soul Bearers

Partly inspired by real life events, this is a story of courage, the gift of friendship and unconditional love. The story involves three people whose lives cross for a short period of time and the profound effect which results from their interaction. Alex Dorian, freelance travel writer and victim of child abuse, arrives in Sydney in an attempt to exorcise the ghosts of her past. She shares a house with Steve and the disturbing Matthew, a homosexual couple. Alex finds herself inexplicably attracted to Matthew, and she must battle with her repressed sexuality and her fear of intimacy. Matthew, extremely good looking and an inspiring actor/model, lives with Steve, who is dying of AIDS. Matthew has his own battle, that of dealing with the rejection of his socialite parents, and facing a future without his partner. Steve is the rock to which the troubled Matthew and Alex cling as they examine their lives and beliefs. Steve finally dies, but his legacy lives on in the strength which both Matthew and Alex find to face their own pain. Alex learns to love again, thanks to the gift of friendship from Matthew; and in turn, with Alex's love and support, Matthew learns to forgive the past and move on to follow his dream.

This beautifully told story explores the true meaning of unconditional love--for both one's self and for others. Readers of "The Soul Bearers" will come away with a deeper understanding of human relationships and of what it means to truly love without condition.

Made in the USA
Las Vegas, NV
19 June 2023

73634678R00115